MURDER AT
UNION STATION

Praise for David S. Pederson

Murder on Monte Vista

"A great new mystery!…[T]he way everything is described really puts me in the moment. You feel a part of the story, and the way it is written, even though you know Mason is talking to another character, it's as if he is talking to you personally too, so it is so easy to become emerged in the story and really be a part of it. Most enjoyable, super exciting, and a series I cannot wait for more of! What a fantastic mystery!"—*LESBIreviewed*

Death's Prelude

"I highly recommend this story, introducing Heath and giving more insight to his past, as well as setting up the series nicely. The most fabulous thing though was seeing Heath blossom into the detective I met in *Death Overdue*, and I can't wait to read the next mystery he has to solve."—*LESBIreviewed*

Death Overdue

"Deftly drawn characters, brisk pacing, and an easy charm distinguish Pederson's winning follow-up to 2019's *Death Takes a Bow*. Pederson successfully evokes and shrewdly capitalizes upon the time in which his mystery takes place, using the era's prejudices and politics to heighten the story's stakes and more thoroughly invest readers in its outcome. Plausible suspects, persuasive red herrings, and cleverly placed clues keep the pages frantically flipping until the book's gratifying close."—*Mystery Scene*

"David S. Pederson never disappoints when it comes to twisted and suspenseful mysteries…I highly recommend the Detective Heath Barrington mystery series, and *Death Overdue* in particular is suspenseful and an absolute page-turner."—*QueeRomance Ink*

Lambda Literary Award Finalist *Death Takes a Bow*

"[T]here's also a lovely scene near the end of the book that puts into words the feelings that Alan and Heath share for one another, but can't openly share because of the time they live in and their jobs in law enforcement. All in all, an interesting murder/mystery and an apt depiction of the times."—*Gay Book Reviews*

"This is a mystery in its purest form...If you like murder mysteries and are particularly interested in the old-school type, you'll love this book!"—*Kinzie Things*

Lambda Literary Award Finalist *Death Checks In*

"David Pederson does a great job with this classic murder mystery set in 1947 and the attention to its details..."—*The Novel Approach*

"This noir whodunit is a worthwhile getaway with that old-black-and-white-movie feel that you know you love, and it's sweetly chaste, in a late-1940s way..."—*Outsmart Magazine*

"This is a classic murder mystery; an old-fashioned style mystery à la Agatha Christie..."—*Reviews by Amos Lassen*

Death Goes Overboard

"[A]uthor David S. Pederson has packed a lot in this novel. You don't normally find a soft-sided, poetry-writing mobster in a noir mystery, for instance, but he's here…this novel is both predictable and not, making it a nice diversion for a weekend or vacation."—*Washington Blade*

"Pederson takes a lot of the tropes of mysteries and utilizes them to the fullest, giving the story a knowable form. However, the unique characters and accurate portrayal of the struggles of gay relationships in 1940s America make this an enjoyable, thought-provoking read."—*Gay, Lesbian, Bisexual, and Transgender Round Table of the American Library Association*

"You've got mobsters, a fedora-wearing detective in a pinstriped suit, seemingly prim matrons, and man-hungry blondes eager for marriage. It's like an old black-and-white movie in book form…"—*Windy City Times*

Death Comes Darkly

"Agatha Christie…if Miss Marple were a gay police detective in post–WWII Milwaukee."—*PrideSource: Between the Lines*

"The mystery is one that isn't easily solved. It's a cozy mystery unraveled in the drawing room type of story, but well worked out."—*Bookwinked*

"If you LOVE Agatha Christie, you shouldn't miss this one. The writing is very pleasant, the mystery is old-fashioned, but in a good meaning, intriguing plot, well developed characters. I'd like to read more of Heath Barrington and Alan Keyes in the future. This couple has a big potential."—*Gay Book Reviews*

"[A] thoroughly entertaining read from beginning to end. A detective story in the best Agatha Christie tradition with all the trimmings."—*Sinfully Gay Romance Book Review*

By the Author

Murder on Monte Vista

Murder at Union Station

Heath Barrington Mysteries:

Death Comes Darkly

Death Goes Overboard

Death Checks In

Death Takes A Bow

Death Overdue

Death's Prelude

Death Foretold

MURDER AT UNION STATION

by

David S. Pederson

2022

ISBN 13: 978-1-63679-269-9

This Trade Paperback Original Is Published By
Bold Strokes Books, Inc.
P.O. Box 249
Valley Falls, NY 12185

First Edition: September 2022

Credits
Editors: Jerry L. Wheeler and Stacia Seaman
Production Design: Stacia Seaman
Cover Design by Inkspiral Design

Acknowledgments

Special thanks to all my family, especially my wonderful mom, Vondell, and in memory of my dad, Manford.

And to all my terrific friends who are my chosen family.

And as always, thanks and all my love to my husband, Alan.

Finally, thanks also to all my readers, and to Jerry Wheeler, my editor with the most-est, as well as everyone at Bold Strokes Books who have helped me so much, especially Radclyffe, Sandy, Cindy, and Ruth, Stacia, and Sheri.

Thanks to Thomas MacDonald for being a beta reader, and for his friendship.

Chapter One

Late evening, Monday, May 6, 1946
The baggage room, Union Station, Phoenix

Leland Burrows was in his mid-forties, on the shorter side, and solid. He was as strong as an ox, and rather resembled one, too, with a wide nose, thick eyebrows, small, dark eyes that were usually bloodshot, short brownish red hair, and a bushy red mustache that seemed to grow out of his deep, oversized nostrils. He wore dingy, oily bib overalls with an old blue work shirt underneath, stained below the arms from months of perspiration. Upon his feet were heavy, well-worn brown leather work boots. He had been employed at Union Station in the baggage room for almost twenty years and had seen his share of fellow handlers come and go. Most of them couldn't adjust to the long hours, the heavy lifting, and the oppressive heat of the summers, and moved on to other jobs within a year or two. The latest, Alfred Brody, had been there only a few weeks but so far seemed to be working out okay, in Leland's opinion. Leland wiped his brow with a soiled red kerchief and stared at the younger man now, watching him feed part of a ham sandwich to a rail-thin dog near the large street-side doors. "You know, son, that mangy old pooch wouldn't keep hanging around here if you'd stop feeding it," Leland said with a slow drawl as he stuffed the kerchief back in his pocket and hooked his thumbs on the straps of his overalls.

The younger, handsome dark-skinned man looked over at Leland, an annoyed expression on his clean-shaven face. He was in his mid-twenties, tall and lean, with short black hair, large, bright brown eyes, and long, muscular limbs. "I am *not* your son, Mr. Burrows. My name is Alfred, Alfred Brody, as you well know. And he's *not* a mangy dog. He's a fine hound, just down on his luck, like a lot of us these days."

Leland bristled. "He's a mutt, and he probably has fleas and God knows what else. You know Mr. Dawson doesn't like animals in the baggage area unless they're crated cargo."

"And I suppose you're going to run and tell him. You'd like to tell the station manager on me, I think, sir," Alfred Brody said. His eyes narrowed a bit.

Leland spat a wad of chewing tobacco into a tin bucket with amazing accuracy. "I ain't got no mind to presently, but that don't mean I won't. I ain't no stool pigeon, but that dog is a pest."

"By saying you 'ain't no stool pigeon,' to use your colorful English, you're actually saying you *are* a stool pigeon. That is what is known as a double negative," Alfred said, getting to his feet as the hound finished the bit of sandwich and wandered off toward the center of the baggage room.

"Bah, uppity, you are. Just 'cause you're supposedly college educated don't make you any better than me," Leland said, running a coarse, calloused hand through his hair.

"Doesn't make me any worse, either, Mr. Burrows."

"Yeah, well, you report to me, and don't forget it."

"Yes, sir, but only until I get a job teaching."

Leland laughed and wiped his nose on the sleeve of his dirty shirt. "They ain't gonna hire a dark-skinned fella like you to teach children, no matter how much schooling you have. You're lucky old man Dawson gave you a job here. Now get moving and finish tagging those bags for the Golden State Limited. And get that damned dog away from that there trunk before he goes and lifts his leg on it."

Alfred looked over at the old, thin dog who was now sniffing and whining relentlessly at a large steamer trunk. "What's the matter, pooch? What do you smell?" Alfred said, ignoring the senior baggage handler and walking over to the hound.

"Go on! Shoo!" Leland said loudly. He clapped several times, but the dog wouldn't move away. Instead, he started circling the trunk slowly, keeping his head down and sniffing at the corners as he continued to whine and growl.

Alfred walked still closer and examined the luggage tag attached to the handle. "Belongs to a Miss Charlotte Castle. Hmm. That's the trunk I picked up with those suitcases this afternoon from that apartment over on Roosevelt."

Leland clapped his hands again, this time with more force. "Dammit, get him away from there. That trunk's going on the Golden State Limited to Los Angeles, along with all those bags over there, and I don't want to have to explain to the owner why it's soaked in dog piss. Get him away from there and get back to work."

Alfred bent down and inspected the area of the leather trunk the dog seemed most interested in. "There's some fluids leaking out, Mr. Burrows, and a bit of an odd odor. That's what's gotten Barkly's attention."

"Jesus, now you've named the mutt," Leland said, moving over to the trunk also and bending down awkwardly for a look. He put on his glasses, squinted, and sniffed. "Hmpf, I've seen this before. Contraband deer meat inside, most likely. Folks are always trying to smuggle it to the West Coast. Looks like that old dog may be worth something after all."

"Good boy, Barkly," Alfred said, giving him a pat on the head and a scratch behind his ears, which was rewarded by several thumps of Barkly's scraggly tail.

Leland straightened himself up with a groan and took off his glasses, wiping them somewhat clean with his soiled kerchief before putting them back in his shirt pocket inside the overalls. "Yup, contraband, most likely. This trunk's been sitting here in the heat awhile. They didn't pack it well enough, I guess, and the meat's started to rot. Looks like the lock's busted, too. Best go get Mr. Dawson, son, and let him know what I found. This Miss Castle's going to be in a heap of trouble."

"Once again, I am not your son, Mr. Burrows, and for that I am thankful."

"Bah, uppity. And best get that mutt out of here before old man Dawson sees him and blames me for it."

"Right." Alfred led the dog outside through the track-side doors, where he had placed a bowl of fresh water earlier, and then returned. "I'll inform Mr. Dawson right away about the trunk." He took out his watch and studied it. "It's eleven thirty. The Limited is due in fifteen minutes. You'll have to finish tagging those other bags yourself, sir." He didn't wait for a reply but instead hurried out the east door into the main headhouse of the station, which contained the passenger waiting area, telegraph office, newsstand, snack bar, and railroad offices, the largest of which belonged to Edgar Dawson, the station manager.

Chapter Two

Late morning, Tuesday, May 7, 1946
Mason Adler's apartment

Mason Adler had been more or less awake since seven, drifting in and out of consciousness. The heat had caused him to toss and turn all night, in spite of the electric fan he had set up with a bowl of ice placed in front of it. Finally, at a quarter after eight, he forced himself to get up, realizing any attempt at further sleep was futile. He raised the window shade and dumped the melted ice down the drain of the bathroom sink before washing up and shaving. He put on his gray silk robe and then went to the bedroom window, where he glanced out at the thermometer attached to the building just outside. It was eighty-four degrees, clear and sunny, just another spring morning in Phoenix, Arizona.

On the sidewalk below, he saw Eliza Woodburn and her little black-and-white dog, Scruffy, walking slowly west, probably on her way to visit her sister, who lived nearby. Mrs. Woodburn, an elderly widow, had a small place on the first floor of Mason's apartment building, next to his friend Lydia. With a sigh, he turned and headed to the kitchen, where he had a light breakfast of fresh grapefruit, toast, juice, and coffee with just a little cream and sugar. After he'd done up the scant dishes, he returned to the bedroom and dressed in clean white boxer shorts, a French cuff shirt, onyx cufflinks, and a gray two-piece suit with a dark green tie. He had just finished putting on his socks and black oxfords when he heard a knock at the door of his apartment.

Mason walked to the entry and swung the door open to reveal his friend and downstairs neighbor, Lydia Dettling, standing there on the balcony hall overlooking the courtyard of the El Encanto apartments. She was barefoot and wearing a light blue sleeveless cotton dress, her long red hair swept up and back.

"Good morning, love. Sleep well?" she said, a soft smile on her lips as she looked up at him.

"Good morning, Lydia. No, I didn't, not really. You?"

"Not so much. I've been up since six. I think a nap may be in order this afternoon."

Mason stifled a yawn. "Same for me. Not working at the store today?"

"Nope, I don't have to be back to Penney's until tomorrow morning. I'm working the day shift. At least they have refrigerated air in the store."

"That helps, I'm sure."

"Most certainly. Makes me *almost* want to work every day," she said with a light laugh.

"And it makes me almost want to *shop* every day, which is why they do it, of course."

"Of course. They've little interest in keeping the employees happy," she said, laughing again.

"Not likely, though you're not *unhappy* there, are you?"

"No, not usually. The pay's not bad, and the discount is nice. I think all my furniture and most of my clothes have come from Penney's."

Mason smiled. "Nothing wrong with that. What's in the bag?"

Lydia glanced down at the white wax paper bag in her right hand. "Oh, I brought us doughnuts, one plain and one with chocolate sprinkles."

"How nice. You know I love doughnuts with chocolate sprinkles. But, er, were we meeting this morning? Did I forget something?"

"No, I just decided to stop up and visit since you're not working on a case at the moment. I thought you might like a little company, and besides, I haven't seen you in a few days."

"I see. And would that happen to be my newspaper tucked under your left arm?"

Lydia glanced down at the folded-up *Arizona Republic*. "Why yes, it is. I happened to notice it was still on your doorstep just before I knocked."

"And I saw Mrs. Woodburn was up early today," Mason said. "I saw her and Scruffy heading west."

"Oh?" Lydia said innocently.

Mason folded his arms across his chest and squinted at her. "Don't 'oh' me, Lydia. I know you don't get your own newspaper. You always read Mrs. Woodburn's before she's awake, but you didn't get a chance today since she was up early. So, you decided to read mine."

"You *are* a brilliant private detective, Mr. Adler. Guilty as charged. But you know I'm always curious to read *Hedda Hopper's Hollywood* gossip column over my morning coffee. And Mrs. Woodburn never notices. I always fold it back up and return it to her doorstep before she realizes it's gone."

"That, Miss Dettling, is stealing, even if you *do* put it back."

"I prefer the term borrowing. She's normally a late sleeper, but I think she's been getting up earlier because of the heat."

"As have we all."

"Yes, that's true. But at least I brought us doughnuts, and since I'm holding your paper hostage, are you going to invite me in for coffee or leave me standing out here?"

Mason laughed and uncrossed his arms. "By all means, entrez-vous," he said, standing aside and ushering her in. "Come on into the kitchen and I'll make a fresh pot as a ransom payment for my newspaper while you tell me what old Hedda has to say today in her column about all our favorite Hollywood celebrities."

"Deal," Lydia said, sweeping into his living room. "Ah, the tile feels much better on my bare feet than that cement of the balcony."

"You really should wear shoes," Mason said, closing the door to the balcony hall once more.

"Oh, pooh, why? It's too hot for shoes and certainly too hot for stockings. In fact, when I'm home alone, I don't wear much of anything."

Mason raised his brows. "You live on the first floor, you know. I hope you keep your shades drawn."

"I do, most of the time, but mainly just to keep the heat and the sun out. If someone wants to look, let them look."

"Lydia Dettling, you are something else."

"Thank you, and likewise, in your own stuffed-shirt, buttoned-down way."

"I have my unbuttoned moments," Mason said as he headed to the kitchen.

"Oh, I know you do. I know you well. I've been your downstairs neighbor and your friend for six years now," she said, following behind him and swinging the wax paper bag in her right hand.

"And we keep each other's secrets," he said over his shoulder.

"Of course. That's what friends do, love."

"Then I'm glad we're friends."

"Me too. By the way, I must say I was surprised you hadn't yet retrieved your paper. It's almost nine thirty already."

"And already eighty-nine degrees, heading to a high of one hundred and four, supposedly, according to Wendy the Weather Girl on the radio."

Lydia handed the wax paper bag to Mason, sat on a dining chair, and curled her bare legs up, the newspaper on the table in front of her. "Ugh, I can't stand Wendy the Weather Girl. She's so perky, and I just know she's a big-chested, slim-waisted blonde in her twenties with an IQ to match."

Mason laughed. "Probably, but she gets good ratings. Anyway, you're right. I usually do get my paper off the doorstep earlier than this. I normally read it over breakfast, but since I have the morning free, I thought it might be more comfortable to wait and do it in my reading chair by the window, where there's always a chance, albeit slight, of a light breeze."

"And always a chance you may nod off for a catnap," Lydia said.

Mason chuckled and stifled another yawn. "More than a slight chance of that, especially today. As you said before, you know me too well. By the way, I like the red hair," Mason said as he filled the percolator with cold water from the tap. "When did that happen?"

"Thanks. I had it done a couple of days ago. I got tired of being a brunette, at least for now. Besides, Thad mentioned he likes redheads."

Mason added some ground coffee to the percolator basket, put the lid on, and set the pot on the stove, turning the burner on medium heat. "Thad O'Connell, you mean."

"Naturally."

"Since when do you change your appearance to please a man?"

"Since never, love, as you well know. But I felt like making a change, and since he likes redheads and I haven't been a redhead in a while, I figured, why not?"

"Well, it looks good on you. Goes well with your green eyes. I'm sure Mr. O'Connell appreciates it."

"He actually hasn't seen it yet. He's been so busy at the bank, what with everyone needing loans for all this post-war building going on. But we have a date for Saturday night."

"That's good to hear. Sounds like things are going well between the two of you, then."

Lydia shrugged her shoulders and massaged her neck. "I guess so. It's only been a little over three weeks since Thad and I met at Walter's party. It seems so strange to be dating again at my age."

"What do you mean? You're only forty, and ten years younger than me."

"I prefer to think of myself as thirty-nine."

"A female Jack Benny, eh? Eternally thirty-nine?"

"Why not? It works for him," Lydia said with a twinkle in her green eyes.

"Except you play the bass fiddle quite well, compared to his awful violin playing."

Lydia giggled. "Oh, that's all just a part of his act. I've heard he actually plays quite beautifully."

"Could be, I suppose."

"And that bass fiddle doesn't exactly help me in the dating department, you know. It's hard to look feminine with that big thing between my legs."

"I'd say you manage quite well. And besides, you make it sound like you've been locked away in a convent someplace. You've had lots of dates since I've known you."

"Oh, I've had a few, here and there. When my mom died, I was only nineteen and the twins were just seven. Dad was no help at all, so I ended up raising them, more or less, *and* taking care of him. I was thirty when the kids turned eighteen."

"I remember you telling me that. Not really fair to you."

"No one said life's fair, I guess. Anyway, I love the twins, and I almost feel like they're my own kids rather than my brother and sister, so I guess I didn't mind too much, though I did miss out on a lot of things other young, single women do. When I'd meet a guy back then and I told him I lived with and took care of my dad, was raising my two younger siblings, and played the bass, they usually ran the other way and never looked back."

"Their loss. But I've known you about six years now, and I recall several men who've come and gone."

"I wouldn't say several, Mason."

"All right, a few, then. There was that waiter fellow, I forget his name, and that man with the annoying laugh, the clerk at Penney's, and of course, Dennis, the door-to-door vacuum cleaner salesman."

"Yes, Dennis O'Keefe. We went out for almost six months."

"I recall, one of your longest. You never really did say what happened with him."

"Oh, I suppose it doesn't really matter if I tell you now. He had a problem with *you*, actually, so I had a big problem with him, and I ended it."

"He had a problem with *me*?"

"Well, yes. Of course, I never discussed your personal life or anything with him, but after a while he kind of figured it out. He put two and two together, and it bothered him. He said you were mentally ill, because you're a…you know."

"A homosexual. Gee, I didn't know he felt that way. I'm sorry."

"As you said, his loss, the jerk. Besides, Mr. Zester didn't like him much. I should have known right then Dennis was all wrong for me."

"Mr. Zester didn't like him? Your cat likes just about everybody."

"Not everybody. Remember when Mr. Ferguson came over to fix my bathroom faucet last month? I had to lock Mr. Zester in the bedroom, he was so angry."

"Who was angry? Mr. Zester or Mr. Ferguson?"

"Both, actually. Mr. Ferguson doesn't like cats, and he doesn't like to work, so he was grumpy to begin with, and Mr. Zester definitely didn't like Mr. Ferguson. He was hissing and growling at him something fierce."

"Animals are smarter than most people think, and smarter than some people. They can sense things. And I must say I agree with Mr. Zester. Dennis O'Keefe is clearly an idiot, and Roy Ferguson is not a nice man."

"But Mr. Zester *does* like Thad O'Connell, and Thad likes Mr. Zester," Lydia said.

"And *you* like Thad O'Connell, too."

Lydia blushed a deep cactus flower pink. "I do. He's a good man, I think."

"And a handsome widower with a good job at the bank."

Lydia cocked her head coyly. "You think he's handsome?"

"Of course he is, and you know it. Quite an eligible catch."

"But I'm not fishing."

"That's usually when it happens. When you don't look, you find. Anyway, you two make a nice couple."

"Don't rush it, please. I've enjoyed the few dates we've had, but I'm in no hurry to settle down, and I doubt Thad is, either. I've never subscribed to the ridiculous theory that every girl should be married, though my father certainly does. He brings it up nearly every time I talk to him."

"Some parents are like that, I suppose. Fortunately my mother gave up on me getting married many years ago, and my dad's been gone a long time. Still, I'm glad you're getting out and about with someone besides me."

Lydia smiled softly as she stared at him. "I know, but I must admit I miss seeing you and spending time with you."

"Thanks. And I must admit I've missed our little dates the past couple of weeks. I'm glad you stopped up this morning."

"Me too. Thad knows we're just friends, and he doesn't mind if you and I still go out once in a while."

"Does he know anything else?" Mason said, as he retrieved two clean cups and saucers from the cupboard and put the doughnuts Lydia had brought onto a plate.

"You mean about you being the way you are?"

"You can say homosexual."

"I don't like that word, and I only use it when absolutely necessary. It just sounds so clinical. There needs to be a better word, a happier word, something light and gay."

"I'll get to work on that," Mason said with an impish grin.

"Good. Of course, you know *I* don't mind that you are, and I never have, ever since you moved in and I heard you stomping around up here."

"And you peeked in the window off the balcony hall to see me doing the tango with Gregory Banning."

She laughed. "I'll never get tired of thinking about that, and you with that red rose in your teeth."

"And I cut my lower lip on that damned thorn."

"Oh my, I'd forgotten that part. But to answer your question, no, he doesn't know that you're a, you know, a homosexual. I think he'd be okay with it, though, unlike that awful Dennis O'Keefe."

Mason shook his head. "Still, best not to take chances."

"Of course. I'd never say anything to him or anyone without your approval. But he *has* asked me if you've ever been married or if you're seeing anyone. I think he does wonder. I mean, you *are* fifty now."

"Yes, I know I'm fifty. You don't have to remind me. So, what did you tell him?"

"The truth and *only* the truth. That you're a confirmed bachelor, married to your work as Phoenix's best private detective, and that you don't have much time for dating."

"That's kind of you, but I don't think I'm the best P.I. in Phoenix."

"Well, you're the best one *I* know."

Mason chuckled. "I'm the *only* private detective you know."

"So? You're still the best. And quite handsome yourself. Over six feet tall, slender, dark hair that's just kissed with whisps of gray, steel blue eyes, a Roman nose, strong jaw..."

"Stop, you're embarrassing me," Mason said with a gentle laugh. The coffee had just begun to bubble into the glass globe atop the percolator lid, so he lowered the heat, let it percolate a couple more minutes, then took the pot off the stove before it could overheat. He removed the basket with the wet grounds and set it in the sink, and then poured two cups. Later, when they were finished reading the newspaper, he'd wrap the grounds up in the paper and place them all in the trash.

"Gee, that coffee smells good," Lydia said. "And I'm sorry, I didn't mean to embarrass you. By the way, if Thad ever did find out about you, and if he *did* have a problem with it, I'd end it just as fast as I did with Dennis."

"That's sweet of you."

"You're a big part of my life, and we're a package deal. Besides, someone who'd have a problem with you isn't someone I'd want to be with. But I do wonder, are you ever going to settle down, darling?"

"You mean with a man?"

"Well, yes. You are a...you know."

"A homosexual. Yes, I know. If I'm not, I've been doing things all wrong."

"Wise guy."

"Oh, maybe I'll find someone someday. I can't say the thought hasn't crossed my mind," Mason said.

"You've had your share of relationships since I've known you, too, you know. Gregory Banning, Bryce, Gary, Roger Sinclair..."

"I wouldn't exactly call them relationships. Just fellows I dated, for a time."

"Yes, you date them for a while and then it ends, and you're usually the one who ends it."

"True. Maybe I'm just too independent. Maybe you and I are *both* too independent."

"Or maybe you just haven't met the right one yet."

"And maybe you have?"

Lydia shook her head. "It's too soon to tell. I've never really believed in 'the right one,' and I certainly don't need a man to complete me. I'm happy with my life, but I must admit I enjoy Thad's company."

"I agree, I don't need a man to complete me, either."

"You don't. But maybe it's time you met someone else, someone's company you could enjoy, at least. You know, Thad has an older brother in Tucson who's never married. I believe Thad said he's forty-eight."

Mason squinted his eyes. "Lydia, don't go playing matchmaker."

"I'm not. I'm just saying, darling. He may not even be a...you know. Thad never said, only that his brother's never been married."

"Not every unmarried man over forty is a homosexual."

"I know that, silly, but I just got that feeling from the way Thad talked about him. I haven't met Toby yet, but if he's as kind, smart, and witty as his brother, I think you'd adore him."

"Read your newspaper or *my* newspaper, as the case may be. And drink your coffee and eat your doughnut," Mason said, setting a cup and spoon down before her along with the creamer and sugar bowl. The plate of doughnuts he set in the middle of the small table.

"Fine." She took the plain doughnut. "You know, Thad showed me a photograph of Toby the other day."

"Oh? What's he look like?"

Lydia grinned devilishly. "All I can say is, ooh la la!"

Mason shot Lydia a look. "He's attractive, huh?"

"Only in a Cary Grant sort of way."

"Nice. And you say he lives in Tucson? What's he do for a living?"

Lydia put two sugar cubes and a spoonful of cream into her coffee and stirred. "Oh, now you're interested? He's the head clerk at a men's clothing shop."

"The head clerk, eh?"

"Yes. And he lives alone," she said, picking up the plain doughnut and dunking it gently into her cup. "Thad tells me Toby had a roommate for over ten years, but the man moved out a year and a half ago. Apparently, Toby was pretty upset about it."

"That's interesting. But still, that doesn't mean—"

"Thad says Toby's a great fellow. So even if he isn't a...you know, what's the harm in meeting him? At the very least, you could make a new friend."

"All right, you win," Mason said, adding cream and sugar to his own coffee. He picked up the doughnut with chocolate sprinkles and sat down across from Lydia at the small table. "Next time this Toby fellow is in Phoenix, perhaps the four of us can meet for coffee or something."

"Deal!"

Mason suddenly looked thoughtful as he nibbled the edges of his doughnut. "You know, if you and Mr. O'Connell continue to hit it off, I'll be left without a female escort. People will think you jilted me, and I'll have to find another single lady to take to the movies and out to dinner."

"We can still go out," Lydia said. "Thad doesn't mind."

"Yes, but it wouldn't do for me to be out sashaying with a woman who's going steady with someone else. What would people say?"

"Most folks assume you and I are a couple."

"They do, and I guess I've gotten used to the security of that, of people not gossiping about my private life. But I truly am happy for you and Thad, and I really do hope it works out for you. Say, maybe I'll ask Eliza Woodburn from downstairs to go to the movies with me some time," Mason said with a sparkle in his eyes. "Maybe she could be my new lady friend."

Lydia gave Mason a mock horrified look. "Mrs. Woodburn is nearly eighty and is usually in bed by eight thirty."

"We could go to the matinee."

"And have dinner at five?"

"Why not? I've heard it's good for the digestion to eat early."

"Very funny, Mr. Adler. Besides, now that you're fifty, you don't necessarily *need* to be seen out with a woman. You can just be a confirmed bachelor. There's nothing wrong with that."

"Ugh, I hate the sound of that. Of being fifty, I mean. But I suppose there is something to what you say. Mothers stopped trying to fix me up with their daughters years ago."

"That's because the mothers are all in old age homes by now, and their daughters are already married with grown children of their own."

"Gee, thanks," Mason said, taking a full bite of his doughnut and washing it down with a swig of coffee.

"Of course, darling," she said, laughing. "Oh, you made me spill coffee down my chin."

"I'll get us some napkins."

"Not to worry, I can get them." She sprang to her feet and yanked a couple of white linen napkins out of a kitchen drawer. She handed one to Mason and wiped her mouth and chin with the other as she took her seat at the table once more and picked up the newspaper.

"Thanks," he said. "Are you going to share any of my newspaper with me?"

"Hmm? Oh, yes, here, you can read the sports section while I peruse the local news and *Hedda Hopper's Hollywood*," she said, handing over a section of the paper to him.

"Gee, thanks," Mason said, taking it from her. "But I only look at the pictures in the sports section."

"Of course you do."

"Nonetheless, I'll have to get my reading glasses just in case you're generous enough to let me read another part. I must say I always enjoy the funnies. I wonder what Dagwood Bumstead is up to today." He got up from the table, retrieved his eyeglasses from the bedroom, then sat down across from her again. He picked up his coffee cup and the sports section, and he scanned a mildly interesting article on the recent Detroit Tigers game as Lydia perused the main page.

She took a sip of her coffee, set it down again onto the saucer, and took another bite of her doughnut as she continued to scan the headlines. Suddenly she sat bolt upright, putting both her bare feet on the floor, her green eyes as big as the doughnuts as she stared at the printed page.

"Good gracious, this is simply horrific. Just ghastly. I can't believe it."

Mason set his cup down and looked across the table at the top of Lydia's red head, just visible over the newspaper. "What is it?" he said with mock concern. "Are Cary Grant and Barbara Hutton getting back together? Does Hedda say Randolph Scott is heartbroken about it?"

"No, I'm serious. They found a woman's body in a trunk at the train station late last night," she said, her voice shaky as she lowered the paper and stared at Mason across the table.

Mason's eyebrows went up in surprise. "That is indeed horrific. Here in Phoenix?"

"Yes, Union Station. I simply can't believe it. How horrible!"

"Agreed," Mason said, leaning forward. He took off his reading glasses and put them in his shirt pocket. "What else does it say?"

"Hmm?" She raised the paper again. "Oh, well, it says the trunk and a few other suitcases belonged to a Miss Charlotte Castle of Phoenix, who had purchased a one way ticket to Los Angeles on the Golden State Limited. The body was discovered by the station manager, Mr. E. Dawson, who was alerted by a baggage handler, Mr. Burrows, to a foul odor and fluids leaking from the trunk."

"Probably left out in the heat too long."

"That's disgusting," Lydia said. "Oh, this is interesting. It says Detective Hardwick of the Phoenix police is investigating."

"Our Emil? That *is* interesting."

"I can't imagine there's more than one Hardwick on the force. Your old friend and former school roommate is apparently on the case."

"Good ol' Emil. Does it say who the body in the trunk was?"

Lydia read a bit more, her eyes darting back and forth, her lips moving silently, before shaking her head. "No. I can't believe it. How could something like that happen here?"

Mason sighed, leaned back, and picked up his coffee cup once more. "Things like that happen everywhere, unfortunately. Still, it's tragic and sad."

"And frightening."

"And also curious. I remember a similar murder, or murders, as it were, back in 1931. A woman killed two of her friends, shot them to death, I think, and hid their bodies in trunks and suitcases, which were then loaded onto a California-bound train. The bodies were discovered in L.A. by a baggage handler, if I'm not mistaken."

"Yes, I remember that, just awful. The whole thing gave me nightmares for weeks," Lydia said. "At least they caught that woman."

"They did, out in California. I believe she was committed to an insane asylum."

Lydia shuddered. "A fitting place for her. Well, hopefully they'll catch whoever did this, too. It says this Miss Castle, the owner of the trunk, was questioned by the police, but she's claiming she's innocent. How could she be innocent when a woman's body was found in her trunk?"

"That's a good question," Mason said, taking another sip of his coffee and a small nibble of his doughnut. "But it's possible."

"I don't see how. Oh, I don't think I'll be able to sleep at all tonight. That poor woman, murdered and stuffed in a trunk like that. I hope it's no one I know."

"Doubtful," Mason said. "Phoenix is a good-sized town."

"Yes, but still. It could have been a customer I waited on at Penney's. Or a coworker. Or someone from church, or—"

"Or someone else altogether that you've never met. I don't think it's likely you knew the victim. After all, you don't know this Miss Charlotte Castle, do you?"

Lydia shook her head. "No, I don't believe so. I don't think

I know any Castles, though I do know a Castlebach, and I knew a Charlotte Plum from school."

"Not the same, my dear. Please don't fret about it," he said, as his telephone began to ring. "Oh, there's my phone." He set his cup down onto the saucer and got to his feet. "Excuse me, won't you?" He didn't wait for an answer as Lydia had once more buried her nose in the newspaper article. He walked quickly to the niche by the front door and picked up the telephone receiver on the third ring. "Mason Adler."

"Good morning, Mr. Adler. This is Adam Castleberry, Charlotte Castleberry's father. Charlotte's the woman who owned the trunk discovered last night at the train station. I assume you've seen the morning *Arizona Republic*."

"Oh, yes, Mr. Castleberry. I did see the paper. I thought the woman who owned the trunk was named Charlotte Castle, though, not Castleberry."

"My daughter shortened our surname recently for, ah, business purposes. And it may have been her trunk, but I assure you she had nothing to do with that young woman's death."

"I see. Well, what can I do for you?"

"The police are investigating the case, of course, but I've heard about your reputation at solving crimes, and I'd like to engage your services to find out what really happened and prove Charlotte is innocent."

"I must admit it's an intriguing case, Mr. Castleberry. I take it the police suspect your daughter was involved in the woman's death?"

"Yes, only natural, I suppose, since it was her trunk, and the woman inside was my daughter's former roommate, Gertrude Claggett. But Charlotte is completely innocent, believe me."

"You say this Miss Claggett was your daughter's *former* roommate?"

"That's right, as of just recently. Charlotte decided to move out and head to Los Angeles, where my sister lives. She wants to try her hand at acting and break into the movies. Charlotte just vacated the apartment yesterday afternoon. She was absolutely shocked to find Miss Claggett's body in her trunk at the station last night."

"I'm sure that was indeed shocking, Mr. Castleberry. I must admit I was rather disturbed and shocked to hear about it myself."

"As was I," Mr. Castleberry said.

"Yes, well, I'm willing to take on the case, but of course I can make no guarantees as to the outcome or of your daughter's innocence. My fee is thirty dollars a day, plus expenses. One full day due in advance."

"I understand, and your terms are acceptable. I'm not a wealthy man, but I'm not impoverished, either. I'm an auditor for the city of Phoenix, and I do all right for myself and my family."

"Fair enough. Where and when may I meet you to discuss everything?"

"How about your office?" Mr. Castleberry said. "I could stop by after I'm finished here if you give me the address."

"I'm afraid I work out of my home, Mr. Castleberry. It keeps the overhead down, but you can certainly stop by my apartment later if you prefer."

"Hmm, no. Why don't you come to my office, then, in city hall? It's at 140 North Third Avenue. I have an opening at two o'clock this afternoon if that's acceptable to you."

"Yes, two o'clock should be fine, I'll see you then," Mason said, putting on his eyeglasses once more and jotting down the address and time on the notepad next to the phone. "Good day, Mr. Castleberry."

"Good day."

Mason returned the receiver to the cradle, tore off the paper with the address on it, put it in his wallet, and walked back into the dining area, where Lydia was still reading the paper.

"Does the article say anything else?" he said, taking off his eyeglasses once more and putting them back in his shirt pocket.

Lydia shook her head again as she set the newspaper down onto the table and sat back in her chair. "No, not really. It all sounds so grisly. It does say the victim was reportedly known by Miss Castle."

"Yes, she was."

Lydia stared up at Mason. "What do you mean?"

"I mean she *was* known by her. The victim was her former roommate."

"Have you gone psychic all of a sudden?"

Mason beamed. "No, that was Miss Castle's father on the phone. He wants to hire me to investigate. He believes his daughter is innocent."

"Of course he does, and he wants to hire you because you're the best private detective in Phoenix. What did you say?"

"I said yes, naturally. Because it's an interesting case. I'm to meet him downtown at his office in city hall at two this afternoon."

"And I'll be waiting for a full report at three. What does he do there?"

"He says he's an auditor."

"Interesting. Well, I want to know everything this Mr. Castle has to say," Lydia said.

"His name's Castleberry, actually. His daughter, Charlotte, shortened it, apparently. And you know I can't discuss my cases while the investigation is ongoing. I believe in client confidentiality."

"I know you do, and yet you do discuss them with me, most of the time, anyway. Because a woman's point of view can be very helpful, and I'm excellent at keeping secrets. I'm like Dr. Watson to your Sherlock Holmes."

Mason chuckled. "Only you're much more attractive than old Dr. Watson. Lydia Dettling, what would I do without you?"

"Let's hope you never have to find out."

Mason shook his head, his lips pursed. "Now what would Thad O'Connell say if he heard you talk like that?"

"Oh, you know what I mean. You and I are the best of friends. I can't imagine my life without you, Mason T. Adler, but I must admit Thad has certain charms you don't possess."

"I wouldn't say that, I think I can be quite charming. But I will admit he has interests I don't share."

"Like kissing me good night under the stars or going for a drive up Camelback mountain to look at the moon."

"And neck in the moonlight."

"Exactly."

"Naturally." He glanced at his watch. "It's coming eleven. I have to meet Walter at Diamond's downtown at one. I should be able to meet him and then go to Mr. Castleberry's office right from there."

"Whatever are you meeting Walter at Diamond's for?"

"He's going to help me pick out some new clothes."

"Walter? He has rather colorful taste."

"I know, believe me I know. But maybe he's right. Maybe my wardrobe could do with a bit of color. Besides, I'm trying to be more of a friend to him, and this was his idea."

"All right, but don't let him talk you into anything too outlandish."

"I'll do my best."

"And you can pick out something to wear Toby O'Connell would approve of."

Mason chuckled. "Perhaps, though that could be difficult. You did say he's the head clerk at a men's clothing store."

"I did, and he is. Want me to come with for moral support and a woman's opinion?"

"Thanks, but I don't think I could handle you *and* Walter in Diamond's at the same time, no offense. I'm meeting Emil after work for drinks at the Cactus Cantina later, too."

"My, you've certainly got a busy day."

"Yes. I set the meeting up with Emil just yesterday because I want to tell him about old Mr. Blanders's cabin. But the fact that Emil is the police detective on the case and we're meeting for drinks may actually be fortuitous."

"You mean, you may be able to pump him for information on this murder at Union Station."

"Possibly, Dr. Watson," Mason said with a sly grin.

"Well, you two are old friends, but you know Emil doesn't like you sticking your nose into police business, Sherlock."

"I do know that, but it's also *my* business, isn't it?"

"I suppose it will be when you meet up with Mr. Castleberry this afternoon."

"Exactly. By the way, when I went to answer the telephone, I had half a doughnut still on my plate, which is now empty."

"Oh, you must be mistaken," Lydia said innocently. "You probably ate it and just forgot."

Mason shook his head. "Not hardly, I'm not *that* old. You ate your doughnut *and* the other half of mine. Yours was plain but mine had chocolate sprinkles, and there are now chocolate sprinkles on your plate."

Lydia looked down at her plate and laughed. "Guilty as charged, once again. Like I said, you are a brilliant detective."

"Flatterer. Anyway, I'll just clean up these dishes and read that newspaper article for myself while I take a few notes, then I'll freshen up before I have to leave."

"Meaning my cue to exit, stage left. All right, love, call me later," she said, getting to her feet and smoothing out her dress.

"I will. And feel free to read my paper any time. Far better than stealing Mrs. Woodburn's."

"Borrowing, if you don't mind."

Mason laughed. "Like you borrowed the other half of my doughnut." He leaned down and gave her a peck on the cheek. "Have a good day, my good Watson."

Chapter Three

Early afternoon, Tuesday, May 7, 1946
Diamond's department store

Mason parked his slightly sun-faded blue 1939 Studebaker Champion on Second Street between Washington and Adams and walked into Diamond's department store on the corner of Second and Washington. He paused briefly inside to catch his breath and enjoy the conditioned air, which had been installed in 1931 at great expense and much fanfare. He hadn't shopped there in a while, but the directory showed him the men's department was still on the second floor, so he strode across the terrazzo floor and took the stairs two at a time, sidestepping an elderly woman in a peacock blue dress and matching hat as she made her way down slowly and cumbrously, clutching her new purchases.

When he reached the top of the stairs he noticed Walter Waverly Wingate perusing a display of imported neckties and silk handkerchiefs. Walter looked up as Mason approached. "There you are, Mason! It's almost one thirty. You're late."

Mason glanced at his wristwatch and then back at Walter, a solidly built little man, standing almost five foot six, though he claimed five foot eight. He was a bit thick around the middle and had light brown eyes, an average nose, and a well-trimmed, short brown mustache, turned up slightly at each end, that complemented his wavy brown hair, parted on the left side and combed over the top and back to cover a small bald spot on the crown of his head. "I'm not that late, Walter. We were supposed to meet at one, and it's just now five minutes past. I'd hardly say that's *almost* one thirty."

"Well, five minutes past is still late in my book. And *I've* been here nearly thirty minutes already." Walter looked Mason up and down. "Oh my, what a surprise, you're wearing a gray suit. What a refreshing change from all your other gray suits."

"Funny, Walter. I know you're always criticizing my lack of color in my wardrobe, which is why I'm here, so don't complain. And I see you're nattily dressed in your usual array of colors."

Walter beamed. "Thank you, I'm so glad you noticed."

"It's hard *not* to notice crimson trousers, a red and green plaid jacket, and a bright orange tie."

Walter did a brief twirl. "Isn't it, though? Anyway, enough about me for the time being, we're here to see what we can do with *you*."

"That's what I'm afraid of," Mason said with a grimace.

"Oh, tut, tut. You're in good hands, my darling. You're what, a forty-two long?"

"Generally, yes, and a fifteen and a half neck, thirty-five sleeve, thirty-three waist, and a thirty-five inseam."

Walter stuck his right thumb in his mouth. "Hmm, nothing directly off the rack, then. They don't stock clothes for you giraffe types, all neck and limbs and hardly any midsection at all."

"I happen to think giraffes are majestic, graceful, and quite attractive."

"So do other giraffes, I suppose, but regardless, we'll have to have everything fitted. Fortunately they do marvelous alterations here." He removed his thumb and gestured toward a small pile of clothes stacked on a nearby counter. "I took the liberty of picking out a few things before you arrived, since you were late." Walter picked up the stack of clothes and handed them to Mason, draping them over his left arm as he pointed across the department. "The dressing rooms are over there, next to that delicious-looking young man in the light blue jacket. Try these on for size and see what you think. Or better yet, I'll let you know what *I* think."

"Honestly, Walter," Mason said, moving the clothes from his left arm to his right.

"What?"

"Delicious-looking young man?" Mason said, his voice just above a whisper as he stepped closer to Walter.

"Well, he *is*, darling. Just look at him. Simply scrumptious."

"Yes, and he's all of twenty-three, I'd guess. You're going to get yourself into trouble in a multitude of ways if you're not careful."

"Yes, darling, of course. But I'm as careful as a long-tailed cat in a room full of rocking chairs, as they say. Now hurry up, I don't have all day, you know."

"Fine, but behave yourself out here," Mason said sternly, taking off his fedora. "Here, hold my hat."

"Do I look like a hat rack?"

"Only if hat racks are short, squat, colorful, and temperamental."

"Oh, you're hilarious. They have hooks in the dressing room you can hang your hat on."

"Where's yours?"

"I left mine in the car. I find it just gets in the way when I'm shopping. Now scoot, I want to see how these lovely clothes look on your giraffe body."

"All right, I'll be out in a few minutes." Mason walked over toward the dressing rooms while managing to steal a closer look at the handsome young man in the blue jacket. He was indeed attractive, Mason had to agree, but too young for his taste. When Mason sought out male company, he preferred the more mature ones. Still, the young man gave Mason a smile which Mason returned, knowing Walter was watching and probably green with envy. But before the fellow could strike up a conversation, Mason stepped into the first vacant dressing room on the right and closed the door behind him. A few minutes later Walter rapped upon that same door.

"Well? How's it coming? Don't keep me in suspense," Walter said.

"I'll be out in a minute, Walter."

"Oh fiddlesticks, I can't wait." Walter yanked open the dressing room door and stared at Mason's lower half. "Really, darling," he exclaimed. "What happened to the pants I gave you to try on? Bright white trousers before Memorial Day? And such a glaring shade of white, it hurts my eyes. Wherever did you get them? They weren't in the pile I gave you to try on."

Mason gave him a withering look. "Oh, Walter, you're so very droll. I haven't put the trousers on. These are my bare legs, and you know it. I just took my own trousers off."

Walter shook his head. "Oh dear, you really *do* need to get some color. You're as pale as a corpse. Say, I've a smashing idea. Why don't we spend a weekend soon in Palm Springs, California? Just the two of us."

"Please shut the door, Walter," Mason said as an older woman walked by, staring in at him, her mouth agape as Mason stood in his underwear.

Walter squeezed himself into the dressing room and closed the door. "All right, if you insist, but it's crowded in here, not much bigger than a phone booth."

"I *meant* step out and close the door behind you, and you know it."

"Fine, be modest if you like, but it's not like I haven't seen you undressed before. But do hurry up. I'm just dying to see how everything looks." Walter opened the door once more and backed out into the store before closing it again.

After a few minutes, Mason stepped out, too, now dressed in bright, pea green trousers, a black jacket, and a burnt orange tie decorated with little black diamonds. He glanced down at Walter. "Well?"

Walter's shiny brown eyes lit up like a new copper penny. "Ooh! I love it! The jacket is perfect—flapless pockets, and no vest. And the trousers with the single pleat and the three inch high waist are right in style."

Mason turned and looked at himself in the three-sided mirror. "Really? I don't know. The pants are awfully bright and flashy. They seem more you than me."

"Well, I *am* awfully bright, it's true, and you're rather dull, but we're trying to change that, aren't we? That's why I brought you to Diamond's. They have the best men's clothing department in Phoenix, you know."

"Yes, I do know. I've shopped here before, though it's been a while."

"Ugh, you mean you've shopped in the bargain basement, where all the ugly, boring clothes go to die. *This*," Walter said, gesturing at Mason's attire, "is fashion!"

Mason looked doubtful. "I'm not sure fashion and I go together. Besides, Lydia told me not to get anything too outlandish."

"Oh good grief, Miss Dettling likes anything that doesn't show the hair from that nasty cat of hers, Mr. Zut."

"Mr. Zester," Mason said. "And he's a sweet kitty."

"A kitty that sheds so much I'm surprised he's not bald. The last time I was over to her place with you, I had to send my entire wardrobe out to be cleaned and de-haired afterward, and I had a cardigan sweater made from the hair they removed."

"You're exaggerating."

"Perhaps, but I wouldn't take wardrobe advice from Lydia. That outfit you have on is divine!"

Mason studied himself in the full-length mirror once more. "Hmm, you really think so? But where would I wear it?"

"Every place you now wear your boring gray suits, my dear. Heads will turn."

"Of that I've no doubt, probably completely around. I don't mind the tie and the jacket, but I'm not sure about the pants, though they're better than the yellow and green plaid ones you gave me to try on. Those are *definitely* out."

"Your loss. Personally, I think they'd look smashing on you with a deep blue jacket and a patterned tie in yellows, greens, and blues, but trust me, you'll be the hit of Palm Springs in this getup you're wearing now."

"What's this about Palm Springs?" Mason said, still staring at his reflection.

"Honestly, weren't you listening? You need color, and not just in your wardrobe. You're as white as a ghost. And you need a little time away. A weekend in Palm Springs with yours truly will do you wonders. I happen to know the night manager of the Triada Palm Springs Hotel, you know."

"Do you now?"

"I do, intimately."

"Of course you do, and knowing you, biblically. Probably several times."

"Oh hush, we're just old friends, so to speak. I'm sure he can get us a charming room at a discounted rate. You know, Dinah Shore, Ginger Rogers, George Burns, Gracie Allen, and Howard Hughes all stay at the Triada, along with scores of other Hollywood movie stars."

"Really? Howard Hughes? He's rather dashing," Mason said quietly.

"And rich. Filthy, stinking rich, though rumor has it he's not one of us, at least not entirely."

"So I've heard, and keep your voice down," Mason said, glancing about.

"You are such a worrywart, honestly."

"And you don't worry enough. Phoenix is a small town, people talk."

"Which is exactly why we should get away to Palm Springs, of course, where we can make merry without worrying about anyone hearing or seeing us. We'll stay at the Triada, a room with two beds, of course, and dine at the Racquet Club and lie by the pool all day, while handsome young waiters in white jackets bring us drinks with little umbrellas in them, and little club sandwiches with fancy toothpicks stuck in the middle."

"Sounds nice, but expensive."

"Oh, who cares? You can afford it, I know you can. Besides, my friend the night manager will get us an excellent rate."

"So, I'd be footing the entire bill."

"Of course, darling, but it was my idea, and I *am* getting us the excellent rate. Or at least I will be."

"I see. Let me think on it. And let me think on these trousers. But the jacket and tie I'll take, I suppose."

"There's nothing to think about. I'll call Marvin at the Triada this afternoon when I get home. I think he gets on duty at four."

Mason turned to Walter and held up a hand. "Whoa, not so fast, my friend. I just signed on a new client today, or at least I will. I have to be to his office at two, and it's twenty minutes to already, so I need to hurry this up."

"A new client? Really? Do tell! Who's been cheating on who now and who's been sleeping with whom? Anyone I know?"

"It's nothing like that. Didn't you see the morning paper? The late edition?"

"Yes, of course I did. Why?"

"The headline about the woman in the trunk."

Walter's eyes grew wide, and his mustache twitched. "Oh! You don't mean that awful business down at the train station? Murder at Union Station? That poor woman decapitated, dismembered, and stuffed inside, with her head in a matching hatbox?"

"That's the article, Walter, but I don't recall it mentioning anything about the victim being decapitated or dismembered, or any matching hatbox with the head in it."

"Oh, well, no, perhaps not, but I seem to recall that's what happened with a similar case a few years ago. You know, that woman who murdered her friends back in the early thirties and took them with her on the train to California in her luggage? Anyway, when the bodies are dismembered, it just makes it easier to fit it all in."

Mason raised a brow as he stared at Walter. "You sound like you're speaking from experience."

Walter gave a half laugh, half giggle. "Oh, of course not, but I do read those thrillers, you know, and I've seen all those movies that keep me up at night and give me nightmares."

"I have a feeling this case is going to give me nightmares. That poor woman. As long as I live, I'll never understand how people can do such heinous things to each other."

"Oh, I know. It's almost enough to make me want to move to the mountains and live in a shack, well-decorated and furnished, of course."

"Of course. I'm afraid you wouldn't last long in a shack in the mountains, though, Walter. You're far too sociable."

"I could if I had someone to keep me company. I wonder where that delicious young man in the blue sport jacket wandered off to," Walter said, standing on his tiptoes and looking about.

"He probably hightailed it for the nearest exit when he saw you leering at him."

"Me? You're the one who was grinning at him like an idiot as you approached the dressing rooms. Don't think I didn't notice."

"Amazing you could see me smiling through the back of my head," Mason said.

"You turned your head to smile at him. And you nodded, too. I saw you."

"Then you also saw that *he* smiled at me first, and rather than engaging him, I went directly into the dressing room. He's not my type."

"Pity," Walter said. "He probably never noticed me over here, and when you brutally rejected him he went sulking off before I had a chance."

Mason rolled his eyes. "Yes, I'm sure that's the case."

"Of course it is. So anyway, who's your new client? A relative of the dismembered woman in the trunk?"

"Honestly, Walter, they never said she was dismembered. And no. The father of the woman who owned the trunk is the client. He works at city hall, and I'm to meet him there shortly."

"City hall? Impressive. In the mayor's office?"

"I don't think so, no. He told me he's a city auditor. Anyway, I'll just take the jacket and the tie, I think," Mason said, looking at his watch again. "I need to get going, I don't want to be late. And after I meet my new client, I'm supposed to catch up with Emil at the Cactus Cantina for drinks at four. Want to join us?"

"Thank you, but no. You know Emil annoys me, and besides, I have a potential new client consult of my own this afternoon with an irritating woman who wants me to decorate her husband's office. He's a lawyer, and quite successful. I'm picturing doing his office in something unexpected, something Greek, revolving around a replica of Michelangelo's statue of David, only he'd be holding a law book instead of a sling."

"That would be unexpected, all right," Mason said.

"Wouldn't it just? But sadly I have a feeling they'll both want something more traditional and boring. You know, like your apartment."

"I happen to like traditional, and I don't think my apartment's boring."

"Of course not, because *you're* traditional and boring. Anyway, I'm sure they're going to want me to do something stale, stuffy, and dark, with lots of old books on big, carved bookcases, oil paintings of dead barristers, etchings of horses, a massive mahogany desk, and large, oversized leather chairs everywhere."

"Which you'll give them if the price is right."

"Most certainly, darling, I always give my clients what they want. But I still might throw in a little something unexpected. After all, it's what I do. And speaking of that, you simply *can't* take the jacket and tie without the trousers. They're a package deal, and the trousers are unexpected." Walter whipped his head around, spotted a sales clerk, and snapped his fingers above his head. "Oh clerk! Over here, please."

Mason rolled his eyes. "You know I hate it when you do that."

"When you're my size, you do what is necessary to get attention."

"Yes, sir?" the clerk said, coming up to them.

"My friend here will take it all, on his account. Mason T. Adler."

"I don't have an account here, Walter."

"That's not a problem, sir," the clerk said, looking at Mason. "It's a simple matter to set one up."

"It is," Walter said. "I have accounts all over town. Naturally, the jacket sleeves will need to be let down, the trousers hemmed, and the waist taken in."

"Of course, sir. Did you want cuffs on the trousers, Mr. Adler?"

"Heavens no," Walter said, answering for Mason.

"But I like cuffs, Walter."

Walter gave Mason a stern look. "You won't see Cary Grant in cuffs this season."

"I'm sure I won't see Cary Grant at all this season. Or any other season, except on the movie screen."

"You might, when you whisk me off to Palm Springs for a fun-filled, sun-filled weekend. But nonetheless, no cuffs."

Mason sighed. "All right, Walter, no cuffs."

The clerk raised his eyebrows ever so slightly. "Very good, sir. If you'll just turn and face the mirror, I'll pin the jacket and trousers for you."

"Fine, but I'm in a hurry," Mason said, turning once more toward the mirror.

"Of course, sir. Everything should be ready by Thursday afternoon."

"Great, but I meant I'm in a hurry right now. I have an appointment at city hall at two."

The clerk looked suitably impressed. "Oh, I see, sir. Very well, this shouldn't take but a few moments. Please stand still until I'm finished."

"All right," Mason said.

"I'll take care of setting up your account, Mason, while you get fitted and then change back into your dull, gray outfit. And since you're such a busy man, I'll even pick the clothes up on Thursday and deliver them to you personally at your apartment."

"Actually, sir," the clerk said to Walter, "we ask that the customer try the items on after alterations in case any last-minute adjustments are needed."

"If any last-minute adjustments are needed, we'll come back, but I'm sure they'll be fine," Walter said. "Now hurry up and do your markings or whatever it is you do. My friend here has an appointment at city hall!"

CHAPTER FOUR

Mid-afternoon, Tuesday, May 7, 1946
Phoenix City Hall

At ten minutes to two, Mason and Walter exited Diamond's together, Mason putting his hat back on and tugging it low as he handed his claim check for his new clothes to Walter, who put it in an inside pocket.

"Thanks for saying you'll pick up my new clothes, Walter. The idea of trying them all on again and having that clerk make a fuss drives me mad."

"Happy to do it, darling, but of course you *will* have to try them all on again when I bring them over on Thursday, and I *will* make a fuss, you can count on it."

Mason chuckled. "At least I'm used to your fusses."

"Good, I think," Walter said, shading his eyes with his right hand as he looked up at Mason. "Oh, I shouldn't have left my hat in the car. This sun and heat are beastly, and all this squinting will give me crow's feet."

"The price you pay for not bringing it in with you."

"I suppose, but it's just always in the way. Oh well, I can hardly wait to see you in that outfit when the alterations are finished."

"It will be a sight, I'm sure."

"You'll be absolutely divine. Where did you park?"

"Just up the street here. You?"

"The same," Walter said, still shading his eyes with one hand while he fanned his face with his other. "Honestly, it's too early in the year for it to be this hot."

"Supposed to be a high of 104 today, so try not to melt," Mason said as they started down the sidewalk.

"I'll do my best, darling. It was worth the trek out, though, I suppose, to get you some decent apparel. And it was nice seeing you, even if we were rather rushed." Walter tried to keep pace with Mason's long stride while also staying in his shadow and out of the sun as best he could.

"Yes, sorry about having to hurry off. This new client just came up this morning."

"Of course, after that grisly murder last night."

"Right. Anyway, it was good seeing you again, too, Walter. Oh, and, uh, thanks for the fashion advice."

"You're most welcome, my tall friend. You needed it."

"I suppose it wouldn't hurt to add a little color to my wardrobe," Mason said, stopping as they came alongside his Studebaker. "Here's my car, and just in time. It's almost two o'clock."

"Yes, you have an appointment at city hall. The clerk at Diamond's was suitably impressed."

"Well, it's the truth. I didn't say it to impress him."

"Of course you didn't, but it did nonetheless. Anyway, do let me know how it goes, won't you? I'm just dying to hear what you find out. That poor woman, all chopped to bits."

Mason shook his head. "Honestly, Walter, what am I going to do with you?" he said, stepping out into the street to the driver's side door.

"Whisk me away to Palm Springs for a fun-filled weekend, I hope," Walter said, still shielding his eyes.

"We'll see. I must dash," Mason said, climbing in behind the wheel.

"All right, call me. Ta."

Mason gave him a wave, started the engine, and drove off hurriedly, driving the short distance from Diamond's department store to Phoenix City Hall, which was a beautiful brick and terra-cotta structure completed in 1928 and located at 125 West Washington

Avenue. He parked in the relative shade of two towering palm trees on Washington, left the car windows down a few inches, and walked around the corner. He couldn't help but notice a decent-sized group of men, many of them with cameras about their necks, milling about the Third Street doors, talking with each other and smoking cigarettes. They stared at Mason, shook their heads, and then went back to what they were doing. Mason found their behavior odd, but since he was short on time, he pressed forward through the glass doors, held open by a middle-aged man in a security uniform. His name badge read *Clarence Grimm.*

"Thank you," Mason said to him. "Who are all those men outside?"

"Reporters, sir. They've been out there all day in this heat, since early this morning. I have to admire their determination, tenacity, and steadfastness, but they are a bit of a nuisance."

"Ah, because of last night's murder at Union Station and Mr. Castleberry's connection to it."

"Yes, sir."

"I'm here to see Mr. Castleberry, actually. I have an appointment with him at two. Do you know where his office is?"

Clarence eyed Mason suspiciously. "How do I know you're not one of those reporters?"

Mason shrugged. "You don't, I suppose. But trust me, I'm not."

"Hmm. There's a directory over by the elevators. You'll find him listed."

Mason looked where the man was pointing and tipped his hat. "Thanks."

"You're welcome, sir. But if I find out you *are* one of those reporters, being sneaky…"

Mason didn't wait for him to finish but instead hurried across the shiny terrazzo floor to the directory and found Mr. Castleberry's office listed as being on the third floor. With no time to waste, he bypassed the elevator and hurried up the two flights of stairs, two at a time. He walked quickly to the city auditor's office, room 304, arriving at exactly two p.m., just slightly out of breath.

"Good afternoon," he said to the youngish woman seated at the desk in the outer office as he removed his hat. The nameplate next to her typewriter read *Miss Gleason*. "I'm here to see Mr. Castleberry."

"You and everyone else today," she said dryly, looking up at him with a curious frazzled expression as the telephone on her desk began to ring. She held up one finger in Mason's direction. "One moment, please." She picked up the receiver and stabbed a button on the base of the telephone with her index finger. "Mr. Castleberry's office. Who's calling? No, he's not in, and I don't expect him back today. *No.*" She hung up the receiver firmly, shook her head, and looked back up at Mason suspiciously. "Are you a member of the press?"

"Please believe me, I'm not," Mason said.

"Is he expecting you?"

"Hmm? Ah, yes, yes. I have an appointment at two o'clock," he said.

"Your name?"

"Er, Mr. Adler, Mason Adler. As I said, I have an appointment, so I'm confused if he's left for the day."

She shoved a strand of dyed-black hair behind her right ear and let out a breath. "Right, sorry, Mr. Adler. It's been a madhouse here today. He told me to expect you. Just a moment." She picked up the telephone receiver again, pushed another button, waited, and then spoke in that same, exasperated tone. "Mr. Adler to see you, sir. Right." She hung up the telephone and looked up at Mason again. "Go right in." She pointed with her pencil over her left shoulder.

"Thank you, miss," Mason said, giving her a smile that was not returned as her telephone began to ring again.

He walked past her and entered the door marked *A. Castleberry* in gold letters on the glass, closing it behind him. A middle-aged man with silver hair and a round, pale face sat behind the small, cluttered desk. He got quickly to his feet and extended his hand.

"Ah, Mr. Adler, right on time."

"Good afternoon, Mr. Castleberry," Mason said, taking the man's soft hand in his, giving it a brief shake, and then dropping his own hand to his side.

"Yes, good afternoon. Thank you for coming. This is all most distressing. I honestly don't know why I even came into the office today. I can't focus on anything, I just keep thinking about my poor daughter."

"That's understandable, of course. And of poor Miss Claggett, I'm sure."

"Hmm? Oh, yes, of course, of course. Simply horrible. I just can't understand why anyone would do such a thing," Mr. Castleberry said.

"Nor I, but I hope to at least discover who did."

"Yes, exactly. That's why I'm hiring you."

"Did you know Gertrude Claggett?"

"No, not really. I only met Miss Claggett once or twice, but she always seemed pleasant enough. Please, have a seat."

"Thank you." Mason sat on one of the wooden chairs opposite the desk and placed his hat on the other, while Mr. Castleberry seated himself once more in his own oversized leather chair, his back to the solitary window. He leaned forward toward Mason, his elbows on the desktop, his hands supporting his double chin. He looked weary and tired.

"What is the current status of your daughter, Mr. Castleberry?"

"Her status?"

"I mean, how is she holding up, where is she staying, that sort of thing."

"Oh, yes. She's quite upset, naturally, and she's staying with her mother and me, back at home in her old room. I know Charlotte is innocent, Mr. Adler. She and Miss Claggett didn't always get along, and they did have a little disagreement not long ago, but Charlotte would never kill anyone."

"The same has been said about many killers over the years, Mr. Castleberry."

"What's that supposed to mean?"

"No offense, sir, but most killers were thought not to be killers initially. And most anyone *could* kill, under the right circumstances."

"That may be so, Mr. Adler, but I assure you it doesn't apply to my daughter. I want to hire you to find the real killer, not suggest that she actually did this horrible thing."

"Of course, and I hope to find the murderer, but naturally I can make no guarantees."

"What if the murderer is never found? Or if the police solve the case before you do? What happens then?"

"You may terminate our agreement at any time, Mr. Castleberry. However, my fee is payable up until then regardless of the outcome of the investigation. And speaking of that, as I told you on the telephone, my fee is thirty dollars a day plus expenses, and the first day is due in advance."

"All right, that's agreeable to me. I have the thirty dollars here in this envelope," he said, pointing with a well-manicured finger to a white envelope atop a pile of papers. "I assume cash is acceptable?"

"Of course. Do you wish a receipt?"

"That won't be necessary," Mr. Castleberry said, picking up the envelope and handing it to Mason, who placed it in his inside jacket pocket. "I trust you, as a gentleman."

"Thank you."

"I noticed you didn't count it," Mr. Castleberry said.

"I trust you, as a gentleman."

"Indeed. Then we understand each other. Since it's two o'clock already and the day is half over, how do you determine your complete fee, if I may ask?"

"A fair question. I charge by the twenty-four hour period and any portion thereof. Therefore, if I should conclude my investigation by two p.m. tomorrow or sooner, you would owe no more than the thirty dollars you've already paid, plus any expenses I may incur."

"Reasonable expenses, I assume."

"Of course," Mason said, crossing his legs at the knee and leaning back as he studied Mr. Castleberry. He was clearly suited to his job as city auditor. He was well dressed, in an expensive-looking tan suit with a dark brown and red tie. He was clean shaven and had deep-set, round dark brown eyes on either side of a long, narrow nose.

"I'll present an itemized bill for your perusal at the conclusion of my investigation," Mason said.

Mr. Castleberry took his elbows off the desktop and leaned back in his chair, which creaked accordingly. "Acceptable. I'm sorry to be so particular in regard to the terms. It's just that I want to know exactly what I'm paying for. As I said to you this morning, you have a reputation for solving difficult cases, and I must say this one is completely baffling and shocking, not only to me but apparently to everyone who's heard about it. Miss Gleason has been screening my calls and visitors all day. Reporters from not only the local papers but also state and nationwide have been pestering me relentlessly."

"It is a shocking murder, Mr. Castleberry. I read the story in the *Arizona Republic* this morning, of course, but I only trust what I read so far. I prefer to do my own investigating. I'm skeptical of the press, and of sensationalism."

"I'm glad to hear it. Of course this all brings to mind the similar case from 1931, as I'm sure you remember, which is partly why the press is going crazy over it. That insane woman who shot her two friends to death and stuffed them in her luggage, taking the bodies with her to California."

"It's hard to forget."

"Yes it is, unfortunately. The detective who questioned Charlotte last night couldn't help but bring that case up. He seems to think, or at least he implied, that Charlotte was doing the same thing as that crazy woman. I assure you, Mr. Adler, my daughter is not insane, nor is she a murderer."

"I suppose it's only natural to compare the two cases, though," Mason said, taking out his notebook and pencil. "You mentioned that your daughter and Miss Claggett were roommates. How long had they lived together?"

"Just shy of a year, I think. They met here, actually, at city hall. Charlotte and Gertrude were both working in the typing pool, though Miss Claggett was here just part-time. Charlotte was anxious to assert her independence from her mother and me, and Gertrude was looking for a new roommate, so Charlotte moved out of our house and in with her. We weren't wild about the idea, but Charlotte can be stubborn, and she is over twenty-one, if just barely."

"You mentioned Charlotte and Gertrude had had a disagreement. What was that about?"

"Actually they had several disagreements during the time they lived together, from what I understand, but nothing major. Charlotte told me the latest was about Miss Claggett's boyfriend, John Patterson. Gertrude felt Charlotte flirted with him when he'd come to their apartment to visit Miss Claggett."

"Did she?"

Mr. Castleberry snorted and laughed through his nose. "I highly doubt it. Charlotte's not the type to flirt with other women's men. Besides, she's focused on other things right now, like moving out to Los Angeles and getting settled, which is why she was at the train station last night."

"Did you ever meet Mr. Patterson?"

Mr. Castleberry leaned forward again, resting his elbows once more on top of the desk and placing his fingertips together to form a steeple. "Just once, briefly. He seemed pleasant enough and not a bad-looking sort. Charlotte told me that Gertrude said she hoped he'd propose to her soon."

"I see. He must be devastated over Gertrude's death."

"Mr. Patterson? Yes, certainly, I'm sure. I haven't spoken with him since the, uh, incident, though. I've only met him once, as I said, but I'm sure you'll be talking to him as part of your investigation. Please extend my condolences."

"I'll do that, Mr. Castleberry. Do you happen to know where he lives or works?"

"Not really, though Charlotte probably does."

"All right, I'll make a point to ask her. You mentioned earlier Charlotte was at the train station last night because she was moving to California."

"Yes, that's right. She plans to live with my sister in Los Angeles. She wants to try her hand at acting in the movies. My wife and I tried to talk her out of it, but as I said before, Charlotte is a very stubborn girl. I admit she's pretty and marginally talented, but I'm afraid she'll get her hopes dashed out there. Anyway, she bought a ticket for the night train to L.A., packed her bags and trunk, and I picked her up from her apartment at five."

"Did you go up to the apartment? Did you see Miss Claggett?"

"No, I buzzed from the front door of the building, and Charlotte came down to meet me. I took her to our house, we had dinner, then I drove her to Union Station."

"Along with her bags and the trunk?"

"No, she left those in the apartment. She'd arranged for a porter from the station to pick them up."

"About what time did you leave her at the station?"

"The train was supposed to leave at midnight, so I dropped her off close to eleven thirty. I parked and saw her safely inside. I wanted to wait with her, but she sent me on my way, telling me she wasn't a little girl anymore. So I made sure she had her ticket, told her to be careful, and gave her five dollars for expenses along the way. After she promised to call us when she arrived in L.A., I gave her a kiss on the cheek and I left."

"What happened next?" Mason said, making copious notes.

"I went home. It was late, I was tired, and my wife was waiting up. We went to bed and were fast asleep when the telephone rang. When I answered, I was quite surprised to find it was Charlotte. She was nearly hysterical, asking me to come pick her up and bring her home."

"And you did."

"That's right, Millicent and I both did. Millie is my wife, and she insisted on coming with me. We picked Charlotte up and brought her back to our house, but none of us slept a wink the rest of the night, I'm afraid. I debated not coming into the office at all today, but I had several appointments to attend to, one of which was you, of course, and I thought it best to keep to my normal routine as much as possible, at least for now."

"That's a wise course of action."

"I thought so at the time, but after the barrage of phone calls, telegrams, and attempted visits from members of the press, I'm not so sure. Of course, poor Millicent told me they've been calling the house, too. She's taken the phone off the hook for the time being. If I need to reach her, I have to call the neighbor's and they have to go next door and get her."

"I'm sure things will settle down soon, Mr. Castleberry."

"I certainly hope so. My wife and I, and of course Charlotte, are all nervous wrecks." Mr. Castleberry rubbed his bloodshot eyes and picked up a pitcher of water, pouring it into a tumbler next to his telephone. "Would you care for some water, Mr. Adler?"

"No, thank you. I would like to speak with your daughter at some point, though."

Mr. Castleberry took out an aspirin tin from his desk drawer, retrieved two tablets, and popped them into his mouth, followed by a drink of water. "Yes, I assumed you would. I asked her to meet with us here at two thirty." He glanced at his watch. "She should be here by now, actually."

"You are a thorough man, Mr. Castleberry."

"Being an auditor requires me to be, and it carries over to all aspects of my life, for better or worse." The telephone on his desk buzzed just then, and he picked up the receiver abruptly. "Yes? Good, send her in." He replaced the receiver and looked at Mason. "This is her now."

Mr. Castleberry got to his feet as Mason did the same, both looking expectantly at the door to the outer office, which was opened by a tall, pretty blonde with broad shoulders. She was dressed in a short-sleeved green print dress with a white collar and belt, and she wore a wide-brimmed white hat with a green velvet ribbon.

"Hello, Charlotte, thank you for coming, please come in and close the door." She did as instructed and then looked blankly at her father and Mason. She was clearly tired and nervous, like her father.

"Hello, Father," she said. "Sorry I'm a few minutes late. I took a cab here, and there were a few reporters outside the house shouting questions at me and taking pictures. Then when I got here I had to come up the service elevator. Clarence was kind enough to come to my rescue."

"Rescue?" Mr. Castleberry said, puzzled.

"There are several overeager reporters outside here, too, that

Clarence is keeping at bay, or trying to, anyway. The moment I stepped out of the cab they rushed toward me, shouting questions, taking pictures, and trying to follow me into the building. I'm not sure how they knew who I was."

Adam Castleberry scowled. "Someone tipped them off, like they were tipped off that I'm your father. Maybe someone at the train station, or perhaps Mrs. Wilson across the street from our house. She's such a busybody."

"I did notice her peeking through the curtains when I got into the cab," Charlotte said.

"I'm sorry about all that, my dear, I should have warned you to come in the back way. The reporters have been outside all day."

"And buzzing about the house like nasty little flies. I just wish they'd leave us alone."

"So do I, dear," Mr. Castleberry said, pointing at Mason. "This is Mr. Adler, the private detective I was telling you about."

"How do you do, Miss Castleberry?"

"Clearly not all that well, to be honest, Mr. Adler, and it's Miss Castle. I shortened it recently for the movies."

"Oh yes, your father mentioned that. Charlotte Castle has a nice ring to it. I'm sure it would look smashing on a theater marquee."

"Thanks, I think so. Charlotte Castle and Tyrone Power, starring in a new adaptation of *Wuthering Heights*. Wouldn't that be wonderful?"

Her father cleared his throat. "Yes, well, first you have to get to California and see what happens. Won't you sit down, dear?"

"All right." Mason retrieved his hat, and she took the empty chair next to him, and then Mason and Mr. Castleberry took their seats as well, Mason now holding his hat on his lap.

"As I told you this morning, Charlotte, I've hired Mr. Adler to investigate Gertrude's death. He of course wants to ask you a few questions."

"I suppose," she said. "if you feel it will help." Her eyes were deep blue, like the ocean, her lips bright red, like fresh drawn blood, and she had fingernails to match. She had long, shapely legs and quite a curvaceous figure.

"I'll try to be as brief as possible, Miss Castleberry, er, Miss Castle," Mason said. "I'm sure this has all been, and continues to be, traumatic. I'm so sorry for what happened to Miss Claggett, your friend."

"Thank you, but Gertrude wasn't really my friend, Mr. Adler. We were roommates, and acquainted, of course. We also worked together in the typing pool here, but we were very different people. Nonetheless, it has been indeed stressful and traumatic."

"Of course. Would you mind telling me exactly what happened last night?"

"Well, I finished packing my bags and the, uh, trunk, with my clothes and belongings and left them in the living room of my apartment. I called Union Station and asked them to send someone over for them. Gertie told me she'd be home and would let the porter in to get my bags. I gave her a quarter for the tip, then Dad came just a few minutes before five, and we went back to the house so we could all have dinner and I could say goodbye to Mother."

"And when your father buzzed from the building's front door, you went down to meet him, is that right?"

"That's right. Mom and I did up the dishes after dinner, then we played cards and listened to the radio until it was time to go to the station. Mom cried and hugged me, I cried, too, I must admit, then Dad and I left. He dropped me at Union Station a little after eleven."

"And then what?"

"Well, I was sitting on one of the long wooden benches, reading the *Life Magazine* I'd bought and waiting for my train. Then I heard my name being called from the loudspeaker overhead. It was so surprising and strange. I got up and went to a porter and identified myself, and he told me to wait while he hurried away. At the same time the Sunset Limited was arriving, and I didn't know what to do or what to think. Then an older man who identified himself as the station manager came up to me and asked me to come with him to the baggage room, as there was a question about my trunk. I was most annoyed at first, as I was afraid I was going to miss my train, but he was insistent, so I reluctantly followed him. When we got to the baggage room, he asked me what was in my trunk, which seemed ridiculous. I told him it contained my clothes and personal items, not that it was any of his business. He asked me to open the trunk and that's when I noticed the lock was broken. Still, I opened it, and I couldn't believe it, I still can't. Poor Gertrude. She was all blue and bloated, her hair all matted down, and dead."

Charlotte shuddered at the memory and dabbed at her eyes with a handkerchief she had produced from her white handbag. "I nearly fainted from the shock, and I think I screamed. It's a sight I'll never forget, unfortunately. It made me quite sick to my stomach, and I had to use the ladies' room. When I came out, the station manager took me back to his office, got me some water, and called the police and some detective, who questioned me at length. Of course, I missed my train. When they finally released me, I called my father and told him to come and get me."

"Yes, your father told me. Did Miss Claggett have any family that you know of?" Mason said, scribbling away on a fresh page of his notebook.

"Only her younger brother, Josiah. He'd been sleeping on our sofa until recently. Gertrude's boyfriend, John Patterson, eventually took him in. Gertrude always worried about her brother."

"Oh? Why is that?"

"He's a bit different. He's smart but not very bright, and he's easily influenced. He goes from menial job to menial job, sometimes gets himself in trouble, and Gertrude always helps him out. I'm not sure *what* he's going to do now, or if he even knows what's happened yet. Poor J.P."

"J.P.?" Mason said.

"Yes, J.P. That's her brother, Josiah. His full name is Josiah Paul Claggett. I'm told that as a child Gertrude had trouble saying Josiah, so she called him J.P., and it stuck."

"Ah, I see. That was kind of her boyfriend to take him in. Had Mr. Patterson and Gertrude been courting long?"

"About seven or eight months. He was dating another girl who works here, but he dumped her when he met Gertrude. She got him a job in the office of the Lost Souls Mission over on Nineteenth Street. Gert worked there full-time Wednesday through Sunday, and part-time here at city hall in the mornings, Monday through Friday, which was fine by me 'cause I had the apartment to myself most of the time."

"Sounds like she kept herself pretty busy."

"She always said something about idle hands and the devil. That's just how she was."

"Interesting. Do you happen to know where Mr. Patterson lives?"

"Some place on Third Street, a little stucco house. I can't remember the exact address, though. Oh, wait! Gert had me drop her off there last week after work when she was running late. I wrote his address down in my notebook." She opened her white handbag once more and rummaged around before taking out a brown leather notepad and flipping it open a few pages. "Yes, here it is, 127 South Third Street."

"Thanks," Mason said, jotting it down into his own notebook. "What about Gertrude's parents?"

"She never talked about them. I think they're dead, but I'm not really sure."

"Any friends?"

She shook her petite head, her wide-brimmed hat moving with it. "Not many. She kept to herself mostly, and she was difficult. Not well liked, I'm afraid."

"Difficult in what way?"

"Oh, Gert was very critical of nearly everyone. She didn't approve of smoking or drinking, or too much makeup, or revealing clothes, or staying out late, or girls going out on their own, or popular music, dancing too close, or just about anything fun."

"Charlotte, really. I hope you're not doing any of those things," Mr. Castleberry said, shocked.

"Oh, Dad, honestly. This is 1946, not 1916. Things have changed since you were in your twenties."

"That may well be, but still—"

"So, she didn't have any friends that you know of, Miss Castle?" Mason said, interrupting Mr. Castleberry.

"No, not really. Though she was friendly with Julia Powell for a time. Julia works in the typing pool here, too. She started about a year ago. The three of us, Julia, Gert, and me, got to know each other, more or less. Julia's the one Mr. Patterson was dating before he met Gert. Julia actually introduced Gertie to John, and then John broke up with Julia to date Gert."

"I see. That must have created some hard feelings. By the way, I understand you and Miss Claggett had a disagreement about Mr. Patterson," Mason said.

"Who told you that?"

"I, uh, may have mentioned it, Charlotte," Mr. Castleberry said, reaching for his glass of water once more.

"Really, Father, I'd hardly call it a disagreement."

"What would you call it, Miss Castle?" Mason said.

"I don't know. It was nothing, really. She thought I was interested in John, in Mr. Patterson, I mean, and vice versa, and it annoyed her."

"Were you, are you, interested in him?"

"Don't be ridiculous. He's not my type. But like I said, she seemed to think he had the hots for me."

"But you don't think he did?"

"I don't know, maybe he did, but I assure you I wasn't interested in him, in spite of what Gertrude thought. She was just jealous, that's all. If I so much as said hello to him when he came to visit Gert, she'd get her nose out of joint, so she preferred going to his place rather than him coming to ours, and she was over there pretty much anytime she wasn't working or sleeping. John's neighbors probably assumed she was his wife."

"Okay. Can you think of anyone who may have wanted to harm your roommate, Miss Castle?"

"Not really, no. She was just your average, typical girl, a little on the dull side, actually, and like I said, rather severe. She would have been prettier with a little makeup and some nicer clothes, but she refused. She had nice enough hair, too, but she never did anything with it, which made her look older than she was."

"Quite different from you, it sounds like."

"Most definitely, and don't start, Dad," she said, shooting her father a look before turning back to Mason. "Gertrude was very religious, pious, proper. She didn't approve of me wanting to be an actress and a singer, and she didn't approve of some of the men I dated, the clothes I wore, or some of the things I did."

"Did she get along with her brother?"

"As a brother and sister do, I suppose, though I'm an only child, so I wouldn't really know. He's a bit on the dim side, as I believe I mentioned, but he could also be super smart. I know she got frustrated with him from time to time. She told me J.P. was going to come over Monday because she wanted to talk to him about something. He and Gertrude fought a lot when he was staying with us, and I'm told the neighbors complained about the noise."

"What did they fight about?"

"Oh little things, usually. His lack of responsibility, his drinking, things like that. Oh, and his gambling. He's addicted to alcohol and to gambling, I think, and that infuriated Gert. She made him promise to stop, and he swore he would."

"Did he?"

"As far as I know, at least for a while. You know, I kinda like him. Not in a romantic way, but he can be funny, and to be honest, I enjoyed that he irritated Gertrude so much. He was always quoting statistics and facts, too, and that's another thing that drove her bananas."

"You said he was going to go to see his sister on Monday afternoon because she wanted to talk to him about something. Do you know what that was about?"

"No, sorry, I don't, Gert never said, only that he was coming over sometime after five. I got the impression she wanted to wait until I was gone and didn't want to discuss it with me. She was a private person."

"Was there anyone else you know of that Miss Claggett didn't care for, or that didn't care for her?"

Miss Castle looked thoughtful. "Gee, I don't know. Like I said, Gert and I weren't exactly close, and we didn't talk much. There was a thing with the two women who own and run the building we lived in, though, Mrs. Comstock, and her sister, Miss Lucille Evans."

"What about them?"

"Well, Miss Evans seemed to take a liking to Gertrude, though why she did is beyond me. Miss Evans was very friendly to her, *very* friendly. She was always bringing her baked goods or flowers from her garden or just coming by to chat over coffee. And she let J.P. stay with us, though it was against the rules, and she didn't hound us when we were late on our rent."

"That certainly sounds like she was thoughtful," Mason said.

"I suppose so, but Miss Evans was always touching Gertrude's arm, or stroking her long auburn hair and making comments about Gertrude's figure, what there was of it, and saying things like how pretty she was."

"And that upset Gertrude?"

"Not at first," Charlotte said, "but it certainly bothered Mrs. Comstock. Gert gave Miss Evans a crucifix on a gold chain once, to thank her for all the nice things she'd been doing, and I heard Miss Evans and Mrs. Comstock had quite a row over it."

"How curious," Mason said.

"I was puzzled at first, too. It took a while for me to figure it out, I must admit, and when I did, I didn't dare tell Gertrude, as I knew she'd be very upset."

"What exactly did you figure out, Miss Castle? About Mrs. Comstock and her sister, I mean," Mason said.

"That they weren't *really* sisters at all, of course. I seriously doubt Mrs. Comstock was even ever married. They just pretended to be sisters. It's all so clear now, I'm amazed I didn't see it immediately. They don't even really look alike. Mrs. Comstock is a bit on the manly side, large, and strong, with big hands and short fingernails. Miss Evans is much smaller and softer, more feminine, and obviously much younger."

"I'm afraid I don't understand," Mr. Castleberry said from across his desk. "Why would they pretend to be sisters? For what purpose?"

Charlotte looked across the desk and rolled her eyes. "Oh, Father, really. Sometimes you can be so naïve. Because they're a couple."

"A couple?" Mr. Castleberry said, cocking his head. "A couple of what?"

"A romantic couple, Dad. They don't like men. They like each other, romantically."

"Oh," he said, trying to process this information. "Oh! Oh my, well I never..."

"Really, Dad, honestly. You and Gertrude are two of a kind sometimes."

"But even if they were, as you say, romantic with each other, why would they pretend to be sisters? I'm afraid I don't get that part at all," Charlotte's father said, perplexed.

"To avoid suspicion, Mr. Castleberry," Mason said. "Fairly common. Unmarried sisters living together don't come under the same scrutiny that unmarried non-sisters would, especially older women. The same goes for men. Some homosexual couples pretend to be brothers in order to live together."

"Hmm, I suppose. Seems odd, though," he said, scratching his chin.

"Gertrude thought it was odd, too, and then some," Charlotte said. "She finally figured it out a few days ago and was pretty steamed I hadn't told her when she found out I already knew. She told me Mrs. Comstock and Miss Evans were vile and sick, and that they were going to burn in hell. She also told me, *and* them, that she was going to report them to the police. She told me she wished she'd never given Miss Evans that necklace, because she was a sinner and didn't deserve it."

"And how did the two women react to Gertrude's statement?"

"Like you'd expect, I suppose. Mrs. Comstock got angry and told Gert she'd tear up her lease and throw her out, and Miss Evans cried, I'm sure."

"Do you know for certain that what you say about Mrs. Comstock and Miss Evans is true?" Mason said.

"You mean that they're queer?"

"Honestly, Charlotte, you shouldn't talk like that," Mr. Castleberry said.

"Yes, Miss Castle, that's what I mean, but lesbian is the correct term, not queer. Do you know for certain that they were?" Mason said, ignoring her father.

"I didn't at first, but then Gert showed me a little poem Miss Evans had written her, and it all made sense. And when Gertrude confronted Mrs. Comstock when she came by to fix our stove, she didn't deny any of it. I was in the bedroom at the time and could hear every word."

"Interesting. And how do *you* feel about Mrs. Comstock and Miss Evans?" Mason said, curious.

"Honestly? It doesn't bother me. But what I can't figure out is what Miss Evans saw in Gertrude. I mean, Gert is, was, I guess I should say, no more than five foot tall, and weighed about ninety pounds, with a small bosom and no hips to speak of. She practically looked like a teenage boy going through puberty. And there I was, well, I mean look at me," she gestured with her hands up and down her body, "and Miss Evans never batted an eye in my direction."

"Charlotte, of course you're a lovely girl, but you say that like you're disappointed this strange woman didn't make a pass at you," her father said.

"Well, truly, Dad, it didn't help my ego any."

"Charlotte!"

"Oh, Dad, don't be a knucklehead."

"Don't call your father a knucklehead," Mr. Castleberry said, annoyed.

"Ah, I'd like to have a look around your former apartment," Mason said, interrupting the two of them. "Would you still happen to have the key, Miss Castle?"

She turned and looked at the detective. "No, I gave it and the building key back to Miss Evans just before I left. She was out on the stoop watering her flowers. That was right after I had said goodbye to Gertrude upstairs. That was the last time I saw Gert. Alive, that is," Miss Castle said, with a quiet shudder once more. "But there's an extra apartment key hidden on the ledge above the door to the trash chute in the hall. We put it there just in case we ever got locked out. Our apartment was 3A, in the Evans Comstock Residence for Young Ladies, on Roosevelt, just a few blocks east of Trinity Episcopal Cathedral."

Mason jotted that into his notebook, too. "Good. I'll stop by later today, then, if you don't mind. But first I want to have a chat with a friend of mine." Mason got to his feet and Mr. Castleberry did the same.

"Thank you for coming by, Mr. Adler. I assume you'll be in touch?" Mr. Castleberry said.

"Naturally. I'll keep you posted with any developments. It was nice to meet you, sir, and you, Miss Castle."

"Likewise," she said, looking up at him.

"I'm sure the police have advised you not to leave town at present, Miss Castle," Mason said, putting his notebook and pencil away.

Miss Castle made a face. "Ugh, yes, they certainly did. That nasty police detective clearly thinks I killed Gert, which is absolutely ridiculous. Please bring this investigation to a swift conclusion, Mr. Adler."

"I'll do my best," he said.

She shook her head and bit her lower lip. "I hardly have a thing to wear now, you know. The police don't seem to know what happened to all my clothes that were in the trunk, and they confiscated my suitcases and everything that was in them, too."

"I'm sure you'll get your suitcases back in due time, and perhaps your clothes will turn up yet," Mason said. "Good day." He put his hat back on and left the office, noting the time was four minutes to three.

Mason took the stairs back down to the lobby, where he noticed a fairly attractive platinum blond woman dressed in a tight blue skirt and matching jacket that showed off her curvaceous figure and legs getting off one of the elevators.

"Good afternoon, Miss Powell," Clarence the security officer said to her, tipping his hat.

"Hello, Clarence. I almost dread being finished with work and having to go back outside. Another hot one today," she said.

"Yes, indeed. I wish I had conditioned air at home like they do here at city hall. Sometimes I'm tempted to just sleep here."

Miss Powell laughed. "I know the feeling. And to be honest, I know a couple people who've done just that."

"You know that's against the rules, Miss Powell, so I didn't hear a word you just said."

"Fair enough, and for the record, I've thought about it, too, but I haven't done it. Yet."

"Again, I can't hear a word you're saying," Clarence said with a gentle grin.

She laughed again. "Then read my lips as I say 'good afternoon' to you, and have a pleasant evening. I'll see you tomorrow." She turned and headed for the doors, but Mason moved quickly and cut her off, placing himself between her and the doors.

"Excuse me, would you happen to be Miss Powell? Miss Julia Powell?"

"Oh, it's you again, mister," Clarence said on the defensive, moving between Mason and Julia Powell. "I thought you said you weren't a reporter."

"I'm not, but I do want to know if this is Julia Powell."

"It's all right, Clarence, I can handle him," Julia said as she stepped out from behind Clarence and eyed Mason up and down. "Who wants to know?"

"Private Detective Mason Adler. I'm working for Mr. Castleberry. Charlotte Castle's father," he said, handing her a business card from his silver case.

She took it, studied it, and dropped it into her rather cavernous handbag as Clarence watched, ready to step in again if necessary. "So?"

"So, I was just talking to Miss Castle and her father upstairs in his office. She mentioned that Gertrude Claggett was friends with a Julia Powell who works here."

"So?" she said again.

"So are you aware of what happened yesterday to Miss Claggett?"

Miss Powell grimaced. "Yes. Horrible. Unbelievable, actually. We've all been talking about it."

"How did you hear about it?"

"It was in the papers, wasn't it?"

"Yes, but they didn't mention Miss Claggett by name."

She shrugged. "I suppose not, but when she didn't show up for work today or call in, some of us started wondering. Gert was always on time and never called out. I don't think she ever missed a single day, not since I've worked here anyway, and I've been here about a year. Anyway, on our coffee break Mr. Castleberry's secretary, Wanda Gleason, told us what happened, and how the reporters had been calling all morning and trying to get in to see Mr. Castleberry. She said Mr. Castleberry told her the body in the trunk had been identified as Gertrude's, and of course the papers said it was Charlotte's trunk the body was found in, and she and Gert were roommates."

"Oh, I see. Word travels fast."

"Yes. It was all we could talk about the rest of the day."

"I can imagine. Well, if you are indeed Julia Powell, I'd like to ask you a few questions, if I may."

"What's in it for me?"

"The chance to help me find whoever killed Miss Claggett. I would think that would be sufficient, to find your friend's killer."

"I'm sorry about what happened to her, and I truly can't imagine who would have done such a horrific thing, but Gert and I weren't exactly friends, Mr. Adler."

"That seems to be a common consensus. But nonetheless, I would like to talk to you."

She shrugged again. "I can spare a few moments, I suppose. It beats going out in the heat and waiting for the streetcar. And maybe later you could give a girl a lift home."

"Maybe."

"Or maybe not," she said. "Maybe you're the killer, and you're looking for your next victim."

"I assure you, I'm not."

"Well, of course you'd say that. How do I know your name's really even Mason Adler?"

"You can check with Mr. Castleberry, if you like. He hired me."

She studied him critically. "Naw, it's fine. You look like a dick. And you're a big one, tall and lean."

"*I'm* going to check with Mr. Castleberry, Miss Powell," Clarence said. "Don't you go anywhere with this fella until I find out."

Miss Powell winked at the man in uniform. "Thanks, Clarence, but I think he's okay." She turned back to Mason. "Well, if we're going to chat, let's go over by the windows and sit down where Clarence can keep an eye on us. My feet are killing me, and I need a cigarette."

"Lead the way, then, Miss Powell." They crossed the lobby to a couple of easy chairs and made themselves relatively comfortable in them.

"So, you got a cigarette, Mr. Adler?" she said, hiking her skirt up a little and crossing her legs.

"Hmm, no, sorry. I don't smoke."

"Figures." She opened the cavernous handbag she'd placed on her lap, rooted around inside it, and produced a package of Lucky Strikes and a book of matches.

"If you had your own cigarettes, why did you ask me for one?"

"Why not? I'm doing you a favor by answering your questions, the least you could have done is provide me with a cigarette, if you'd had one," she said, lighting up.

"Right, sorry about that."

She took a deep drag and exhaled. "It's all right, doesn't hurt to ask. Are you married, Mr. Adler?"

"What? Um, no, no, I'm not."

"Widowed?"

He shook his head. "No."

"Divorced?"

"Really, Miss Powell, my personal life is none of your business."

"And my personal life is none of yours. Yet I have a feeling you're going to be asking me about it anyway, so why shouldn't I ask *you* a few personal questions?"

"I'm investigating a murder. The murder of your friend Miss Claggett."

"I know, you said that. And I told you she and I weren't exactly friends." She took another drag on the cigarette, crossed her legs the other way, and leaned back as she looked at him. "So I'm guessing you're not divorced, and never married. Odd. You're not a bad-looking sort, for an older man, attractive even. You must have been quite dashing when you were young."

"Thanks," he said, setting his hat on a nearby table and unbuttoning his suit coat.

"No thanks necessary," she said, and then pointed with her chin to his abdomen. "I see you pack heat."

Mason glanced down and noticed his shoulder harness and Colt .32 Pocket Automatic were now visible. "Yes. Equipment of the trade," he said, buttoning his jacket once more.

"Guess you're a dick, all right. A big dick with a little gun. Anyway, I'm just stating facts, as I see them, about you not being bad looking, I mean. Funny, though. You haven't looked at my legs once, and they're not bad, if I do say so myself. And you didn't exactly light up at the thought of giving me a lift home. Most men find me fairly attractive, you know."

"I'm sure they do, Miss Powell, but about Miss Claggett..."

"She didn't care for queers, you know. Went against her beliefs."

"I'm not sure what you mean by queers, or how you define that exactly, nor do I really care to know."

"I suspect you know exactly what I mean. I'm astute that way. Call it my women's intuition."

"I don't believe in women's intuition."

She blew a cloud of smoke toward the ceiling and then looked him in the eye. "No, I don't suppose you do."

"Where were you yesterday afternoon, Miss Powell? Around five o'clock? It appears you get off work fairly early in the day."

"I do, because I start early in the day. I'm here Monday through Friday seven to three."

"I wasn't aware there was a need for typists at seven in the morning."

"So, you know what I do for a living. I suppose Charlotte told you that."

"She did."

"Yeah, well, I do work in the typing pool, but I do other things, too. Besides, you'd be amazed at the number of reports and documents that need to be typed around here on a daily basis. There's always a stack waiting for me when I come in each morning."

"I suppose so. Why say something with one page when ten pages will do?"

Miss Powell laughed and blew smoke out her nose this time. "Or twenty."

"I'm sure. That's city hall for you."

"You're right, Mr. Adler, it never changes."

"Government usually doesn't. So, you got out of work at three yesterday, as usual. Where did you go from here?"

"Home, as usual."

"Do you live alone?"

"No, with another girl. But she plays bridge on Monday afternoons, so she wasn't home. She didn't get back until nearly six thirty. Why? Do you think I killed Gert?"

"I don't know, did you?"

"Why would I do that? Because I was jealous of her and John? He was my fella first, as you probably know. Gert and I worked together here at city hall along with Charlotte until she quit recently to try to become a movie star."

"So, you and Mr. Patterson were going steady before he dated Gert."

"That's right. Nothing too serious, but I liked him. We had some laughs, some good times, and he's easy on the eyes. He was out of work, and I mentioned him and his situation to Gert one day. She works part time here at city hall, but her full-time job is at the Lost Souls Mission over on Nineteenth. Anyway, she told me they were looking for someone to help out in the office and with fund-raising, which I thought would be perfect for Johnny. His last job was raising funds for Councilman Monroe's campaign, you see? Anyway, Johnny stopped by here one morning and I introduced him to Gert. She got him the job at the mission, they hit it off, and the next thing you know I'm out the door like yesterday's newspaper. But I suppose you already knew all that."

"No, not all of it, actually."

"Then you're not much of a detective, are you?"

"I wouldn't say that. After all, I just got you to tell me all that, didn't I?"

She laughed again. "I guess so."

"It sounds like you had a good reason to be angry with Miss Claggett."

"I did. And with Johnny boy. The two of them really did me over. But I didn't kill her, if that's what you're driving at. If I was going to kill anyone it would have been him."

"I'll make a note of that."

"Go right ahead. Did you ever meet Gert, Mr. Adler?"

"No, I never had the pleasure," Mason said.

"It wouldn't have been much of a pleasure. She was as entertaining and sweet as sour milk. Pure, proper, pious, and as attractive as Popeye's Olive Oyl. No, I take that back. Olive Oyl was a regular Miss America compared to Gert, though if Gert had done something with her hair, and wore a little makeup and lipstick, she would have looked better, even kind of pretty."

"I understand she was quite different from Miss Castle," Mason said, taking out his notepad and pencil and jotting a few things down.

"You can say that again. If Johnny had dumped me for Charlotte I could understand it, but Gert? I just didn't get it. I was pretty steamed and hurt. I'm usually the one who does the breaking up, ya know? But then I realized she may not be the liveliest girl in the world, but she was better suited to him," she said as she ground out her cigarette in a nearby ashtray.

"Oh?"

"Yeah, he's a churchgoer like her, all religious, which is another reason I thought he'd be a good fit at the mission. Personally I don't go for that kind of stuff, though Johnny was always wanting me to. Anyway, after the two of them hooked up, Gert and I didn't talk much. She did her work, I did mine."

"What about Miss Castle?"

"What about her? Charlotte and Gert were like oil and vinegar."

"So I understand. Did Miss Castle and Miss Claggett argue?"

"Not at work that I ever saw. They didn't talk much at all. In fact, Gert didn't talk much with anyone. She was a bit of a loner. Still, before the whole Johnny thing she seemed to like me, for some reason. Maybe because I'm one of the few people who put up with her. She was always telling me about the things Charlotte had done that she didn't approve of, such as coming home at all hours of the night, wearing her skirts too short, drinking, going out with a different fella every weekend, wearing too much makeup. All the stuff I do, too. But Gert didn't live with me, thank God."

"Mr. Castleberry mentioned that they argued over Mr. Patterson. He seemed to think Miss Claggett thought Mr. Patterson was interested in Miss Castle, and she in him."

"I doubt it. Still, if Gert thought that was the case, I bet it did make her plenty mad. She had a mean green jealous streak in her that would make jade look pale."

"I suppose it would be only natural for her to be upset if that were indeed the case," Mason said.

"And it would have served her right after what she did to me, but like I said, I doubt it. Anyway, I think Gert was glad when Charlotte told her she was going to move to California, for a variety of reasons."

"Yes, it sounds like it. Well, I guess that's all my questions for now. I thank you for your time, Miss Powell."

"Sure, happy to help." She dug once more into her cavernous handbag and produced a pad and pencil, along with a small atomizer. "Oh, and, just in case my intuition's wrong about you, here's my number. Call me sometime. You're kinda cute, for a dick." She jotted it down, tore off the paper, and handed it to Mason, who took it and put it in his pocket while she spritzed herself. "My new perfume, Taste of Midnight," she said. "Covers the cigarette smoke smell, you know?"

"Nice. A friend of mine wears that, too. The French name for is it is Goût de Minuit."

"Fancy," she said.

"I suppose. Still want a ride home?" he said, putting his pencil and notebook away.

"Naw, with you I think that's all it would be." She dropped the pad, pencil, and atomizer back into her bag and snapped it shut. "I'll take my chances with the guys on the streetcar. See ya in the funny papers, Mr. Adler," she said, getting to her feet and smoothing out her skirt before walking away, swinging her handbag in her hand. Clarence, Mason noticed, was watching the two of them carefully, from a distance. Miss Powell stopped to talk to Clarence, while Mason picked up his hat and went out the Third Street doors, noting the reporters were still hanging about the entrance, probably waiting for Charlotte or her father to leave. He walked past them and returned to his automobile, glad of the shade the two palm trees had afforded. Still, the steering wheel was hot to the touch, and Mason used his handkerchief to grasp it as he pulled away from the curb and headed to the Cactus Cantina on the other side of town.

CHAPTER FIVE

Late afternoon, Tuesday, May 7, 1946
The Cactus Cantina

Mason arrived at the small café at a quarter to four, after circling the block several times until a parking spot in the shade finally opened up.

"Good afternoon, sir," the waiter said as Mason entered the colorful little place and removed his fedora, wiping the sweat from his brow.

"Afternoon. Table for two, please. The other gentleman should be along shortly."

"Yes, sir, right this way." The man led Mason across the dining room, zigzagging through clusters of small tables covered with plaid tablecloths, to a four-top in the back left corner next to the jukebox. "I'll bring over some water for you. Anything else to drink right now?"

"Draft beer, please, and an order of chili con queso."

"Yes, sir, right away." He walked off toward the bar while Mason put on his reading glasses and perused the simple menu, realizing he was hungrier than he had thought, having basically skipped lunch.

It was ten minutes to four when the waiter brought the water, beer, and chili con queso, the latter of which Mason devoured quickly. At five minutes past four, Mason spied his friend Emil across the small café and gave him a wave.

"Hello," Emil said, striding up to the table, his hat in his hand. "Been waiting long?"

"One beer and an order of chili con queso long," Mason said, wiping some of the chili con queso from his lips.

"So about fifteen minutes."

Mason laughed. "Yup, more or less. I got here a little early. You know me well. Thanks for meeting me, Emil."

"Sure, always happy to have a beer with a friend, and it looks like you're ready for another."

The waiter came up as Emil took a seat opposite Mason and set his hat on one of the empty chairs next to Mason's.

"Two fresh beers for the table," Emil said, holding up two fingers, "and two more orders of chili con queso. Oh, and bring me some tortillas de maíz, I'm hungry."

"Yes, sir," the waiter said, and then looked at Mason. "Anything else to eat for you?"

"Actually yes, I'm still hungry, too. I'll have your regular supper for sixty-five cents. The tamales, enchilada, frijoles, tortillas de maíz, and sopa de arroz."

"Yes, sir," he said, making a notation on his pad. "I'll get your beers out right away, and the food will be ready shortly." Emil stared at Mason as the waiter walked away toward the bar in the adjoining room.

"I'd say you're hungry," Emil said, taking out his pack of Lucky Strikes and lighting up a cigarette. "Where do you put it all, Mason? I seem to gain weight just looking at food, and you eat like a horse, yet a strong wind would blow you away."

"I'm not *that* thin. Besides, I haven't really eaten since breakfast, and that wasn't all that much."

"Well, you should eat more," Emil said, rubbing his eyes and rolling his head about on his thick, red neck.

"I'll see what I can do. What about you? A little chili con queso and some tortillas de maíz isn't going to fill up a big guy like you."

"No, but Shirley will have supper waiting for me by the time I get home, and there would be hell to pay if I showed up without an appetite." He undid the top button of his suit pants and let out a deep breath, once more rubbing his eyes with his left hand as he held his cigarette in the right.

"I suppose so," Mason said. "And Shirley's a good cook."

"One of the best, if I do say so myself."

"No arguments from me," Mason said as he studied Emil carefully. "You look tired today."

"I *am* tired. I've had a long day at the police station."

"Couldn't have been that long, it's only a little after four o'clock."

"But I was there a little before seven this morning, and I'd probably still be there if I didn't have plans to meet you. And it was a late night last night, too. I got called out a little after midnight and didn't get back home until almost three this morning, so I'm basically going on about three or four hours of sleep. I almost canceled on you."

"I'm glad you didn't."

"I would have, but I was hungry and thirsty."

"Glad you wanted to see me," Mason said sarcastically.

"You know what I mean," Emil said as the waiter brought over two more glasses of beer with foaming heads.

"Your food will be out shortly, gentlemen," he said, as he picked up Mason's empty glass and dish and hurried away.

"Cheers, my friend," Mason said, raising his glass and clinking it against Emil's.

"Cheers," Emil replied, taking a large drink.

"And I do know what you mean, Emil. I'd be tired, too, after a night and a day like that."

Emil sighed. "Yes, and of course Shirley got woken up, too, when the phone rang, and again when I got back home and crawled into bed early this morning, so she wasn't in the best of moods today, either. But I am glad to see you, actually, Mason. It's been a long, hard day, and a friendly face and a mug of cold beer is just what I needed." He took a long drag on his cigarette and blew a cloud of smoke toward the ceiling.

"Long and hard because of the woman's body found in the trunk down at the train station?"

Emil nodded. "I figured you'd know about it."

"It *was* in the morning paper, and they did say Detective Hardwick was investigating."

"Yes, I saw the article, those damned reporters."

"They're just doing their jobs, Emil."

"I know, but they make pests of themselves. When and if the department has something to say on this case, we'll notify them."

"So, you don't have any leads?"

Emil picked up his beer and took another healthy swig before setting it down again, wiping the foam from his thick upper lip. "You know I can't divulge police business and information to you, Mason. You're a private dick."

"I'm just asking a simple question, is all," Mason said.

"But there's no simple answer. Why do you want to know, anyway?"

Mason leaned back in his chair, his cold beer in hand. "Because Miss Castle's father hired me to investigate the murder."

Emil snorted. "Of course he did. I should have known."

"He told me the body belonged to a Gertrude Claggett, Miss Castle's former roommate."

"That information hasn't been released to the public yet, Mason."

"I'm not telling anyone, though apparently Mr. Castleberry is. It sounds like everyone at city hall knows Miss Claggett was the victim."

"Figures. So, the old man has a big mouth."

"He told his secretary, she told everyone else."

"Naturally. How does the saying go? Telephone, telegraph, tell a woman?" Emil said.

"That's not fair or accurate. It was Mr. Castleberry who spilled the beans first. A *man*. And Lydia would slug you if she ever heard you say something so derogatory."

"Sorry. How is Lydia?" Emil ground out the remains of his cigarette in the metal ashtray on the table and took another swig of his beer. "I know you two are like brother and sister, joined at the hip, practically."

"She's fine, and she's a friend is all."

"Of course she is. I like Lydia, she's a good egg. I suppose you've already discussed the case with her."

"Some of it. She was there this morning when Mr. Castleberry called to inquire about enlisting my services. But don't worry, Lydia knows when to keep her mouth shut. Besides, I never gave her the name of the victim, just that it was Miss Castle's roommate."

"Still too much information, if you ask me. I don't share details with civilians unless absolutely necessary, you included. Hell, I don't even talk about my cases with Shirley, and she's my wife."

"I know, and I know she hates it that you don't. So were you first on the scene last night? At the train station, I mean. Surely you can tell me that much, anyway."

Emil nodded. "I suppose, and yes, I was first on the scene, along with two uniforms and the coroner. I was on call, and the station telephoned me at home, like I said. Woke me and Shirley both up. I got dressed and drove over straight away, and when I arrived, I spoke with Miss Castle at length. She claims she's innocent, but I have my doubts."

"Understandable, I suppose."

"That she claims she's innocent or that I have my doubts?"

"Well, both, actually."

"Right. Her father came and picked her up when we were through with her, around one in the morning. I talked to him briefly. He seems like the type who'd hire a private dick."

"He is, not that there's anything wrong with that."

"And he also has a big mouth, apparently."

"Yes. So, once again we're both working on the same case."

"Yup," Emil said, taking another healthy swig of his beer. "I suppose you remember that case back in 1931. Eerily similar."

Mason nodded. "Hard to forget that one, and just a few weeks before Halloween. A woman shoots her two friends to death, hides their bodies in her luggage, and boards a train to California."

"Exactly. And Miss Castle was heading to California, and her roommate's body was in her trunk. Spooky, if you ask me," Emil said. "Maybe that's where she got the idea, from that case in '31."

"She couldn't have been more than five or six back then," Mason said.

"Doesn't mean she didn't remember it or hear about it later. It made national headlines."

"True. Her father certainly remembers it, and so does Lydia."

"I'm sure. So, what all have you found out so far, Mason? Do *you* have any leads or suspects?"

"I doubt I've found anything out you don't already know, but I've only just begun. You've got a head start on me."

"And I intend to keep that head start this time," Emil said.

"We'll see about that. What about the official cause of death? Can you tell me that?"

"It wasn't suicide," Emil said, staring at Mason over the top of his beer glass, which was now almost empty.

"Funny."

"It could have been, you know. We don't rule anything out until proven otherwise. She could have overdosed, then climbed into that trunk and died."

"So, it was a drug overdose?"

"No."

"Come on, Emil. I'm trying to do my job, too."

"And it's not part of *my* job to supply you with information."

Mason shrugged. "Fair enough. So, it wasn't suicide. And I take it that it wasn't accidental."

"It could have been that, too. She may have been fooling around, trying to play a prank on her roommate or someone, climbed into the trunk, got locked in, and accidentally suffocated."

"But I take it she didn't," Mason said, almost finished with his beer, too.

"No, she didn't."

"So, it was definitely murder," Mason said, leaning forward once more.

"A brilliant deduction, detective. And they pay you thirty bucks a day?"

"Thank you, and yes, they do. How *did* she die?"

"Oh, for crying out loud, Mason. I told you I can't discuss this with you. I've already said too much."

"Okay, if that's the way you want to be."

"That's the way I want to be," Emil said as the waiter arrived, laboring beneath a heavy tray, which he sat down on a vacant neighboring table. He distributed the food, most of it in front of Mason, and Emil ordered two more beers for the table. Then the waiter, having ascertained nothing else was needed, picked up the now-empty tray and walked away, his heels clicking on the terra-cotta tiles.

Mason took a few bites of his enchilada while he studied Emil across the table once more. "Sure you don't want some of this? It's delicious."

"I'm sure. It looks and smells wonderful," Emil said, "but I'd better not. Shirley's making pot roast tonight, and the chili con queso and tortillas de maíz is already more than I should be eating."

"Okay, let me know if you change your mind before I eat it all."

The waiter delivered the two fresh beers and whisked away the empties as Mason continued to eat and Emil devoured his scant food.

"By the way, Emil, did I tell you about that older fellow who lives in my building, Mr. Blanders? He has a charming little cabin up in the mountains."

"No, you didn't. And what of it?" Emil said, wiping his mouth with his napkin, having finished his food already.

"It's partly why I originally wanted to meet you today for drinks, to discuss it. I'm told the cabin is right by a creek, teeming with fish, and set off in the woods, which are loaded with wildlife. No one else around for miles."

Emil raised a bushy eyebrow. "Sounds nice."

"Doesn't it? He told me last week he's going to be selling it now that his wife's died and he's getting up in years himself. He wants it to go to someone who appreciates that kind of place, though."

Emil laughed. "Then why did he mention it to you? You hate

fishing and hunting, and I don't think you've ever set foot in a cabin, or the woods, for that matter."

"True, but I happen to be friends with someone who loves all that," Mason said, starting in on the tamales and the sopa de arroz. "Someone whose company I'm enjoying right now."

"Yeah, so?" Emil said, his tone suspicious.

"So, I mentioned you to him. He said he'd be happy to let you use it for a weekend, free of charge, to see if you like it. And I could probably persuade him to let it go cheap if you decide you want to buy it. I've done a few favors for him and his wife over the years."

Emil crossed his arms over his still-empty stomach as he watched Mason continue to eat. "Interesting. And in return all you want is a little information, is that it?"

"I wouldn't object," Mason said, wiping his mouth clean, "but I'm not necessarily making it a condition. Mr. Blanders tells me it's a nice little place, one room but fully furnished, sleeps two comfortably. No electricity or telephone, but there's a front porch with rockers, a fireplace, a pump, and a privy out back."

"Sounds nice all right."

"I thought it might. The icebox runs off a small generator, and it's got a wood-burning cookstove, too. I was puzzled as to where one bathes, but he said he rinses off in the creek if he has to, but most of the time he said he doesn't bother."

"I wouldn't, either. I'd only stay for four or five days at a time, tops, and Shirley would never go. So. why take a bath?"

Mason raised his brows ever so slightly. "Why indeed? I'm glad the cabin appeals to you."

"It does. And you're not making this a condition, eh? The cabin in exchange for information about the case?"

Mason looked offended. "Of course not. You're my friend, and friends help each other, don't they?"

Emil scowled, reached over, and grabbed a tamale off Mason's plate, dropping it down onto his own. "Dammit, Mason. You're as irritating and pesty as those reporters. No, *more* so. Fine, Miss Claggett died from strangulation. A man's green necktie with a hula girl painted on it was found wrapped tightly around her neck."

Mason raised his eyebrows even farther this time. "Hmm, interesting. Suspects?"

"Besides Miss Castle, of course, there's an Alfred Brody as of right now. He works at Union Station in the baggage room. He's the one that retrieved the trunk and bags from her apartment yesterday. We questioned him at length last night, too, as he was on duty when the body was found."

"What motive would he have?" Mason said. "Did he know Miss Claggett?"

"Not that we're aware of, and he claims they never met. But it may have been a crime of convenience. He says no one was home when he arrived at the apartment, but that may be a lie. Maybe she was there alone when he picked up the luggage."

"So what? Why would he kill her? Robbery? Did he ransack the place?"

Emil shook his head as he started in on the tamale. "No. We were over at the apartment this morning, one of the landladies let us in. It actually looked like everything was in its place, nothing out of order or out of the ordinary that we could see. We took a few pictures and lifted a few prints, but there really wasn't anything there, or not there, that should have been."

"Then why would this Mr. Brody kill Miss Claggett?"

Emil shrugged. "He's a young man, she's a girl. Maybe he made improper advances and she rejected him, and things got out of hand. It's been known to happen, and his prints were all over that trunk."

"Which is only natural since he picked it up and brought it back to the train station. Are there any other suspects on your list besides him and Miss Castle?"

"Not at the moment. And frankly I'd be shocked if it was anyone else but one of those two," Emil said. "I just have to figure out which one."

"I'm told Miss Castle nearly fainted when she opened that trunk and saw her roommate inside. And she was quite distraught when you questioned her. She nearly vomited."

"She did vomit. But that doesn't mean she's not a killer."

"True," Mason said. "I suppose you know she and Miss Claggett worked together in the typing pool at city hall as well as being roommates."

"Yes, I know, she told me that last night," Emil said. "I asked all the standard questions: 'Did you know the victim? How did you meet?'"

"And don't forget 'How long had you known the victim?'" Mason added.

"Exactly. All questions right out of the police detective handbook."

"Which you know backward and forward," Mason said.

"I ought to, I've been a police dick long enough."

"Right. Anyway, Miss Castle was present when I met with her father this afternoon. She told me she was on her way to California with hopes of becoming an actress, though her father seemed doubtful as to her prospects."

"I know she said she was heading out west. She didn't mention anything about wanting to be an actress, though. She said she was going to be staying with her aunt."

"Her father's sister, yes. Because she wants to break into show business."

"I see. So maybe she was just playing the part last night of a shocked, concerned friend."

"That's possible, of course," Mason said.

"It is. I've seen it before. I'd put money on either her or this Mr. Brody being the murderer."

"Don't close any doors you may need to open again," Mason said.

"And don't tell me how to do my job. I told Miss Castle and this Brody fella not to leave town. We'll probably bring them both into the station for a more thorough interrogation."

"Get one of them to confess?"

"Well, yeah, whichever one of them did it, anyway. It's really kind of an open and shut case once we figure that out. I'm not sure of Miss Castle's motive yet, though, unless it was some kind of jealousy over a man. But I know this Brody had motive *and* opportunity."

"Perceived motive, Emil, nothing more."

"True, but right now there are no other suspects besides the two of them. No one else had a motive, perceived or otherwise, or opportunity."

"What about the boyfriend, John Patterson? You said Miss Castle's motive may have been some kind of jealousy over a man, and rumor has it Mr. Patterson, Miss Claggett's boyfriend, was interested in Charlotte."

Emil stared at Mason over the top of his beer. "My, you have been busy."

"His name came up when I was talking to Miss Castle."

"Naturally. We talked to him earlier today. He seemed in shock. He had no motive for killing her, and he's apparently gained nothing from her death, as she didn't have much, only eighty-four dollars in a bank account. Besides, he seemed to really love Miss Claggett, and I think the rumor about him and Miss Castle was probably just a rumor. And if he *was* interested in Miss Castle, it would be more of a motive for Miss Claggett to kill *her*, not the other way round."

"That's true, I suppose. And what about the brother? Miss Claggett's brother?"

"Josiah Claggett, you mean. I suppose his name just came up, too."

"It did, actually."

"He's been staying at Patterson's place but took off after hearing about his sister and hasn't been back yet. I told Patterson to let us know when he shows up. We're on the lookout for him in all the usual places, but no luck so far. We want to talk with him, of course."

"Curious he'd take off like that," Mason said.

"I'm told he's not quite right in the head. Those types do unpredictable things."

"Like murder."

"Eh, you read too many detective novels. He's probably holed up somewhere, scared and upset because his only sister, his only relative, apparently, was killed."

"Possibly. Were you aware he was planning on going over to his sister's apartment yesterday afternoon, sometime after five?"

Emil raised a bushy brow. "No, who told you that?"

"A source. Apparently his sister wanted to talk to him about something, but my source wasn't sure what it was about."

"Your source. You kill me, Mason. Whatever it was, if he actually went there, it was probably just to drop off his laundry or something. We'll ask him about it when we find him, but like I said, Alfred Brody and Charlotte Castle are our strongest suspects right now."

"Sounds like your only suspects, in your opinion."

"It only takes one," Emil said, "And right now I'm leaning toward Brody."

"Actually out of those two, my money would be on Miss Castle."

Emil shot Mason a look across the table. "Didn't her old man hire you to prove she's innocent?"

"He did, and I intend to do just that, if she is indeed innocent. I don't know that yet for a fact. Miss Castle is a tall woman, and it sounds like she outweighed Miss Claggett by quite a bit, and they didn't exactly get along. If the rumor that Miss Claggett's fella had a thing for Miss Castle *is* true, maybe it was reciprocated, and they decided to get Miss Claggett out of the way for some reason."

"For *what* reason?" Emil said. "If Patterson and Castle had a thing for each other, he could have just dumped Claggett. Why kill her?"

Mason shrugged. "Who knows? But maybe Miss Claggett was already dead and inside the trunk when Miss Castle's father picked her up at five. After all, he never went up to the apartment when he picked his daughter up, she went down."

"Well, you go ahead and bark up that tree if you want, but my money's still on Alfred Brody. After all, she was strangled with a man's necktie."

"That means nothing. Every man wears a tie, and they're not hard to come by. And Miss Claggett's brother had been staying with them for a while. He may have left a tie behind that Miss Castle, or anyone else, may have used to strangle her."

"Maybe, but not likely."

"But maybe," Mason said. "You may also want to talk to a Miss Julia Powell."

Emil squinted at Mason across the table. "Who's that?"

"She also works at city hall in the typing pool and was friendly with Miss Claggett at one time, until she introduced her to John Patterson, who *she* was dating, who then dumped her for Miss Claggett."

"You don't say? That could certainly be a motive. How'd you find all that out?"

"Just doing my job. And since you were kind enough to share some information with me, I thought I'd return the favor."

"Thanks." Emil took out a notepad and jotted down the name. "I'll have a talk with her tomorrow. You think she may have killed Miss Claggett?"

"Maybe."

"Or maybe not," Emil said. "Still, I'll have a talk with this Miss Powell." He glanced at his watch. "I'd better get going, it's getting late."

"Yes, I need to go also, and just in time. That lady in the pink hat just put a nickel in the jukebox."

"I thought you liked music?" Emil said.

"I do, but not right now, and this place is too small. Anyway, thanks again for the information about the cause of death."

"Sure. I guess I don't mind sharing a few details with you, seeing as how we go back a long way and all, but if anyone asks you, didn't hear anything from me, understand?"

"Not a word, Emil," Mason said as "New San Antonio Rose" began blaring forth from the jukebox speakers.

"Good, 'cause you know I'll deny it," Emil said, raising his voice. "I've got some free time coming up the end of the month, by the way, the 25th, 26th, and 27th. I could use a little mountain getaway."

"I'll talk to Mr. Blanders about it tomorrow," Mason said, also raising his voice.

"Right, thanks. And thanks for the beer and the chili con queso and tortillas de maíz."

"*And* one of my tamales."

"Yeah. I assume you're footing the bill," Emil said.

"Glad to. Since this was a business discussion, I'll ask for a receipt and I can charge it to Mr. Castleberry under expenses."

"Of course you will. If I'd known that I would have had another beer. And by the way, once we pick up this Mr. Brody and Miss Castle and get a confession from one of them, I don't want you claiming credit."

Mason wiped his mouth clean once more. "*If* you do. And not to worry, Emil. Not to worry."

CHAPTER SIX

Early evening, Tuesday, May 7, 1946
The Evans Comstock Residence for Young Ladies

It was nearly six when Mason and Emil left the Cactus Cantina, and dusk was upon them.

"Say hello to Shirley for me," Mason said, shaking Emil's hand as they stood on the sidewalk in front of the plate glass window of the Cantina. "And enjoy your dinner."

"I will, on both counts," Emil said, lighting up another Lucky Strike. "And believe it or not, I'm still hungry. You heading home now?"

"More or less," Mason said. "I have an errand or two to run first."

"I see. Well, let me know if you find out anything else regarding the case."

"I will. Have a good night."

"Right, good night." Emil turned and ambled up the sidewalk toward his car, trailing cigarette smoke behind him as Mason went in the opposite direction toward his Studebaker.

The interior of his automobile wasn't as hot this time, so he didn't need his handkerchief to hold the wheel as he steered toward Roosevelt Street and the Evans Comstock Residence for Young Ladies. Mason found the building without too much trouble, a three-story brick and stucco place set back from the street, neat, tidy, and well maintained, just a few blocks east of the Trinity Episcopal Cathedral, as Miss Castle had said, on the south side of Roosevelt.

He parked his Studebaker near the front door and climbed the steps to the entrance, which was flanked with clay pots of desert honeysuckle and orange bells. As he suspected, the main door to the building was locked. Undeterred, Mason walked around to the rear, but the back exit off the alley was locked also, and he didn't see anyone who might let him in. He returned to the front door, where a directory and a bank of buttons was set into the wall on the left. He pressed several of the apartment buttons randomly, one at a time, starting with 3B, then 3C, followed by 3D, and then working down to the second floor, each time waiting a few moments for a response. There was no answer from anyone on the third floor, nor from 2D or 2C, and Mason was beginning to wonder if the whole building was vacant, when finally a young woman's voice from apartment 2B answered over the tinny speaker.

"Yes? Who is it?" the disembodied voice said.

"It's me, Mike, let me in," Mason said, figuring it was a pretty common name and the resident of 2B most likely knew at least one fellow named Mike.

"Oh hi, Mike, I wasn't expecting you. Come on in." He heard a buzzing sound, then Mason yanked on the door and he was in. The lobby of the building was small, really just a hallway that ran from front to back, but it was clean, with a black and white tile floor, a group of brass mailboxes on the right, and a door marked Manager, 1A on the left, just before the stairs.

Since the building had no elevator, Mason took the stairs up to the third floor, and, as Charlotte had said, he found a key above the door to the trash chute room. After retrieving it, he walked down the hall to Charlotte's old place at the front of the building, inserted the key in the door, and opened it. Mason stood in the doorway and peered cautiously about the living room. As Emil had said earlier, everything looked pretty ordinary, tidy, and in its place, as far as he could tell. Mason put the key in his pocket, entered the small apartment, and closed the door quietly behind him.

"Hello?" he called out, not really expecting an answer. When none was forthcoming, he turned on the overhead light, noting it was a few minutes past six. The sun would be completely down in just over an hour, and since the apartment faced north, it was already dark and gloomy inside.

Mason walked slowly around the living room, not really sure what he was looking for. He peered out each of the two windows, which led to a fire escape and looked down on Roosevelt. A young couple with a baby carriage ambled by on the sidewalk below. A small piece of blue cloth clung to a sharp edge of the fire escape, and it caught Mason's eye. He unlocked and opened one of the windows, and he was able to reach out and retrieve it, putting it in his pocket next to the apartment key. He closed and locked the window once more and had a look in the closet, which held a few overcoats, some ladies' galoshes, hats, scarves, and a couple of board games.

From there he moved on to the kitchen, where he found a few dirty dishes in the sink and scant groceries in the icebox, but not much else of note. He checked the bathroom off the hall next. It was filled with the usual grooming accoutrements of a single young woman, though decidedly devoid of makeup, perfumes, and hair products. Many of the other items were a complete puzzlement to Mason, and he wondered what exactly women did with them.

Finally he went into the small bedroom, where two twin beds stood opposite the door. There, too, things seemed to be more or less in order, though one of the beds was unmade. Mason turned on the overhead light and inspected the small closet, which held three or four dresses, an overcoat, a few blouses, and some women's trousers. On the shelf were a few hatboxes, and on the floor, several pairs of small-sized shoes. The dresser held pretty much what he expected, mostly unmentionables and a few scarves and socks, so he went on to the nightstand between the two beds. In the second drawer of the nightstand, shoved in the back beneath a black sleep mask and a lace handkerchief, was a small, red leather-bound diary.

"Interesting," Mason said quietly to himself as he took it out. He turned on the bedside light and opened it carefully. On the inside cover, written in ink in a feminine script, were the words *Property of G. Claggett, private.* The word *private* was underlined twice. He turned the pages to the last entry, which was from the day before she died, Sunday, May 5: *J.P. is coming over tomorrow to discuss what I found out. I'm still upset and troubled, and unsure of how to proceed. It goes against everything I believe to be true and right. I telephoned and arranged for a meeting here after five, after Charlotte has gone.*

Mason took out his own notebook and copied down the entry verbatim, as well as one written three days prior, on Thursday. *Found out something disturbing today about J.P. I almost can't believe it's true.*

He put the diary back where he'd found it after making some notes, and then he got down on his hands and knees to peek under each of the beds. A couple pairs of slippers were tucked under the one nearest the window, but the other one was packed with women's clothes, shoved here and there every which way and crumpled into balls up against the wall where the headboard was. The mystery of what happened to the clothes from Charlotte's trunk had been solved, anyway.

He'd just gotten to his feet when he heard a noise coming from the kitchen. Mason switched off the bedside and overhead lights, cursing the fact that he'd left the light on in the living room. He looked about, wondering what to do. At last he decided on the window and the fire escape beyond it. Mason undid the latch as quietly as he could, raised the sash, and had one leg out and on the escape when he felt a firm hand clamp down on his left shoulder.

"Who the hell are you, and just what do you think you're doing?" a deep voice said from behind him.

Instinct kicked in, and Mason whirled about, shoving the body that belonged to the voice away and trying to get out the window. But the fight had only just begun. Two strong hands now grabbed both his shoulders, thrusting him back and throwing him roughly to the floor. Mason grabbed a trouser leg and yanked as hard as he could. His opponent stumbled, which gave Mason a chance to get to his feet. He now abandoned the idea of escaping out the window and made for the door to the hall, but the other guy blocked his way and slammed Mason backward against the dresser, causing a sharp pain in Mason's lower back.

He cried out instinctively and turned once more toward the door but soon found himself in a firm headlock, his fedora falling to the floor. Mason struggled and elbowed the person's gut, at the same time stomping down hard on his assailant's foot while swinging his left hand up and connecting with their mouth. That broke the headlock and gave Mason just enough time to draw his gun. He whirled about and stepped back into the corner by the door, shaking and breathing hard, but holding the revolver steady, pointed directly at his attacker. "I have a gun, don't move," Mason said breathlessly.

The attacker, whom Mason could now see in the shadows, was about five foot eight, stocky, and solid. The person froze, eyes wide, staring at the barrel of Mason's gun.

Mason took several deep, short breaths, his chest heaving. He felt like he might throw up, and his neck and lower back ached. He felt for the light switch and flicked it on with his free hand. Immediately the room was bathed in light once again, and both he and his attacker blinked several times as they stared at each other.

"What the...? Who are you?"

"I'd ask you the same question if you weren't pointing that gun at me."

"You're a woman," Mason said, surprised. He was perspiring heavily, using the back of his free hand to wipe his brow while keeping both eyes on the accoster.

"Of course I am. And you're a man, more or less."

"What's your name?"

"Puddin' Tane. Ask me again and I'll tell you the same."

"Funny," Mason said. "And I suppose you live down the lane."

"That's right, and if you ask me my number I'll say cucumber."

"May I remind you, Puddin', that I have a loaded .32 Colt automatic aimed right at you? So, I'll ask you again, what's your name?"

"Fine, big shot. I'm Mrs. Comstock, Mildred Comstock," she said, wiping sweat from her face with a white handkerchief she'd extracted from her trouser pocket. Her chest heaved up and down as she struggled to catch her breath. "I own this place, along with my sister."

"Okay," Mason said, unsure exactly of what to do next.

"And I suppose you're returning to the scene of the crime, eh? Or are you one of those damned reporters that won't leave us alone?" Mildred Comstock said. "And how did you get in here?"

"I'm Mason Adler, a private detective. Miss Castle's father hired me to investigate Miss Claggett's murder. I'm here on her authority, and she gave me access."

Mrs. Comstock used her handkerchief to dab at her lower lip now, which Mason could see was bleeding. "Miss Castle doesn't live here anymore," she said. "She turned in her keys and moved out the day before yesterday."

"Yes, but she's paid up until the end of the month, isn't she? Until the end of the lease? Legally she's still a tenant, so legally she has a right to grant me access. She told me where a key to the apartment was hidden, and I was able to get into the building without too much difficulty."

"If what you say is true, and you're here with her permission, why were you sneaking around?" Mrs. Comstock said, taking in gulps of air and holding the handkerchief against her lower lip. "Why were you trying to escape out the window?"

"A fair question, I suppose," Mason said, still breathing heavily himself. He studied Mildred Comstock carefully. She was a stern-looking woman in her late forties or early fifties, dressed in a white long-sleeved shirt and brown trousers. Her brunette hair was worn short and flecked with gray, and she had oval brown eyes on either side of a prominent nose that appeared to have been broken once or twice. She looked like a linebacker, and she might have easily won that fight with him if Mason hadn't drawn his gun.

"So, what's the answer to my fair question?"

"I wasn't expecting anyone else to show up here, that's all. When I heard you in the kitchen, I assumed you were the murderer."

"So you panicked and decided to run away? Even though

you've got a gun? Not much of a man, are you?" she said, her plain brown eyes narrowed and glaring at him.

"I beg your pardon, Mrs. Comstock, but the measure of a man has little to do with his willingness to fight, gun or no gun."

"That's your opinion."

"It is. And I wasn't running away. I figured it was better to hide on the fire escape and observe the murderer than to be caught by him, or her, as the case may be."

Mrs. Comstock looked Mason up and down. "I suppose that makes sense. You're not much of a private dick, either, though. You left the light on in the living room. The moment I opened the door from the hall, I knew something was up."

"Like I said, I wasn't expecting company."

"Surprise."

"Definitely a surprise," Mason said, relaxing a bit.

"The police and some detective were already here this morning, looking everything over. And we've had reporters by the dozen. One actually offered me five bucks to let him in here to take pictures."

"Did you?"

"Of course not. I nearly decked him."

"I'm sure you could have."

"So, what are you doing here, anyway?"

"Talking to you, obviously," Mason said.

"Oh, a wisecracker."

"I prefer the term clever. And as I said, I'm here because I'm investigating Miss Claggett's death privately, apart from the police."

"And sloppily," she said.

"That's your opinion."

"It is," Mrs. Comstock said, also relaxing a little.

"Touché. I believe Miss Castle said you live with your sister, a Miss Evans."

"That is correct. We own and run this place together. She does the books, the rentals, that kind of thing, and I take care of the maintenance, the grounds, and whatnot."

"I see. And your husband?"

"I'm a widow, and my sister never married. We bought this place about ten years ago, and we haven't had a single problem until now."

"So you both run the Evans Comstock Residence for Young Ladies."

"That's right. That's what it says over the front door downstairs, don't it?"

"Fair enough. I understand your sister was friendly with Miss Castle and Miss Claggett."

Mrs. Comstock bristled, still holding the bloody handkerchief to her lip. "What do you mean by that?"

Mason shrugged. "Just that I heard she seemed fond of the two of them. And of Miss Claggett especially."

"Lucy's fond of most of our tenants, Mr. Adler. They're all nice young ladies. And would you put that damned gun away? From the looks of you I'm willing to bet you don't even know how to use it properly, and it could go off accidentally."

Mason studied her again. "All right, but take a few steps back before I do, and don't make any sudden moves."

"Don't make any sudden moves? Did you hear that line in a movie?"

Mason scowled. "Just do it. Please."

"Fine," she said, taking several steps back, which put her almost up against the bed along the window wall.

Mason holstered his gun, but he left his jacket open and unbuttoned, just in case.

"There. And for your information, I *do* know how to use it, and I have."

"Bully for you."

"So, you were saying your sister is fond of most of the young ladies that live here?"

"I'm not sure I'd use the word fond, exactly. But friendly. That's part of her job, that's all. Keep the residents happy and all that."

"Of course, it's only natural, I'm sure. By the way, what are *you* doing here?"

"I own the place, remember?"

"I *do* remember. But this is a crime scene. And even if it wasn't, by law you can't enter a tenant's apartment without giving them proper notice, which I'm sure you haven't done."

"Hard to do when the tenant is dead, Mr....Sorry, I forgot your name."

"Adler. Mason T. Adler, and only one of the tenants is dead, Mrs. Comstock. As I said earlier, Miss Castle is still on the lease until the end of the month, so in order to enter here legally, you should have notified her in writing yesterday, and I highly doubt you did that."

She cocked her head and looked at Mason through narrowed eyes. "Did you say you're a private detective or a lawyer?"

"A private dick, but I also know a thing or two about the law. So, why are you here, in this apartment? Unlike me, you don't have a legal reason to be."

"I don't *have* to answer that, you know, but I will. I was just checking to make sure everything was okay since no one's living here now. You know, making sure the water was off, the windows closed and locked, that sort of thing. It wouldn't surprise me if one of those damned reporters tried climbing up the fire escape to get in here if they noticed one of the windows was open. As the owner of the property, I have a right to protect my investment."

"Or were you just being nosy? Or perhaps were *you* actually returning to the scene of the crime, like you accused me of doing?"

She snorted and half chuckled. "Do I look like a murderer to you?"

"What's a murderer look like, Mrs. Comstock? They come in all shapes, sizes, and ages."

"I suppose that's true." She removed the handkerchief and ran her tongue over her lip. "Guess it's stopped bleeding, but it dripped down onto my shirt, dammit," she said, glancing down at her white blouse. "You got in a lucky punch."

Mason arched his back. "So did you. I'm gonna have a hell of a bruise on my lower back from where you slammed me into that dresser."

"Good. I could have taken you if you hadn't pulled that gun, you know."

"Probably. You're pretty strong."

"I grew up with five brothers who like to wrestle. I know how to take care of myself."

"Obviously."

"Hello?" a soft voice called out from the living room. "Is anyone here? Mildred?"

"Oh Christ, that's Lucy," Mrs. Comstock said. "Button your coat so she doesn't see that silly little gun. She's sensitive, you know."

Mason buttoned his jacket, retrieved his hat from the floor, placed it back on his head, and opened the bedroom door.

"We're in here, Lucy," Mrs. Comstock called out.

"Who's we, Mildred? And what are you doing in here?" Lucy replied as she came down the short hall toward the bedroom. She stopped short at the sight of Mason. "Oh, hello."

Mason took off his hat and nodded. "How do you do?"

"Fine, thank you. Who are you?" Lucy said. Her voice displayed just a touch of nervousness as her eyes went from Mason to Mildred and back again.

"Mason Adler, Miss Evans," he said. Lucy Evans was a pretty woman, in her mid-thirties, small in stature but with a nice figure, long, wavy russet-colored hair, and big brown doe eyes on either side of a delicate nose, which appeared to be dripping. She wore a green and yellow plaid housedress, with simple brown shoes upon her small feet, and a tiny gold cross hung on a gold chain about her delicate white neck.

"How do you do, Mr. Adler? So you know who I am," she said, dabbing at her nose with a white handkerchief she clutched in her right hand.

Mason nodded. "Your sister here mentioned you to me. She and I were discussing what happened to Miss Claggett."

Lucy shivered and shuddered and blew her nose gently into the handkerchief. "Oh, wasn't that just too awful? I've barely slept since it happened. I just can't imagine. It's all just too awful."

"I agree," Mason said. "I'm a private detective, Miss Evans. Miss Castle's father hired me to investigate the murder."

"Oh, how interesting!" Lucy said, brightening. "I've never met a private detective before."

"Did you need something, Lucy?" Mrs. Comstock said.

"Hmm?" Lucy said, looking critically now at Mrs. Comstock. "Mildred! What happened to your lip? It's red and swollen, and there's blood on your blouse."

"I bumped it, is all. I'll be fine."

"You should put an ice pack on it right away," Lucy said, moving closer to her with a concerned look on her face.

"I will, when we get back downstairs."

"And change out of that shirt so I can soak it," Lucy said.

"What are you doing here, Lucy?" Mrs. Comstock said.

"Oh, well, Wanda Porter in 2A called down to our apartment a little bit ago and said she heard a lot of noise coming from up here, stomping about and whatnot. I couldn't for the life of me think what was going on since no one's supposed to be in here. It scared me something fierce. I didn't know where you were, Mildred, so I figured I'd better take the passkey and come see for myself."

"I'm afraid that was just me and Mr. Adler practicing some dance moves," Mrs. Comstock said.

"Dance moves?" Lucy said, a slightly puzzled look on her pale face.

"Your sister jokes, Miss Evans. I'm sorry we frightened you," Mason said, smiling again.

She blew her nose once more. "Oh. That's okay, I guess. I'm just glad it was you two and not something else. Or *someone* else. Lavinia Stutgard in 2B said a man claiming to be her friend Mike LaMont buzzed her apartment a little while ago. She let him in, but he never showed up at her door, so finally she tried telephoning him at his house and found out he was still at home and had never come over today. I thought maybe whoever that was pretending to be this Mike person was actually one of those reporters again, nosing about and being sneaky."

Mrs. Comstock shot Mason a look. "Someone pretending to be

Mike, eh? Gee, I wonder who that could have been? Someone who didn't have a key to get in the building, perhaps? Which is how they managed to gain access without too much difficulty?"

Mason looked back at her. "Perhaps, Mrs. Comstock. You should warn your residents to be more careful as to who they buzz into the building."

"We'll do that," Mrs. Comstock said flatly.

"Yes, of course we will. Especially after what happened to poor Gertrude," Lucy said. "It's just too awful."

"Yes, it certainly is," Mason said. "By the way, did either of you see anyone the afternoon of the murder?"

"See anyone? What do you mean?" Miss Evans said.

"In relation to Miss Claggett or Miss Castle," Mason explained.

"I didn't, but I believe you said you did, didn't you, Lucy?" Mrs. Comstock said.

Lucy nodded. "That's right, I did. I was out front watering the flowers in the pots on the stoop when Mr. Castleberry arrived to pick up Charlotte."

"I understand she came down to meet him rather than him going up," Mason said.

"That's right. He only waited a few minutes, she came right out, said goodbye to me and gave me the keys to the building and the apartment, then they drove away. Shortly after that, I saw Miss Claggett's brother, Josiah, arrive. He had been staying with the girls for a short while but moved out a couple of weeks ago, thankfully."

"Why thankfully?" Mason said.

"The ladies are not allowed to have overnight male guests, but since he was Miss Claggett's brother, we made an exception," Mrs. Comstock said, "on Lucy's insistence. But it was only supposed to be for a few nights."

"That's right," Lucy said. "I wanted to help Gertrude, but those two fought all the time, and some of the other ladies complained about the noise. Josiah was only working part-time and always hanging about the place. He'd stop me in the hall or in the laundry room and patter on about something, spouting statistics or facts of some kind or another. He's not right in the head, and I don't mind telling you he made me uncomfortable. So, we were both glad when he finally moved out, and I think Miss Claggett and Miss Castle were, too."

"Where did he go?"

"Gertrude's boyfriend, Mr. Patterson, took him in until he can find another place," Lucy said, dabbing at her nose again.

"That was kind of Mr. Patterson. So, you saw Josiah arrive shortly after Miss Castle left with her father?" Mason said.

Lucy nodded. "Yes. I saw him get out of a car and come up the sidewalk, then the car drove away. Josiah's always particular about his appearance, I'll give you that. His hair was combed, his face shaved, and he was wearing a clean shirt and a yellow tie with a brown jacket and tan trousers. Even his shoes were shined. He *looked* quite respectable and normal, but as he got closer and I said good day to him, he didn't answer, as if he didn't even hear me. I could see trouble in his eyes. I didn't like the look of him one bit."

"About what time was that, Miss Evans?"

"Oh, I think it was a little after five. I always wait until a little after five to water this time of year, because it's so hot, you know."

"Yes, it certainly is. So, he came in to the building?" Mason said. "Josiah, I mean."

"He did. *I* wasn't about to let him in, but his sister must have opened the door, because he went in and up the stairs without a word to me, which is unusual for him, but like I said, he didn't seem to notice or even hear me. He looked troubled, distracted, and upset. I finished up outside and went back to Mildred's and my apartment. Then, a short while later, a young lady arrived, Miss Audrey Allen, to inquire about an apartment. Of course at the time we didn't have any vacancies, but now we have this one, I suppose."

"You never told me we had a prospective tenant on Monday," Mrs. Comstock said.

"Oh, with everything that happened, I guess I just forgot. She's not looking to move in until the fall, anyway. She's going to be going to college here. She's a real pretty girl, peroxide blonde, just like Jean Harlow, remember her? Gee, Miss Harlow's been gone a while now, but I always loved her movies. She had on perfume, too, a real pretty scent, but kind of strong and overpowering."

"Jean Harlow did?" Mason said.

Lucy laughed lightly. "No, silly, this girl looking for an apartment, Miss Allen. But I imagine Miss Harlow wore perfume, too. So sad about her."

"Yes, she died much too young," Mason said. "So, this woman wanted to see an apartment?"

"She was really just looking for information and wanted to know if I thought we'd have any vacancies come fall. I thought at first maybe she'd be a potential new roommate for Gertrude, Miss Claggett, I mean, but Miss Allen was kind of flashy for Gertrude. She had lots of questions, though. Gee, we must have talked for forty-five minutes or more. I gave her a tour of the building, too. She was worried about security, but I assured her we keep the building locked up tight. I even showed her the back door and how it's always kept locked, too. No one goes in or out of the building that's not supposed to. Well, most of the time, anyway, except for whoever that was pretending to be Mike earlier."

"I think you'll find, Lucy, that person is a tall, skinny, sneaky private detective," Mrs. Comstock said, staring squinty eyed at Mason.

Lucy's own eyes got big. "Oh? Oh! You mean it was you?" she said, also looking at Mason. "I'm so relieved, Mr. Adler. I just couldn't imagine, and I admit I was worried and a little scared."

"My apologies, again, Miss Evans. It wasn't my intention to frighten you."

"I understand, I think. Anyway, I really liked Audrey, Miss Allen, I mean, and I hope we can find her an apartment when she's ready," Lucy said, now looking at Mildred.

"We'll see," Mrs. Comstock said briskly.

"Sure, Mildred, I know you'll want to meet her first. You'll like her, too, though. She even came in the kitchen with me and helped while I baked a cake, wasn't that nice of her? Of course we had just put it in the oven when the front door buzzer buzzed. When I asked who was there, a man answered and said he had come from the train station to pick up Miss Castle's trunk and suitcases. I told him to buzz 3A, but he claimed no one answered. So, I let him in, thinking perhaps Gertrude was on the phone or something, as she was supposed to be home. Charlotte had said before she left Gertrude had agreed to sign for the bags."

"Was Miss Claggett's brother still here visiting at that point?" Mason said.

"I personally never saw him leave," Lucy said. "I do know some of the other tenants told me later that they heard him and his sister quarreling loudly, just like they used to when he was staying here."

"Do you know what they were arguing about this time?"

"No, sir, just that some of the residents complained there was a lot of shouting and yelling going on, mostly from Josiah. I never heard it myself, but that's because I'd gone back to our apartment."

"You never heard it because you were preoccupied with that pretty young girl," Mrs. Comstock said, clearly annoyed.

"Well, it's my job to be friendly to the tenants and prospective tenants, Mildred."

"But you're getting to be too friendly with them, and I don't like it."

"What happened after you let the man from the station into the building?" Mason said.

"Well, I buzzed this fellow in, but then I thought perhaps Gertrude, Miss Claggett, I mean, might have been in the bathroom or napping or something, and she certainly wouldn't like this man just showing up at her door unannounced. I tried telephoning her, but she didn't answer the phone. Then I got worried and thought I'd better go upstairs and have a look for myself."

Mason turned toward the older woman. "And where were you at that point, Mrs. Comstock?"

"I was in the boiler room pretty much all day, working on the heating system."

"In this heat?"

"Better to make sure it's in working order now before the cold weather arrives."

"Conscientious of you," Mason said.

"I would have made a good Boy Scout," Mildred Comstock replied dryly.

"No doubt," Mason said, turning back to Lucy. "So, Miss Evans, you went upstairs to see what Miss Claggett was doing after you couldn't reach her on the telephone?"

"Well, that was my intent, but Miss Allen was still here, and I had the cake in the oven and all, and anyway, before long that man from the train station had come back downstairs with the trunk and the suitcases and was knocking on the door. He wanted me to sign for Miss Castle's bags. I told him Miss Claggett was supposed to do that, but he claimed the apartment door was ajar when he got upstairs and no one appeared to be home."

"I see. So did you sign?"

"I did," she said, sniffling. "But as I told Mildred later, there was something odd about the man, something sinister."

"How so?"

"He was tall and quiet, mysterious, like he was up to no good. And the fact that he said the door was open and no one was there. Poor Gertrude. Such a nice girl, you see."

"You think this man from the station had something to do with her death?" Mason said.

Lucy nodded, her handkerchief to her nose. "It's certainly possible. As I said, he *claimed* the apartment door was ajar when he got upstairs and no one appeared to be home, not Gertrude nor Josiah, so he just took the trunk and bags and left. But who knows what really happened?"

"That's what I'm trying to determine," Mason said.

"I suppose that is what private detectives do," Miss Evans said, sniffling even more. "Anyway, it wasn't long after that when Mr. Patterson showed up, saying he was here to see Gertrude, Miss Claggett, I mean."

"He buzzed you on Monday afternoon, too?" Mason said to Lucy.

"That's right," Lucy said. "I let him in and met him in the hall."

"What about the young woman who was looking for an apartment?" Mason said.

"Yes, Lucy, what about her?" Mrs. Comstock said, staring hard at the younger woman.

"Oh, when Mr. Patterson buzzed, Miss Allen said she thought she'd better be going as she could see I was busy, so I gave her our business card and told her to check back with us in July, as we require a two-month notice to vacate, and we'd know better then what would be available for September."

"All right," Mason said. "But back to Mr. Patterson. You said you met him in the hall?"

"Yes, I did, since the young lady was leaving anyway. He said he'd tried buzzing 3A also, just like the fellow from the station did, but he didn't get an answer, either. He said Josiah was coming over, and he was concerned he and his sister might get into a fight. I told him Josiah had already arrived, and I told him about the man picking up the trunk, and how no one was apparently home. He thought that was strange, too, and he seemed real concerned so the two of us went upstairs to have a look. The door to the apartment was ajar, just like the man from the train station had said, only who's to say if he found it that way or just left it that way."

"Indeed," Mason said.

"It sent a little shiver up my spine, I don't mind telling you. Mr. Patterson called out a little hello and then pushed the door open and we both went in. Right away I noticed one of the living room windows was open, but otherwise everything seemed normal. Mr. Patterson went to the window and saw Miss Claggett's brother hurrying away on the sidewalk below. He called out to him, but I guess he didn't answer."

"Curious," Mason said.

"Yes. We never saw him coming down the stairs, so we figure he went down the fire escape for some reason, which is why I never saw him leave. It was most peculiar, but then, Josiah is a peculiar man."

"It sounds like it. What did you do then?"

"Well, we had a brief look around the apartment, but as I say, nothing seemed out of place and no one was there. It was all so strange, like she'd just disappeared into thin air." Lucy shuddered again, dabbed at her dripping nose once more, and gave it another blow.

"Only she hadn't just disappeared into thin air," Mason said. "Her body was in that trunk that was taken away."

"I can't even imagine," Lucy said. "Horrible."

"Yes, quite horrible," Mason said, now looking at the older woman once more. "And you were supposedly in the boiler room all that time, Mrs. Comstock?"

"That's right, why?"

"Just wondering if perhaps you didn't go to the boiler room at all that day. Or at least, not at first."

"What's that supposed to mean? What are you insinuating?"

"Just that maybe instead of going to the boiler room, you came up here to see Miss Claggett, perhaps after her brother left but before the man from the train station and Mr. Patterson arrived."

"Why would I do that?" Mrs. Comstock said, clenching her fists now.

"Yes, why would Mildred do that?" Lucy said, puzzled as she looked back and forth at them.

"That's a good question. By the way, I understand Miss Claggett gave Lucy a necklace…"

Lucy's left hand went to her neck, where the simple gold cross hung from a gold chain. "Gertrude did give me this," she said. "It was so sweet of her, not even my birthday."

"What of it?" Mrs. Comstock said, annoyed.

"Just that it was a very nice gesture," Mason said, looking at Mrs. Comstock with a steady gaze. "And I understand your sister here frequently brought Miss Claggett baked goods and fresh flowers, and was often complimenting her on her appearance, touching her arms, her hair, doing favors for her…"

"I was just being friendly," Lucy said. "Gertrude wasn't beautiful in the traditional sense, but she had a way about her, you know? Fresh scrubbed, natural beauty, with long, soft, auburn hair." Lucy blushed. "I, I did like her, but just as a friend, of course."

Mason turned to Lucy. "Of course, part of your job is to be friendly and helpful to the young ladies, I understand."

"Yes, that's right."

"As I said before, you're *too* friendly. Look at all the problems it's caused," Mrs. Comstock said.

Mason looked back at the older woman. "I understand you didn't like Miss Evans being too friendly with the residents. And rumor has it Miss Claggett found out something about the two of you she didn't like. Is that one of the problems you're referring to?"

"I don't know what you're talking about," Mrs. Comstock said.

"Oh, Mildred," Lucy said softly.

Mason pressed on. "I'm told Miss Claggett even said she was going to inform the police about the two of you, and you, Mrs. Comstock, threatened to tear up her lease and throw her out. I imagine if the police found out about all that, it wouldn't have gone over so well with your other tenants and future tenants, would it? In fact, the police might have even shut you down and arrested the two of you."

"Gertrude didn't mean it," Lucy said. "About informing the police, I mean. Gert was a nice girl. She would have never—"

"Oh, I think she would have," Mrs. Comstock said, her voice a low growl.

Mason turned back to Mrs. Comstock. "Perhaps she would have, and I'm sure you were worried about that. Maybe you came up here to see Miss Claggett about it all, to ask her about her intentions, unbeknownst to your sister. Maybe Gertrude said she was going to call the police, you and she argued, one thing led to another, and you strangled her. In a panic, knowing someone was coming for the trunk and bags shortly, you broke the lock on the trunk, removed the clothes, stuffed them under the bed, and put her body in the trunk. Then you left and went to the boiler room to attend to the heating system as if nothing had happened. And perhaps you came back tonight to make sure you didn't leave any clues, or to dispose of Miss Castle's clothes, which, I discovered, are still under the bed."

"How dare you? I would never…" She had both fists clenched and seemed ready for a fight again. Lucy looked horrified.

"Oh, but in a fit of anger, fear, and jealousy perhaps you would, even though you didn't mean to, or intend to, when you first came up here to confront her," Mason said. "Clearly you're quite strong. I think I may need a neck brace after that headlock you had me in, and as I said, my lower back will have a nice-sized bruise on it."

"Headlock? Bruise? What are you talking about?" Lucy said, sniffling fiercely now, her eyes watery with tears.

"You deserved it, and then some, Mr. Adler," Mrs. Comstock said, her voice harsh. "I only wish now I would have punched you right in the kisser. I still might."

"I'd advise against that," Mason said, also bracing for another fight, his right hand ready to go for his gun again if necessary.

"Mildred would never kill anyone, Mr. Adler, never!" Lucy said, her tears now dropping down onto her soft pink cheeks.

"Maybe not, but maybe so," Mason said. "By the way, Mrs. Comstock, you still haven't told me why you really came in here tonight."

"I *did* tell you. I just wanted to have a look around, that's all, make sure the windows were closed and locked in case some reporter tried to get in. I was just being conscientious."

"And yet you never told Lucy you were coming here. She said a short while ago she didn't know where you were when the woman in 2A called to complain about us making noise."

"It was a spur-of-the-moment decision," she said. "I'd been fixing the icebox in 3B across the hall, and as I passed by I thought I'd just stop in and have a look-see."

"Interesting."

"Not really. I guess I've just been a landlady so long I do things automatically, like making sure windows are closed and faucets are off in unoccupied apartments, especially, as I said, with all that's happened. Besides, I saw the light on under the door and found that odd."

"Of course you did," Mason said, though he didn't sound convinced. "Well, I suppose I should let you two get back to things, then, but I would advise against coming in here again without notifying Miss Castle or Miss Claggett's family. I'm sure they'll be wanting to remove her belongings."

"It's really just her brother, and I doubt he'll care much what happens to any of it, unless he can make a buck or two. I'll notify him and Miss Castle tomorrow that we intend to enter and remove Miss Claggett's belongings and put them in storage so we can attempt to rent the place," Mrs. Comstock said, relaxing her left hand but keeping her right fist clenched.

"What of the furniture?" Mason said.

"It's a furnished flat, Mr. Adler. All our apartments come fully furnished," Lucy said, drying her eyes with the damp handkerchief and blowing her nose once more. "Right down to the dishes."

"I see," Mason said. "By the way, would either of you two ladies happen to know where I might find Miss Claggett's brother, Josiah?"

"As I mentioned earlier, he's staying with Miss Claggett's boyfriend, John Patterson, but I don't have an address," Mrs. Comstock said. "I'm sure Mr. Patterson is probably in the telephone directory, though."

"Right, thank you. Well, if you're finished checking the windows and faucets, Mrs. Comstock, perhaps we should head downstairs."

"Yes, Mildred, I have dinner ready," Lucy said. "And a chocolate cake for dessert, but first you need to change out of that blouse."

"Fine," Mrs. Comstock replied. She turned off the overhead light and walked out of the bedroom and through the apartment to the main hall as Lucy and Mason followed behind, Lucy still sniffling. Mrs. Comstock turned off the living room light and locked the door behind the three of them once they were all out in the hall.

They took the stairs down to the first floor and walked to the front entrance on Roosevelt.

"Good evening, ladies," Mason said, tipping his hat in their direction.

"Good evening, Mr. Adler," Mrs. Comstock said tersely before turning to Lucy. "And blow your nose—you really should do something about those damned allergies."

Mason drove back to his apartment and climbed the stairs. He really wasn't hungry, having eaten so much at the Cactus Cantina, nor was he overly tired. It was just coming eight o'clock, much too early for bed, so he poured himself a scotch, neat, and made himself as comfortable as possible in his easy chair, deciding to read a bit of the book Lydia had given him for his birthday last month, *Great Expectations* by Charles Dickens. At ten fifteen, after a refill or two of his scotch and several more chapters, Mason put the book aside, washed out his glass, and filled the bowl on the kitchen counter with ice cubes, which he then carried into the bedroom and set before the electric fan in the corner by his bed. He switched the fan on, brushed his teeth, undressed, and climbed into bed, tired, sore, and puzzled.

CHAPTER SEVEN

Morning, Wednesday, May 8, 1946
Mason Adler's apartment

The morning came slowly to Mason, who was bathed in sweat from another long, hot, sleepless night. He hauled his naked body out of bed, his neck and lower back stiff, sore, and aching, and walked slowly to the bathroom to use the toilet. He flushed, took two aspirin, and decided that in spite of the heat, he would take a hot bath to hopefully relieve the pain. He soaked in the tub until the water cooled, only then pulling himself up and out, noting the time was almost nine thirty.

With a fresh white towel wrapped about his waist, he brushed his teeth and shaved, the various aches and pains at least temporarily somewhat subsided. Mason went from the bathroom into the bedroom and switched off the fan in the corner of the room nearest the bed. Carefully he picked up the bowl of now-tepid water that had been ice the night before and dumped it down the bathroom sink drain. Still clad only in a towel, he went to the kitchen, where he fixed some oatmeal and coffee along with a glass of fresh-squeezed orange juice. When he'd finished, he washed his dishes, set them in the rack to dry, and shuffled slowly back to the bedroom, where he hung up his damp towel, put on a fresh, clean pair of white briefs, and changed into a gray linen suit with a dark blue tie and gold cufflinks. He tugged on a pair of black over-the-calf socks and black cap toe dress shoes, freshly polished, and tucked a clean white handkerchief into his breast pocket before walking over to the telephone near the front door.

As promised, he rang up the police station and asked to be connected to Detective Emil Hardwick, who answered on the third ring.

"Hardwick here."

"Good morning, Emil, it's Mason."

"Oh, yes, good morning. Find anything else out?"

"Maybe. I just wanted to let you know I had a conversation with Mrs. Comstock and Miss Evans last night, the owners and managers of Miss Claggett's apartment building. They, uh, showed me Miss Claggett and Miss Castle's apartment, with Miss Castle's permission, of course."

"Yeah? We talked to Comstock and Evans yesterday morning, as I believe I mentioned. Nice enough women, I guess, though a bit odd. The younger one kept sniffling and sneezing and her nose was dripping like Niagara Falls."

"Allergies, apparently," Mason said.

"Figured as much. All this damned dust in the air. Whoever thought living in the middle of the desert was a good idea?"

"I like the desert," Mason said. "Anyway, I got the impression Mrs. Comstock didn't care for Miss Claggett much. I think they may have quarreled the day she died."

"Women fight with each other all the time, Mason, like feral cats. Means nothing."

"But I can attest to the fact that Mrs. Comstock is rather strong. She could have easily strangled Miss Claggett," Mason said, massaging his neck.

"I suppose. She did look a little on the brawny side."

"More than a little. By the way, I found a bunch of women's clothes wadded up and shoved under one of the beds. I suspect they're the ones taken out of Miss Castle's trunk to make room for the body."

"What were you doing looking under the beds?"

"Searching the apartment, like I thought you said you did yesterday morning."

"We had a look around, took fingerprints and photographs, as usual. But frankly I didn't see the point in getting down on my hands and knees and looking under the beds."

"You never know what you might find, Emil."

"Yeah, apparently. I'll send a crew over this morning to retrieve the clothes and bring them to the lab once Miss Castle makes a positive ID that they are indeed hers. We'll check them for any markings or loose hairs that may belong to the murderer, but I doubt we'll find anything."

"Who knows, you may get lucky and find an intact fingerprint or something."

"Stranger things have happened."

"Indeed."

"If we do find a print, loose hair, or anything else, we'll need to compare it to our main suspects."

"Your main suspects being Alfred Brody and Charlotte Castle," Mason said.

"That's right, though we still want to talk to the brother once we find him."

"But Mrs. Comstock definitely appears to have had a motive, as well as opportunity and means."

"What's her motive, other than that she didn't seem to care for Miss Claggett and they argued? That seems pretty weak."

"If she murdered her, it may not have been premeditated. It may have been in the heat of that argument."

"What did they argue about?"

"I'm not sure exactly," Mason said, which wasn't precisely the truth. "But Mrs. Comstock is quite strong, and she seems hotheaded. Perhaps they argued over late rent or, uh, something more important, and tempers flared. Maybe Miss Claggett struck out at Mrs. Comstock, and Mrs. Comstock strangled her in a rage."

"And she hid the body in Miss Castle's trunk?"

"Why not? It would certainly take suspicion off herself. I wouldn't rule out Mrs. Comstock or even Miss Evans as a suspect, if I were you."

"Fine, I'll check them out more thoroughly and have another

chat with them, a little more in depth. Anything's possible, I suppose."

"And don't forget Miss Powell. Did you speak with her yet?"

"No, but she's on the list for this morning, for what it's worth."

"She's an interesting woman, so prepare yourself."

"Duly noted. What about you? What do you have planned for the day?"

"I want to talk to the boyfriend, John Patterson."

"And Alfred Brody, I'm willing to bet," Emil said.

"Unless you have any objections."

"Nope, it's a free country. If he's willing to talk to you, be my guest."

"Gracious of you," Mason said.

"Did you ask that fella about the mountain cabin yet, by the way?"

"No, but I will today."

"Great, let me know. Listen, I gotta go, Mason, Simons wants to talk to me. But thanks for the call. Let me know if you think of anything else."

"Okay, see ya round, Emil."

"Bye."

Mason's next call was to the city auditor's office. Miss Gleason was still screening Mr. Castleberry's calls, but she put him through after he identified himself.

"Mr. Castleberry speaking."

"Good morning, it's Mason Adler."

"Yes, good morning, Mr. Adler. It's good to hear from you. Find anything out?"

"A few things. I see you decided to go into the office again today."

"Yes, the reporters seem to have backed off a bit. The calls are fewer, both here and at the house, and no one was hanging around downstairs or outside when I arrived, thankfully."

"Yesterday's news," Mason said.

"What's that?"

"Gertrude Claggett's murder. Yesterday's news. I'm sure by

now the reporters have gone on to other events, having come up dry in her death. If something new develops, though, I'm sure they'll be all over it again."

"Yes, I suppose you're right."

"The way of the world, is all," Mason said. "I'm calling because I wanted to let you know I visited your daughter's former apartment yesterday, as I said I would, and I met with Mrs. Comstock and Miss Evans."

"Oh, those two. Those, uh, those…"

"I believe the word you're looking for is lesbians, Mr. Castleberry. And I think your daughter was correct about that, not that it matters in the scheme of things, but it may end up being a motive for murder."

"How's that?"

"Too soon to tell at present. By the way, I also believe I found your daughter's clothes, the ones taken out of the trunk to make room for Miss Claggett's body. They were shoved under one of the beds in the bedroom of the apartment."

"That makes sense, I suppose," Mr. Castleberry said. "I doubt Charlotte will want to go back there, but I could stop on my way home from the office and get them for her."

"That won't be necessary, or even possible, I'm afraid," Mason said. "The police are going to retrieve them, and your daughter will have to identify them."

"Identify them how?"

"I'm not sure, exactly. They may just ask her to describe the items that were in the trunk, or they may have her come down to the station to look at them."

"I hope it's the former. Charlotte's been through so much already. Why do the police want them, anyway?"

"So they can have them taken to the lab and checked."

"Checked? Checked for what?"

"Stray hairs, blood, fingerprints, that sort of thing. Anything that may have come from the person who murdered Miss Claggett. Chances are she was already dead when the trunk was emptied, so it's hard to say what may or may not be on those clothes."

"Oh my. If I tell Charlotte that, she won't want the clothes back anyway, so I guess it doesn't matter."

"Nonetheless, the police will notify you when they're finished with them, and you can decide what to do from that point."

"Sure, thanks. What's your next step, Mr. Adler?"

"I want to talk with the man from the train station who picked up the trunk and suitcases, and also Miss Claggett's boyfriend, John Patterson."

"You think either of them had anything to do with the murder?"

"I honestly don't know, though the police have other ideas. I'll keep you apprised of what I find out. I suppose I should also tell you the police want to question your daughter more fully, which they may do in conjunction with her identifying those clothes."

"I don't like the sound of that, Mr. Adler. She's been through so much already. Isn't there something you can do?"

"I'm doing everything I can, Mr. Castleberry. I would advise that Charlotte cooperate fully with the police and the investigating detective, and keep a cool head about her. Tell her to answer any questions honestly, but not to volunteer information. And of course, if you haven't already, I would suggest obtaining legal counsel."

"Yes, I've already contacted Daryl D. Dupree. He's one of the best in town, and an old friend of the family."

"Glad to hear it," Mason said. "If she has to go to the station for questioning, make sure he accompanies her."

"Thank you, I will."

"Oh, I also had an interesting conversation with Miss Julia Powell yesterday after I left your office."

"So I heard. Clarence, one of the building security guards, telephoned me to check up on you. He said you were in the lobby talking with her."

"City hall has a good man in that Clarence. What's your take on Miss Powell?"

"I don't really know her, to be honest. I mean, she works in the typing pool, and she's a friend of Charlotte's, but my personal interactions with her have been quite limited. Why do you ask?"

"Just following up on all possible leads, Mr. Castleberry."

"Fair enough. I'll be at the office until about five thirty today if you need anything else or find out any other pertinent information. You can reach me at my home after that, 5-2834."

Mason jotted it down on the pad next to the phone. "Got it. If not later today, I'll touch base tomorrow."

"All right, I'm usually here in the office by eight. If I'm not in, you may leave a message with Miss Gleason. Good day, Mr. Adler."

"Good day, Mr. Castleberry," Mason said, hanging up the receiver as he dragged out the telephone directory from a drawer in his nearby rolltop desk. He couldn't find a listing for an Alfred Brody, so Mason put the directory away and headed out into the heat of the day, pausing only to put on his straw boater.

CHAPTER EIGHT

Later that morning, Wednesday, May 8, 1946
Mason Adler's apartment

When he reached the first floor of his apartment building, he crossed the open courtyard to Mr. Blanders's place and rapped on his door. Fortunately, he was at home. Mason let him know Emil was indeed interested in possibly buying the mountain cabin and would like to take Mr. Blanders up on his offer to let him try it out, preferably the weekend of May 25. Mr. Blanders was agreeable and made a note of it on his calendar, thanked Mason, and said he'd be in touch to get Emil the keys and instructions. Mason gave him Emil's home telephone number, bid him good day, and headed out to Central Avenue and around to Encanto, where he had parked his car overnight.

Since Union Station was on his way, more or less, to John Patterson's place, he decided to stop there first and have a word with Alfred Brody before Emil brought him into the station for questioning along with Miss Castle and possibly other suspects. He parked his Studebaker in a somewhat shady spot on Harrison, which was really just a block extension of Fourth Avenue, and walked toward the two-story adobe building, which had single-story wings jutting out on either side. As he approached, he could smell the burned coal hanging in the air from the steam engines, the odor of the new diesels, and the creosote from the railroad ties on the tracks, which were baking in the late morning sun.

He entered the large general waiting room through the entrance on Harrison and looked about. The sounds of a busy depot on a Wednesday morning accosted his ears as people hurried by chattering away, and porters, loaded down with luggage, followed behind, going this way or that. A lunch counter and small newsstand were to his left, and smells of coffee, bacon, cigarettes, and newsprint wafted out to him. Men, women, and children sat on long wooden benches in the center of the waiting room as they waited for their trains, or for passengers arriving on them, Mason supposed. And to his right was a ticket counter manned by neatly groomed men of various ages in blue uniforms with brass buttons. Just before the ticket counter was a short hallway, and the door leading to it had a sign above it marked *To baggage room, employees only.*

He waited until all the clerks at the ticket counter were occupied with passengers and then he walked briskly through the door and down the hall to the large baggage and freight area, which had two sets of double doors open to both the street and the tracks. Piles of luggage of every type and size were scattered around, some on carts or dollies and some stacked precariously, waiting to be loaded onto the next train, or perhaps the one after that. Pallets of crates and containers lined the far wall, headed for destinations unknown. In this area, even with the doors open to the outside, the odors of leather, oil, and sweat hit Mason's nostrils, and the air was still and thick. A couple of brawny men were wrestling with a cart at the far end of the room, sweating profusely, their skin glistening, in sharp contrast to the neatly uniformed men behind the ticket counter in the main waiting room.

A fairly short, heavyset man in his late forties with a squat, wide nose, small dark eyes, short reddish-brown hair, and a bushy red mustache growing out of his nostrils walked over to him. "Employees only in this area, sir. The waiting room is back down that hall, and if you're looking for the men's restroom, it's through the smoking room on the other side of the main entrance." His voice had a bit of a Southern drawl to it, his teeth stained and discolored, most likely from the wad of chewing tobacco in his left cheek.

"Thank you," Mason said, glancing about the cavernous space.

"Don't mention it. You're not the first passenger to wander back here by mistake, mister, so don't feel too bad."

"Right. Actually, though, I'm not looking for the waiting room or the men's toilet, I'm looking for Mr. Brody. Is he working today?"

The man looked Mason up and down. "Oh." He paused, sticking his right hand down inside his overalls and adjusting himself. "Cop, are ya?"

"No."

"You're another one of those reporters, then. If you want pictures or information it will cost you. Ten cents a photograph, and information's more, depending."

"I'm not a reporter, I'm a private detective. It's my understanding Mr. Brody works here, and I was wondering if I could speak to him if he happens to be on duty."

"Mr. Brody, indeed," Leland drawled. "You mean Alfred."

"Alfred Brody, yes. So Mr. Brody."

The bullish-looking man spat his chewing tobacco into a nearby spittoon. "He *did* work here, or at least he was employed here, but he got himself fired. Happened yesterday, when he showed up for his shift. Left me short-handed and overworked, goddammit."

"I'm sorry to hear that. What was he fired for, and why?"

The little man squinted at Mason, one small, dark eye almost completely closed. "What's it to you?"

"As I said, I'm a private investigator looking into the murder of Gertrude Claggett. The name's Adler. Mason T. Adler."

"Ehh, you mean that poor dead woman in the trunk. I'm the one that found her, you know. It was awful. Smelled bad, too."

"I can imagine. Do you know where I can find Mr. Brody?"

He extracted his right hand from his overalls, took out another piece of chewing tobacco from a back pocket, and stuck it in his left cheek. "I figure he done it."

"Who?" Mason said, looking at him quizzically.

"Alfred, of course."

"Oh, and what do you figure he did?"

"Killed her, naturally. He was always acting uppity."

"I don't see how those two things are connected, Mr....? I'm sorry, I didn't catch your name."

"Mr. Burrows. Leland O. Burrows. I'm the senior baggage clerk. Been here nearly twenty years," he said.

"Congratulations," Mason said dryly. "It sounds like you didn't care for Mr. Brody much."

"Eh, Alfred was always acting like he was better than me, smarter than me, smarter than us white folks, ya know what I mean?"

"Ah, I think I do know what you mean. It probably wasn't an act, Mr. Burrows, at least not in your case."

"Huh?"

"Exactly," Mason said. "What happened to Mr. Brody?"

"Like I said, if you want information it will cost you. Twenty-five cents."

Mason reached in the pocket of his trousers and extracted his coin purse, from which he withdrew a quarter and handed it to the little man. "All right, here."

Mr. Burrows took it and dropped it into one of his own pockets. "Thanks. Old Mr. Dawson fired him after he heard about that dead girl in the trunk. Mr. Dawson is the station manager."

"What exactly did happen the night Miss Claggett's body was found, Mr. Burrows?"

Leland moved the tobacco around in his cheek. "Alfred went to her apartment to pick up her trunk and bags. The way I figure it, she was home alone. He made a pass at her, she declined, and he forced himself on her."

"You mean you think he raped her."

"Yes, sir, without a doubt. Then he strangled her and shoved her body in her trunk and hauled it on down here to the station. Some mangy dog he was always feeding started sniffing around the trunk. I investigated, and together with Mr. Dawson, we found her body inside."

"Actually, Mr. Burrows, the trunk belonged to Miss Claggett's roommate, Miss Castle, not her."

"Yeah, well, either way, that's what happened, mark my word."

"Do you have a home address for Mr. Brody?"

"He lives in South Phoenix, of course, with the rest of his kind, on the other side of the tracks, south of the river."

Mason did his best to hold his temper. "Do you have an exact address?"

Leland spat another wad of chewing tobacco toward the spittoon but missed this time. "The exact address will cost you another quarter."

"I'm afraid I'm fresh out of quarters. How about a dime?"

"Eh, I suppose."

Once more Mason extracted a coin from his coin purse and handed it to the man.

"Thanks again, mister."

"Don't mention it," Mason said, annoyed. "Where can I find Mr. Brody?"

"Most likely he's in the county jail by now, but if he's not, he gave his last address as 3842 W. Broadway Road."

Mason jotted it down in his notebook and put it back in his suitcoat pocket. "Okay." He looked at Leland critically. "You know, Mr. Burrows, it sounds like you're convicting the man based on your own particular prejudices."

"The hell you say."

"The hell I do say. Good day."

CHAPTER NINE

Early afternoon, Wednesday, May 8, 1946
Alfred Brody's house

Mason was angry with Leland Burrows, but at the same time he knew he couldn't entirely dismiss Alfred Brody as a suspect without even having met or questioned him. So he decided John Patterson could wait a while longer. When he got back to his car, he headed north on Harrison to Jackson, where he made a right, continuing on to Central Avenue, where he made another right and headed south, taking a right yet again on Broadway Road once he'd crossed the Salt River.

This part of Phoenix was different than the one Mason lived in on Central and Encanto. It had row after row of dilapidated, poorly built shotgun houses, nearly identical in design and built so close together one could almost lean out a side window and borrow a cup of sugar from the neighbor. That is, if the neighbor had any sugar. The streets and alleys were dirty and narrow, and the minuscule plots were nothing more than dust bowls. Litter and garbage were strewn about, having blown free of burn barrels in some of the front yards. Black and Mexican American children played in the streets. They stopped their games long enough to stare at Mason's blue 1939 Studebaker Champion as he drove slowly west, searching the poorly marked shanties for addresses.

Finally he pulled over and parked in the general vicinity, realizing he'd probably have better luck on foot. He put his boater on and got out, stretching his legs and massaging his lower back and his neck as he looked around and up and down the street. The still, hot air smelled putrid, and he tried not to take in deep breaths as he began walking down the narrow dirt path that ran alongside Broadway Road. He paused periodically to check house numbers when there were any, finally coming across 3842.

The black metal mailbox out front, sitting precariously atop a wooden post, had the name *A. Brody* written on its side in neat white paint. The house was a narrow single-story wooden railroad flat with peeling paint, a rusted tin roof, and a stoop made from two cinder blocks. A tired-looking 1930 Ford Model A sat out front, baking in the sun along with everything else. Mason walked up the dirt path, differentiated from the dirt plot of land on either side by stones and rocks, and knocked upon the open door, which was flanked by two small open windows. From within, a dog barked several times, and presently a tall, handsome young man appeared in the doorway, dressed in a clean white short-sleeve shirt and loose-fitting brown trousers. His large feet were bare. A rail-thin dog stood at his side, sniffing and panting in Mason's direction, wagging his tail.

"Yes?" the young man said cautiously, his voice a deep baritone.

"Mr. Brody?" Mason said.

He stared out suspiciously at the well-dressed detective standing on his cinder block stoop. "Who are you?"

"I'm Mason Adler, sir. I'm a private detective, and I'd like to ask you a few questions about the murder of Miss Gertrude Claggett."

The young man sighed and shook his head. "I see. Well, Mr. Adler, I'm afraid I really don't have anything else to say about that to you or anyone else. I've already been questioned by the police and a police detective, and two newspaper fellas were here earlier asking all kinds of questions and trying to take pictures. My dog here didn't take too kindly to them."

"Nonetheless, I'd like to talk to you also, if I may."

"You can talk, but as I said, I don't have any answers to your questions any more than I did those other men's, so why waste your breath?"

"You don't know the questions I want to ask yet, so how do you know you don't have the answers? It took some doing to get here from Central and Encanto and find your house. I'm only asking for a few minutes."

Alfred shrugged his large shoulders up and down, looked at the dog and then back at Mason. "All right, seeing as how you came all this way, and seeing as how my dog hasn't tried to bite you, I suppose I can spare you a few minutes. Come on in, then. It's too hot to stand out here." He stood aside and ushered Mason in to the small, narrow sitting room. Behind it stood a kitchen, and beyond that, through an open door, Mason could see a room with a metal bedstead, and an exterior door beyond that, which also stood open. The sitting room had an old-fashioned davenport on the left, a wood parlor stove on the right, an easy chair next to that, and a small bookcase behind the chair, partially filled with well-used books. In the fairly wide doorway to the kitchen stood a wooden dining table and three mismatched chairs.

"Have a seat at the table, Mr. Adler. You can hang your hat on the hook, next to mine."

"Thanks." Mason did as suggested and made himself relatively comfortable on one of the wooden chairs at the small round table, despite the pain in his lower back. Alfred took a seat opposite him. The old dog, Mason noticed, slouched down onto the bare wooden floor next to Alfred, but kept his gaze on Mason.

"I'd offer you something to drink, but I'm afraid I don't have much," Alfred said. "I could get you a Coke, but it's not cold, or I could make coffee, if you like."

"I'm fine, really, but thank you, Mr. Brody."

Alfred leaned back in his chair and looked at Mason. "It's funny hearing you call me sir and Mr. Brody."

Mason was puzzled. "That's your name, isn't it? Alfred Brody?"

"Yes, but white folks don't typically call me Mr. Brody. To them I'm Al or Alfred at best. I won't mention what they call me at worst. Even those newspaper men that were here. They called me Alfred and insinuated some nasty things."

"Oh, I see. I'm sorry to hear that. People can be, and often are, ignorant and stupid."

"On that we can agree, Mr. Adler. Anyway, my dog chased them off. He's a pretty good judge of character. That's why I invited you in, because he didn't growl or try to bite you."

"I've always liked animals," Mason said, "and I thank you for letting me in."

Alfred gazed about the small room and into the kitchen, where some dirty dishes stood next to a cast iron sink. "If I'd known you were coming, I'd have straightened up a bit."

"I'm sorry about that, I would have phoned first to let you know, but I couldn't find you in the directory."

"That's because I don't have a phone or electricity, though there is running water in the kitchen at least."

"I see, that's a good thing to have."

"Yes. The house isn't much, but it's mine, anyway, for seven dollars a month."

"Of course." Mason glanced about once more. "You keep it quite clean and tidy."

Alfred shrugged. "Except for the dishes. I normally wash them all after supper because I have to heat water on the stove, and it's too much work to do that for every meal. I don't have a hot water heater."

"That makes sense. But you've nothing to apologize for. The floors are swept, the furniture dusted, your clothes hung up, and things put away. It's cleaner than most people's homes I've been in."

"It's not hard to do when the whole place is less than four hundred square feet. Just a sitting room, kitchen, and bedroom. The toilet's out back along the fence. Works out okay, but you have to be careful of scorpions, especially at night. And then there's the snakes. They like to slither into the privy and curl up in a dark corner. Most of the time after dark I use a chamber pot. Living here is challenging sometimes, for a variety of reasons."

"I can imagine."

Alfred snorted and leaned forward again, resting his forearms on the scrubbed table top. "I doubt that. Do you know I've got a small metal tub in the corner of the bedroom that I bathe in every Saturday night? It takes lots of hot water heated on the wood stove in the kitchen. I'm sure where you live you have indoor plumbing, hot and cold running water, electricity, a telephone, a radio, an electric icebox, and probably even a bathtub and shower."

Mason felt embarrassed. "I guess you're right, Mr. Brody, I can't imagine. I'm sorry."

He snorted again. "Don't be. I didn't expect you to understand. It's how things are for now. I want to live in a proper place someday, and I will. And I want to be a schoolteacher. I earned my teaching certificate just before the war."

"Oh?"

"You sound surprised."

"I guess I shouldn't be, Mr. Brody. You're clearly an educated man, well-spoken and knowledgeable. And I couldn't help but notice all those books."

Alfred looked over at the small bookcase by the front door. "I've read them all, some more than once, and I have a library card, too, that I use often. My mama always told me not to just accept life, but to work to change it, and to make it better, for oneself and for everyone."

"Your mother sounds like a wise woman."

"She is. She worked hard to pay for my schooling, and so did I. I want to make her proud, but since the war ended, I've been unable to find a position at a school. So, until I *do* get an actual teaching job, I do other things to pay the bills. I worked as a street sweeper for a while, and before that I picked oranges in the orange groves, but that was seasonal work. Of course I was in the Army during the war, but assigned as a cook at Fort Huachuca. They didn't think we were fit for combat or leadership, for the most part, and it was dispiriting to say the least. Here we were fighting as a country for democracy, while in the United States, I was treated as a second-class citizen."

"I heard about some of that. I'm so sorry."

"Thanks. At least I did my part as much as I was allowed to, and my cooking didn't make anyone sick at the fort. I learned my way around a kitchen from my mother. Anyway, my latest job was in the baggage room at Union Station downtown."

"Yes, I'm aware of that, but I understand the station manager recently fired you."

"Word travels fast. Yes, good old Mr. Dawson. I hadn't worked there all that long, but I was always on time and I did my job well. He had no reason to fire me."

"But he did," Mason said quietly, massaging his neck, which had grown stiff.

"Yes, sir, he fired me when I showed up for my shift yesterday. He said it was because of what happened with that woman's body in the trunk. But I had nothing to do with that, like I told the police and those reporters. I was a good employee before that happened. I put up with Leland Burrows every day."

Mason chuckled in spite of the pain in his lower back and neck. "For that alone you should have gotten a commendation. I met Mr. Burrows earlier this afternoon. He's the one that gave me your address, for a price."

Alfred smiled for the first time that day. "Sounds like him. Mr. Burrows doesn't give anything away for free that he could get money for. He's a tightwad."

"As well as bigoted, ignorant, and belligerent."

"Yeah, well, be that as it may, at least *he's* still employed, and *I'm* out of a job. Again."

"Yes, that's true, unfortunately. But I'm sure something else will come along."

Alfred crossed his arms and leaned back once more. "May I ask you why you care, Mr. Adler? You don't know me from Adam, and I'm not like you."

Mason leaned forward. "You mean you're not like me because of your dark skin?"

"Something like that, yes. And the fact that you clearly have the money to dress well, probably drive that big blue car I saw parked up the street, live in a nice neighborhood, and you don't have to deal with bigoted, ignorant, belligerent people every day."

"I can see your point, but we're all really just the same, Mr. Brody, aren't we? Dark skin, light skin, or any shade or color in between, rich or poor."

"You really believe that?"

"I do, and I know a thing or two about dealing with bigoted, ignorant, belligerent folks, believe me. We're all just people, doing our best to make a go of it however we were born. We're all the same, but we're also all different, each of us, and that's what makes life interesting."

"I'm not sure I'd use the word interesting, Mr. Adler."

"Well, it would be boring if we were all identical."

"Maybe. But maybe it would be enlightening."

"Perhaps. But the fact is we are the same, but not identical. Some folks are born blind, some with twenty-twenty vision. Some are born a bit off, some are born amazingly smart, and some not so much. Some folks are born naturally talented or gifted, and others aren't. Some are just born, well, different. We all work with what we have and try to make a better life for ourselves and our loved ones, as you said earlier."

"That's what my mama always says, too. She tells anyone who will listen that we have to take care of ourselves and each other. Her younger brother, Gus, my uncle, he was born different, too."

"Oh?" Mason took out his handkerchief and wiped the sweat from his brow before returning it to his pocket.

"Yes. I never knew him, not that I can remember, anyway. He died when I was three. He was only nineteen."

"I'm sorry to hear it, that's awfully young."

"Thank you, and yes, it is. He hung himself, you see, and it was my mama that found him hanging from the rafters."

Mason's blue eyes grew wide. "How awful."

"Yes, sir. It's something she never forgot, and never will."

"Why did he hang himself, if I may ask? Was it because he was born different, as you say?"

Alfred nodded, wiping the sweat from his own brow before continuing. "His daddy, my granddaddy, found him in bed naked with a boy from the barbershop and gave him a whipping something fierce, from what my mama tells me. Granddaddy said Uncle Gus had the devil in him, and that he was possessed, but Mama says he was just born that way, different. Uncle Gus hung himself the next day. So, Mama always says we have to look out for each other, and understand that even though we're all different, we're all still just folks."

"I think I'd like your mother."

Alfred nodded. "Most folks do. She never forgave my grandaddy for what he did to Gus, and she blames him for Gus killing himself. I don't really understand about my uncle, but I accept that he was different and couldn't help it. I learned about it some in college, you see. My mother sacrificed a lot to send me to school to be a teacher, especially after she took me and my baby sister and moved out of Grandaddy's house. She moved us here to Arizona, and she got a job as a cook at a hotel in Tucson, and she took in washing, too, and sewing. I graduated high school, first in my family to do so, and at the top of my class. And then, between her jobs and mine, I was able to enroll in a teacher's college eventually. It's her dream and mine for me to one day teach others, as I said before." Alfred grinned broadly then. "If I could teach them half the things she's taught me over the years, the world would be a better place."

"Of that I have no doubt, Mr. Brody, and I hope you get that chance."

"So do I, Mr. Adler, so do I."

Mason stared hard at the proud young man sitting across from him. "What did happen the day Miss Claggett's body was found in that trunk?" He took out his pencil and notepad and opened to a blank sheet of paper.

"I guess you did say you wanted to talk about that. Well, it's a day and a night I'll never forget, I can tell you that. I was at work at the station. I came on duty at four in the afternoon. Around half past five or so, Mr. Burrows took a call from Miss Castle, requesting her trunk and bags be picked up. He told me to go get them, so I took the station truck and headed over to the address he wrote down on a pickup slip, the Evans Comstock Residence for Young Ladies over on Roosevelt near downtown. When I arrived, I buzzed the apartment listed on the piece of paper, but nobody answered. I waited around for a bit, unsure what to do."

"Was there a phone number listed on the paper?"

"No, sir, just the woman's name, the address of the building, and the apartment number."

"And approximately what time did you arrive?"

"About a quarter to six, I think. Anyway, I buzzed the manager, and Miss Evans let me in. She told me Miss Castle had already left but had given permission for her roommate, Miss Claggett, to sign for the bags. As far as she knew, Miss Claggett was home but probably on the phone and hadn't heard the door buzzer. I thanked her kindly and headed upstairs with my dolly. The door to 3A was ajar when I got there. I knocked, then pushed the door open."

"And then?"

"Then I went in. The trunk and two suitcases were all sitting in the middle of the living room, tagged and ready to go. I called out a hello, but there was no answer, so I just loaded up the trunk and the bags onto my dolly and went back downstairs, which was no easy task as they don't have an elevator and I was by myself."

"Did you close the door to the apartment behind you?"

"No, sir, I left it ajar, the way I found it. I figured there had to be a reason. When I got back downstairs, I knocked on the manager's door again because I needed someone to sign that it was okay for me to be taking the trunk and suitcases. The manager, Miss Evans, as I said earlier, answered. She owns the place along with her sister, Mrs. Comstock. Miss Evans said she'd tried telephoning Miss Claggett after I'd gone up, but there was no answer, and she'd wondered if I'd seen her. I told her the door was ajar and no one appeared to be home. I asked her if she'd mind signing for the bags. She seemed hesitant at first, but finally she checked the labels and signed for them. I thanked her again, loaded up the truck, and went back to the station, where I unloaded them and put them with the rest of the bags that needed to be tagged and prepped for loading onto the train when it arrived. It sure gives me the willies to think about that poor woman's body being in that trunk when I loaded it and hauled it away."

"Only natural, Mr. Brody. Did you happen to notice the lock on the trunk was broken?"

"Yes, sir. It was pretty obvious. But the side latches were secured, so I didn't think too much about it. I just hoped jostling it down the stairs, it wouldn't come flying open."

"That certainly would have been unnerving."

"Yes, indeed, Mr. Adler."

"When you first arrived at Miss Claggett's apartment, did anything look out of place or disturbed?"

"You mean were there any signs of a struggle or a fight? No, sir, not that I noticed. Everything seemed the way it should as far as I could tell, fairly neat and tidy."

"Okay. So, you brought the trunk and suitcases back to the baggage room at the station and unloaded them. Then what?"

"Well, a few hours went by. Then I got a call to pick up some luggage from the Westward Ho and the San Carlos hotels downtown, so I did that. I took my dinner when I got back, then a little after eleven I had a sandwich, part of which I fed to ol' Barkly here." Alfred reached down and scratched the dog behind the ears, causing Barkly's tail to thump up and down upon the wooden floor.

"Barkly?"

"That's what I call him. He's an old hound dog that was hanging around the train station the last few weeks. Mr. Burrows didn't like him. Funny, Barkly followed me home yesterday after Mr. Dawson fired me."

"He followed you home all the way from Union Station?" Mason said, raising his eyebrows.

Alfred chuckled. "No, he followed me out to my Model A jalopy. I opened the door and he climbed right on in, wagging his tail like a willow in a cyclone. I intend to keep him, give him a bath, and fatten him up to a good, healthy weight. Him and I are buddies."

"Lucky dog. So, you fed part of your sandwich to Barkly that night."

"That's right. Mr. Burrows was right ornery about it. He didn't care for Barkly much, as I said, and even threw a tin can at him the other day, but luckily he missed. Anyway, Barkly started sniffing around the luggage pile and zeroed right in on the trunk I picked up from Miss Castle's and Miss Claggett's apartment. I went over to investigate and noticed some fluids oozing out the bottom. Mr. Burrows came over to have a look and said it was probably deer meat inside that someone was trying to smuggle to California. He told me to get Mr. Dawson, so I did. I imagine you know the rest."

"Pretty much, yes. Only Mr. Burrows claimed it was he who discovered the trunk, along with the dog's help."

"Figures he'd do that, right, Barkly?" Alfred gave Barkly another scratch, which led to more tail thumping. "Barkly didn't care much for Mr. Burrows, and I can't say I did, either."

"Yes, not surprising, given his personality," Mason said. "By the way, do you happen to own a green necktie with a hula girl on it?"

Alfred looked puzzled. "No, sir. I only have three neckties, and none of them are green, and they certainly don't have hula girls on them. Why?"

"Just curious. What will you do now, Mr. Brody?" Mason said, putting his notepad and pencil back in his inner suit coat pocket.

"I don't know, exactly. I guess it depends on what happens. But I do know this, I didn't kill that woman or anyone. I never saw her alive, I never even met her."

"I have to tell you that so far the consensus is that you did, or at least that you're a strong suspect."

Alfred shook his head and sighed. "I'm not surprised, frankly. What about you? Do *you* think I killed her?"

"People are generally quick to jump to conclusions, Mr. Brody. I try to stick with the facts."

"The facts, yeah. Well, thanks for that, anyway."

"Of course." Mason got slowly to his feet and retrieved his straw boater, his left hand on his back as he grimaced.

"You okay, Mr. Adler?"

"Hmm? Oh, yes, fine. Just ran into a dresser with my lower back last evening and strained my neck, too."

"Sounds like a curious accident. You should see a doctor."

"I'll be all right. Nothing a hot water bottle, some aspirin, and a couple of days won't cure. Thank you for your time today, sir."

"Sure," Alfred said, getting to his feet as well. Barkly did the same, his tail wagging once more. "I hope you find out who did do it."

Mason stepped out onto the cinder-block stoop and put his hat back on, tugging it low. "So do I. And I hope we can meet again under better circumstances. I enjoyed our chat. Good day, Mr. Brody."

"Good day, Mr. Adler."

They shook hands, and then Mason walked slowly back to his car, where a bunch of neighborhood children were gathered about, peering through the windows and gawking at the whitewall tires and snazzy hood ornament. They scattered as Mason approached, and he smiled to himself. Kids will be kids, regardless of race, religion or background. If only adults could be that way.

CHAPTER TEN

Afternoon, Wednesday, May 8, 1946
John Patterson's house

Mason crossed the Salt River on Central Avenue once again, this time heading north. His back was aching, his neck sore, and he was hungry, as it was already after one in the afternoon. He spotted a small drugstore on the corner of Central and Pima, so he pulled over, parked, and went inside, happy to discover it had conditioned air. He purchased a tin of Bayer aspirin from the young clerk behind the counter and then took a seat on one of the red vinyl swivel stools at the soda fountain in the rear of the shop. He ordered a Coke, double cheeseburger, and fries, washing two aspirin down with a glass of water while he waited for his lunch.

As he sat on the stool, his hat on the empty one next to him, Mason contemplated what he knew so far about the case, which, he had to admit, wasn't much. Someone had murdered Gertrude Claggett, but who and for what reason, he really had no idea. Certainly Leland Burrows, and even Emil to some extent, seemed set on Alfred Brody, but Mason just didn't see it. Miss Castle? Possibly. Mrs. Comstock, maybe. Or perhaps Miss Powell or Josiah Claggett. Hell, it could have even been Miss Evans or someone else altogether.

With a sigh he took out a silver dollar, which he left on the counter to pay for his bill plus a fairly generous tip since the soda jerk was attractive in a Spencer Tracy sort of way, and attentive. He put his hat back on and headed out the door into the bright afternoon sunshine and the relentless heat, the tin of aspirin in his pocket. He steered his car north once again to Buckeye Road, where he turned right, and then left onto Third Street, parking in front of a beige adobe house whose address matched the one Miss Castle had jotted down for him. It was a small house, with a sand and gravel yard, a fairly large tree on the left, and various cacti scattered about. Two half-barrel planters holding under-watered flowers flanked the front steps. He left his car windows down and walked up the narrow, cracked cement path to the front door, which was standing open. Mason rapped on the door frame and called out. "Hello?"

Presently an attractive-looking man, probably in his early to mid-thirties, with sandy brown hair, brown eyes, and a small brown toothbrush mustache ambled to the door, peering out at Mason as he stood beneath the striped canopy over the entrance. He was wearing a white long-sleeved shirt, open at the collar, and black pleated trousers, with black leather oxfords on his feet. He wore a black silk band about his right bicep, a symbol of mourning.

"Yes?" he said, his voice low and soft. "May I help you?"

"You're John Patterson? Gertrude Claggett's boyfriend?"

"Who wants to know? Who are you?" He had one hand on the edge of the open door, as if ready to slam it in Mason's face if necessary.

"The name's Mason Adler. I'm a private detective, hired by Miss Castle's father. You *are* John Patterson, aren't you?"

"Yes, that's right. What can I do for you? What do you want? I've already talked to the police and some other detective fellow, and a few reporters have been nosing around."

"I'm sorry to bother you, Mr. Patterson, especially at this difficult time, but I'd like to ask you a few questions, if I may. I'm trying to find the person responsible for Miss Claggett's death."

Mr. Patterson shrugged his broad, bony shoulders. "You say Charlotte Castle's father hired you? I suppose, then, if it will help. Come on in, but it will have to be quick. I'm supposed to work at the mission this afternoon, and I have to leave in about half an hour."

He stepped aside and let Mason enter, leaving the door open behind him.

"I'll try to be brief," Mason said, removing his straw boater, which he set on the table behind the sofa.

"I'd appreciate that, sir. I'm pretty much dressed and ready, though. I just have to put on my suit coat and tie and grab my hat."

"I'm surprised you're not taking some time off work, considering."

Mr. Patterson looked thoughtful. "I didn't go in yesterday, but then I found myself just sitting here staring at the walls and wondering what happened and who could have done such a terrible thing to Gertrude. I couldn't sleep much at all again last night, tossing and turning something awful. I figured today I might as well go into the mission and work my shift, and hopefully take my mind off things, at least for a while."

"That makes sense. What kind of work do you do there?"

"I work in the business office, mostly. But I help out wherever I'm needed. We feed the needy, clothe the poor, and take care of the sick."

"Admirable work."

"It can be rewarding, but sometimes it's simply exhausting. We're always in need of supplies and donations. Old clothes, dry goods, canned goods, blankets, that sort of thing. And of course, we always need money. Part of my job, a big part, is contacting local businesses and wealthy individuals to try and get donations to keep the mission up and running."

"I can imagine that must be difficult at times, but I've found most folks are generous, sometimes to a fault."

"Yes, I've found that to be quite true, also. I don't suppose you'd care to make a donation, Mr. Adler? I'd be happy to accept it in Gertrude's memory."

"I'd be happy to make a donation, though I'm far from wealthy. I didn't bring my checkbook along, however, so I'll have to send it or drop it off later."

"That would be most kind, thank you."

"It's the Lost Souls Mission on Nineteenth Street, is that correct?"

"Yes. How did you know that?"

"I spoke with Miss Julia Powell yesterday," Mason said, as he looked about the small sitting room, with cream-colored stucco walls, a bare wood floor, and a metal ceiling fan spinning creakily overhead. A Spanish-style fireplace stood against the wall at the far end. The place was sparsely furnished, with just two easy chairs flanking the fireplace and a small sofa facing it. The living room was messy, with dirty dishes on the coffee table, magazines and newspapers strewn about, and clothes piled on one of the chairs. A large, dusty crucifix hung on the wall opposite the front windows. To the right of the front door was an arched doorway, which led to a small kitchen and dining area, and directly ahead was another doorway, through which Mason could see a small hallway running left to right, and the door to the bathroom across it. What he presumed were doors to the bedrooms were on either side of the small hall.

"Oh, yes, Julia," John said. "You talked to her, did you? I imagine she had quite a bit to say."

"In what regard?"

"About me, for starters. Please, have a seat, Mr. Adler," Mr. Patterson said, motioning toward the chair without a pile of clothes on it as he sat down onto the sofa.

"Thanks," Mason said, sitting down gingerly as he took out his pencil and notebook. The aspirin had helped, but his neck and back were still sore. "I understand you got the job at the mission through Miss Claggett's recommendation, by the way."

"Did Julia tell you that, too?"

"It may have come up during our discussion."

"Well, yes, it's true, I suppose. I was out of work, and Julia and I were dating at the time. Nothing serious, just some laughs, you know how it is. She's that kind of a girl."

"What kind of a girl would that be, Mr. Patterson?"

"You know. Not the kind you marry, just someone to spend time with, have some fun."

"Ah, I see. Miss Powell is certainly attractive and rather direct, I must say. I imagine she would be, fun, as you put it."

"Oh, I didn't mean it like that, believe me. I'm not that kind of a fellow. We just enjoyed each other's company for a while. Anyway, Julia knew I was looking for work, and she knew my last job was as a fund-raiser for Councilman Monroe when he was running for office. Of course, after he got elected, I was back on the street without a job. Julia heard her friend Gert talking about the Lost Souls Mission over on Nineteenth Street, and that they were looking for someone to help out in the office and with fund-raising, and she thought that would be perfect for me, and so did I. So I stopped by city hall one morning where Julia and Gert worked. Gert worked there part-time, but full-time at the mission."

"Yes, someone else told me that she held down both jobs. Idle hands and the devil, that sort of thing."

Mr. Patterson smiled softly. "That's Gert all right. Poor Gert. Anyway, Julia introduced me to her, hoping she could put in a good word for me at the mission."

"You couldn't just go down to the mission yourself and apply on your own? Surely someone with your experience in fund-raising would have had a good chance of being hired even without Miss Claggett's recommendation."

"That was my first thought, but they only like to hire people who belong to their religion or are willing to convert. I'm a God-fearing Methodist, you see, and my mother would never forgive me if I changed for the sake of a job. Gert had worked there for quite a while and was well respected, so I figured if she recommended me, they might overlook my own religion and give me a chance."

"That makes sense, I suppose."

"Yes, well, anyway, she did help me get the job, and we started working together. Gert worked Wednesday through Sunday, I worked every day but Thursdays and Sundays, so we were together quite a bit. And I got to know her brother, Josiah, too, since he was always hanging around the mission. He works there too, part-time, doing odd jobs and whatnot. He started not too long ago."

"And as you were working together, you and Miss Claggett hit it off, as they say."

Mr. Patterson nodded. "Yeah, that's what they say. It wasn't anything personal against Julia, though. I mean, she's a good kid and all, but me and Gert just were attracted to each other."

"Physically?"

John looked embarrassed. "Well, Gert isn't built the way Julia is, that's for sure. But that's one of the things I liked about Gert. She was pure, and chaste, and smart. And she was pretty, just not the way most girls are. She didn't go for all of that girly stuff, and I liked that about her. It wasn't just for laughs like it was with Julia. We were more like kindred spirits. She's the kind of girl a man marries."

"In your opinion, anyway," Mason said. "How did Miss Powell take the news when you broke up with her to go out with Gert?"

"Eh, women. We hadn't even been going out all that long. But of course, she was angry and hurt, and of course she cried, like women always seem to do."

"I don't think that's a female trait alone, Mr. Patterson. Anyone is going to feel hurt and angry when rejected by someone they care about."

John Patterson looked at Mason queerly. "Maybe, but you don't see guys bursting into tears when some gal dumps them."

"Maybe not, but that may be just because society has taught them not to show their emotions."

"What are you, Mr. Adler, some kind of a mental doctor? I thought you were a private dick."

"I am, I'm just making an observation, that's all. Have you had any contact with Miss Powell since you ended things?"

"I called her a couple of times. I just wanted to check on her, make sure she was okay, but she didn't want to speak with me. Understandable, I guess."

"Still, that was thoughtful of you."

"It seemed like the right thing to do. Even if it was just for fun between me and Julia, I never intended to hurt anyone, and surprisingly she seemed to take it pretty hard. I've heard she's said some pretty harsh things about me since we ended it. Since *I* ended it."

"That's often the case, Mr. Patterson."

"Yes, I suppose so. I guess she was more serious about things than I was. I just didn't realize it."

"That always makes breakups more difficult. I suppose Miss Powell was also pretty angry with Miss Claggett after you started going out with Gertrude."

Mr. Patterson shrugged once more. "I suppose. They had to work together at city hall afterward, and I know Gert felt awkward about it."

"Only natural. I can imagine seeing Gertrude every day kept reminding Miss Powell of what had happened. Maybe the anger built until finally she'd had enough. Do you think that's possible?"

"I know what you're getting at, Mr. Adler, but no, I don't think that's possible. Jules would never have killed Gert. She was upset, but the anger was more directed at me."

"You sound pretty sure of that."

"I think I know Jules pretty well. She was hurt, certainly, when we broke up, and sure, she was angry with me, but she's not the type to hold a grudge or be vindictive. In fact, by now Jules has probably already moved on to some other fella."

"Possibly. Nice place you've got here, by the way."

John glanced around also. "Thanks. It's satisfactory, I guess. I rent it, month to month, fully furnished. I'm fairly new here to Phoenix."

"Oh?"

"I'm from L.A. originally. I've only been in Arizona about a year or so. I came to work on the councilman's campaign."

"I see. You did similar work in L.A.?"

"And other places. I move around. I get restless after a while. Now that the campaign is over and Gert is gone, there's really not much left for me here in Phoenix."

"What about your job at the mission?"

He shook his head slowly. "Too many memories there. Too

many memories everywhere in Phoenix, especially in this house. Gert was over here all the time. We listened to the radio, played cards, she'd cook for me, and we'd talk, just like an old married couple. Now, well, I may head back to L.A. I have friends and family there."

"I hear it's quite a city."

"It is, though the ground shakes a little from time to time."

"That would be unsettling."

"Eh, you get used to it."

"Do you live here alone?"

"Yes, usually, but Gertie's brother, Josiah, has been staying here recently. He'd been sleeping on Gert and Charlotte's couch the last few weeks, after he got kicked out of his rooming house."

"Do you know why he got kicked out of the rooming house?"

"Like I said, he only works at the mission part-time, and I don't think it pays much. Rumor has it he got drunk and angry one night and busted up a few things in the drawing room. Plus, he was behind on his rent, so they threw him out. Gert and Charlotte let him stay at their place for a while. But the two old biddies that run the apartment building didn't like him staying long term, so I offered to let him stay here temporarily. He took the news about Gert's death pretty hard, as did I, of course."

"Of course. Please accept my condolences, by the way. Mr. Castleberry, Charlotte's father, sends his condolences also."

"Thanks, that's kind of you and of him. The funeral will be this Friday morning. I've been making the arrangements."

"What about Josiah?"

"What about him?"

"As her next of kin, shouldn't he be making the arrangements? Or at least assisting?"

"He's of no mind, and of no help."

"That's unfortunate. When was the last time you saw or spoke to Miss Claggett?"

John took a deep, deep breath and nearly closed his eyes before speaking, softly. "She telephoned me the day she was murdered, actually, right about five o'clock. She was upset and angry. She said she'd learned something disturbing about her brother, and she was going to confront him. I told her not to until I could get there, but she said he was already on the way."

"She telephoned you here?"

"No, at the mission. I was working at the time. Anyway, I hung up and rushed over to her apartment as quickly as I could because I was worried about what Josiah might do, how he might react, when she confronted him."

"I see. Gertrude didn't necessarily feel safe around her brother?"

"No, and rightly so, because he has quite a temper, especially when he's been drinking, and he drinks fairly often. Like I said, he busted up the drawing room at the rooming house."

"Hmm, so he gets angry when he's drunk. That would be concerning, I suppose. And about what time was it that you arrived at Miss Claggett's apartment building?"

"A little after six, I think. When I got there, I buzzed her apartment but she didn't answer, which made me even more nervous. Since the building is kept locked, I had to buzz the landlady to get access. The younger one, Miss Evans, let me in and met me in the downstairs hallway, and I told her why I was there. She let me know Josiah had already arrived and that the man from the train station had just been to pick up Charlotte's trunk and bags and that no one appeared to be home in the apartment, which struck me as odd. The two of us went upstairs, and we found the door ajar. We went in, and I noticed one of the living room windows was open. I glanced out and saw Josiah hurrying away down the sidewalk, up Roosevelt. He must have been climbing down the fire escape as I was coming into the building. I called out to him, but he didn't answer. He didn't even look back. He was moving pretty fast."

"Did you see any signs of a struggle or anything out of place when you got to the apartment?"

He shook his head. "No, not at all. Other than the fact that the door was open, everything seemed as usual. Miss Evans and I had a brief look around, but Gertrude was nowhere to be found. We closed and locked the living room window, then we left, closing and locking the door behind us, too."

"Do you have any idea what Miss Claggett found out about her brother?"

Mr. Patterson nodded solemnly. "I think so. Gertrude was a pious woman. She didn't go for gambling, smoking, swearing, drinking alcohol, or anything else like that. Josiah was and is pretty much the opposite, and he's also peculiar. He never finished school, but he's really smart, and he can quote obscure statistics like nobody's business. And he knows facts and figures backward and forward, but he can't carry on a social conversation. He used to drive Gert crazy."

"But those things you mentioned that irritated her are all things she already knew about him. What is it she found out that she wanted to confront him about?"

"Oh, yes, well, I suspect he may have been pilfering funds from the mission, and I think Gert discovered it, though she never told me so directly."

"Why do you suspect he may have been taking money?"

"As I said before, he was broke and needed it. And he was back drinking and gambling, though he'd promised Gert he'd stop. I think she may have found out about that, too. And I believe he had run up a few gambling debts, some big ones. He always thinks he can beat the odds by using logic and statistics, and sometimes he does, but lately not so much, from what I understand."

"Hmm, do you have any proof of that?" Mason said. "Of him taking money from the mission?"

"No, not me personally. But I do know one of the elders mentioned to me that something didn't seem quite right with the finances." Mr. Patterson sighed. "I can't help but feel somewhat to blame."

"Why is that?" Mason said.

"Well, when I got hired and started at the mission, Josiah was doing menial odd jobs there. Cleaning the bathrooms, helping in the kitchen, maintenance, sweeping, that sort of thing. I felt sorry for him. I felt perhaps if he were given more responsibility, he'd live up to it. My father always used to say expect the worst of someone and you'll get it, and conversely, expect the best, and you'll get that, too, you see?"

"Yes, I think I understand."

"Unfortunately it didn't work out that way. I started having him assist me in the front office, helping me make telephone calls, count money, even do the books." John looked Mason in the eye before continuing. "Oh, I know I said Josiah is peculiar, but he's actually brilliant when it comes to math and figures. He's very methodical and organized, too. He's almost fanatical about his appearance. Everything has to match and coordinate, and everything has to be clean and neat, and he's obsessed with facts, organization, and statistics. So I thought he'd be a natural in the office at the mission, and he was, but I think the temptation of easy money was just too great for him. As I said, since he started, I'm told money has turned up missing from the coffers, a fair amount."

"And you think Josiah might have taken it?"

"It stands to reason, Mr. Adler, though he may have altered the books to cover his tracks. He's taken money from me, too, I know he has, here at the house. Not a lot, but enough for me to notice. And my watch has gone missing, as of a couple days ago. It was fairly new, gold, with a black alligator band."

"Yet you continue to let him stay here?"

"What choice do I have? He was Gert's baby brother, and a child of God. He needs help."

"Perhaps more help than you alone can provide, Mr. Patterson."

"Perhaps, but I do what I can. I have to."

"Of course. So you believe Miss Claggett found out her brother was stealing from the mission, and that he was back drinking and gambling, and she confronted him about it?"

"Yes, but he didn't kill her. He wouldn't."

"That remains to be seen, I'm afraid. I understand she referred to her brother as J.P.?"

"That's right. His middle name is Paul, you see."

"But you don't think he had something to do with her death?"

Mr. Patterson looked away from Mason and swallowed hard. "I really don't want to think about that."

"I'm asking you to think about that, please, and to be honest. It's important."

He looked back at Mason, a pained expression on his face. "Josiah's not always in his right mind, you see. If he *did* harm Gertrude, I'm sure he didn't mean to. He may not even be fully aware he did it. I have to protect him, now more than ever, because he's all alone. He has nowhere else to go right now, no family, no real friends to speak of. I can't just turn him out, or turn him in."

"That's extremely kind of you, Mr. Patterson."

"I loved Gertrude. I had planned to ask her to marry me. And she loved me. She also loved Josiah, even though they fought and disagreed on things. She'd want me to care for him as much as I can. And in my heart, I believe he's innocent. I *have* to believe that."

"But what if he's not innocent? What if he did steal that money and kill his sister? Would you protect and care for him even then?"

Mr. Patterson glanced up at the crucifix above the sofa and then back down at Mason, his voice quiet. "I guess I honestly don't know. I'd certainly make sure he got good legal counsel at least, and all the mental help he needs, as much as I could afford, anyway. I suppose that sounds crazy to you."

"I admit it's unusual."

"Gertrude was an unusual woman, Mr. Adler, and Josiah is an unusual man."

"I'm beginning to see that. So, you think she confronted him, they fought, he killed her accidentally, or in a fit of anger, or drunkenness, and then fled in a panic?"

"I *don't* think that, but I suppose it's possible. I truly still feel it must have been someone else, a stranger, or a burglar perhaps."

"But you said you saw him hurrying away down the sidewalk when you looked out the window. If he's innocent, why would he do that?"

"I'm not sure. Maybe when he got there no one was home. Maybe he just got scared when he found Gertrude missing."

"And so he climbed down the fire escape? Obviously he didn't come down the stairs, or you and Miss Evans would have run into him on your way up."

"Maybe Josiah saw me coming into the building, and he was afraid I'd scold him for some reason, so he climbed out and down the escape. Josiah doesn't always do rational things, Mr. Adler."

"It doesn't sound like it. Did you see him at all Monday afternoon, after you left the apartment?"

"No. He didn't come back here until yesterday, after I'd already heard from the police about what had happened to Gertrude. I don't know where he went or where he spent the night on Monday."

"If he did kill his sister, why do you think he would bother taking the time to hide her body in the trunk?"

"Josiah can be rather childlike at times, socially awkward. So I suppose, *if* he did kill her, it was much like how a little boy breaks his mother's favorite lamp and tries to hide the broken pieces under the sofa. He would have realized what he did was wrong, and he'd be afraid and try to hide it."

Mason smiled softly to himself. "I remember doing something similar when I was a boy and broke a favorite figurine of my mother's."

"But your mother found out, of course."

"She did. I couldn't sit down for a week once my father got home."

"Ouch," Mr. Patterson said. "But I just thought of something. By the time I got to the apartment, the trunk and two suitcases had already been picked up, and I saw Josiah just then leaving, so how could he have killed her? Her body was put in the trunk."

"Well, I suppose he may have killed her, then saw the man from the station on the street below or heard him buzz the apartment. Panicked, he hid her body in the trunk, then climbed out on the fire escape out of sight. When the man left with the bags and trunk, he intended to climb back in but then saw you arrive, so he climbed down the escape as you were coming up the stairs with Miss Evans. When you got to the apartment, the trunks and bags were gone and you saw Josiah hurrying away."

"Oh. I hadn't considered all of that," Mr. Patterson said quietly.

"I'm just supposing, Mr. Patterson. It's possible that didn't happen that way at all. It's just a theory."

"Right, just a theory. Poor Josiah."

"You said you and Miss Evans locked up the apartment when you realized no one was there. What happened next?"

"When we got back downstairs, I asked Miss Evans to telephone me at the mission if she heard anything as to Gert's whereabouts, and I told her I'd try calling Gertrude later, also."

"Did you?"

"Yes, of course. Around seven thirty, then again around nine, both times no answer. At ten, just before my shift at the mission ended, I telephoned Miss Evans. Mrs. Comstock answered. She told me neither she nor Miss Evans had seen or heard anything from Gertrude all evening. I was definitely worried by that point. I gave them my home telephone number and said to please call me if they heard from her, no matter what time."

"You came back here to your house after that? After you finished your shift at the mission?"

"That's right. Though I didn't get much sleep. I must admit I was very concerned, and I kept hoping the phone would ring, and I was worried about Josiah, too. As I said, he wasn't here when I got home, and he was still gone when I got up yesterday morning. His bed hadn't been slept in. While I was having breakfast, my phone rang. I thought perhaps it was Gert or Miss Evans or possibly Josiah, but it was the police. I almost fainted when they told me Gertrude was dead. I just couldn't believe it. In some ways, I still can't believe it."

"Understandable."

"Yes, it was quite a shock. They said they wanted to talk to me and that they were also looking for Josiah. I of course told them the truth, that I wasn't sure where he was. But then, a short while later, just before the police came, Josiah showed back up. He was tired and hungry, and looked and smelled awful."

"Did you ask him what had happened the day before at his sister's apartment?"

"I didn't get a chance, really. He went right to his room to change his clothes, and I knew I had to tell him about Gert's death, so when he came back out to the kitchen I told him as gently as I could."

"How did he take the news of his sister's death?"

"When I told him she was dead, he seemed numb, angry. I told him the police wanted to talk to him, and he became very agitated. He put his fist through the kitchen wall and took off again. I think he was fairly intoxicated, as he often was. He hasn't returned since, so that's Monday night and Tuesday night he's spent somewhere else."

"And you don't know where that was or where he is now?"

"No, sorry, I don't. He never said. I left word at the mission to contact me if he shows up there, and the police are looking for him, too."

"Yes, of course. By the way, do you happen to own a green necktie with a hula dancer on it?"

John gave Mason a quizzical look. "No, in my job at the mission I'm required to wear a simple black tie and dark blue suit coat with black trousers. In my personal life I also choose to wear simpler clothes. I'm not a flashy dresser by any means. But Josiah owns a tie like that, why?"

"Just curious."

"It's funny you should ask, actually. He was wearing it on Monday when he left the house before I went to work, but when I saw him out the window from Gertrude's place, he didn't have a tie on at all. Nor did he when he came back here yesterday, which is unusual for him, because as I mentioned, he's always been fastidious about his clothing and appearance."

"Where does he stay when he's here?"

"In the spare room."

"Would you mind if I had a look?"

"I suppose not." They got to their feet, and Mr. Patterson led the way through the archway into a short hall and then left to a small bedroom at the back of the house. "This is it."

Mason glanced about. A single bed, neatly made, a chest of drawers, a nightstand that held a small lamp and a Bible, and a few religious pictures on the wall Mason assumed belonged to Mr. Patterson. "Very clean and tidy."

"Josiah's always been. As I said before, he's very methodical and organized. One of his quirks."

Mason nodded and walked across the tile floor to the small closet. "A brown sport coat, a green one, a few dress shirts, some trousers, and five ties, none of which are green with a hula girl on it," Mason said, mostly to himself. "He wasn't wearing the hula tie the last time you saw him, you say?"

Mr. Patterson looked thoughtful. "No. As I said, he had it on Monday before I left for work, but not later that day. I remember he was wearing this green sport coat here, too, on Monday." John lifted its sleeve. "Funny, I don't remember a button missing from the sleeve, but I may not have noticed, given everything that happened."

"Yes, that makes sense." Mason also looked at the sport coat. "Fairly fancy buttons with an unusual design. Looks like a silver unicorn."

John Patterson chuckled softly. "Yes. Josiah can't afford expensive, tailor-made clothes, so he buys off the rack, usually on sale, then changes out the buttons for more elaborate ones."

"Clever."

"I suppose so, though it seems like a lot of work to me. What's the significance of his hula girl tie, by the way? Why did you ask about it?"

"I'm not really at liberty to say just yet, Mr. Patterson, but I would appreciate your letting me know if and when you see or hear from him. Here's my card," Mason said, extracting his business card from a silver case he kept in his pocket and handing it to him.

"Sure, I'll do that. I'm supposed to let that police detective fellow know, too."

"Of course. By the way, you said he changed his clothes when he stopped back here yesterday. Do you recall what he changed into?"

"Why yes. He put on his tan sport coat, brown trousers, a white shirt, and a red and brown tie. Why?"

"Just wondering where his missing hula tie is, though I'm afraid I might know."

John Patterson cocked his head. "And where do you think it is?"

"All in due time, Mr. Patterson, all in due time. I'd better let you get to work, you'll be late," Mason said, glancing at his watch. "It's nearly two."

"Jeepers. I'll just get my coat, tie, and hat and walk out with you."

Mason retrieved his straw boater from the table while Mr. Patterson hurriedly put on his black tie and dark blue jacket, the black mourning band now about the right arm of the coat. With his black fedora in his right hand, the two of them stepped out the front door and Mason waited while John closed and locked it.

"Thank you again for your time, Mr. Patterson," Mason said, shaking his hand as they both put their hats on.

"You're welcome. And please believe me, I don't think Josiah would ever hurt his sister. And if for some reason he did, it was accidental."

"Of course," Mason said.

"I'm afraid I must hurry, Mr. Adler. Good day," he said, stepping around Mason and hurrying out to the sidewalk before turning south.

Mason watched him go and then ambled slowly down the walk to his car, where he paused, pulling his hat lower to shade his eyes from the unrelenting sun overhead. He was about to open the car door when he saw another man looking at him, peering out from the side of the little house underneath the pergola off the kitchen. He looked bedraggled and nervous, and he was dressed in a rather dirty tan sport coat, brown trousers, white shirt, and a red and brown tie, a brown felt fedora atop his head. Mason nodded to him and gave him a friendly wave, but the man didn't move or flinch. Slowly Mason went back around the car and up onto the sidewalk.

"Hello," he called out as cheerfully as he could. "I'm a friend of Charlotte Castle. I believe you know Charlotte?"

The man blinked, still staring at Mason, but he didn't run away. Slowly, Mason approached until he was about ten feet away from him.

"You're Josiah, aren't you? Josiah Claggett? You live here with John Patterson."

"Who are you?" the man said at last, staring at Mason with big, dark eyes. "What do you want?"

"My name is Mason. Mason Adler. I'm a friend of Charlotte's, and I'm trying to help her."

"Help Charlotte? Help her how? Is she in trouble?"

"Some people think she had something to do with your sister's death. I'm so sorry about Gertie," Mason said gently.

"Me too," Josiah said softly, still staring at him, unwavering. "Very sorry. She's dead. She died on Monday."

Mason inched a couple of steps closer. "Did you see your sister on Monday afternoon?"

"Yes."

"At her apartment?"

"Yes. I went to her apartment. I left here and stopped to say hello to Mr. Granger. Mr. Granger gave me a ride to Gert's place."

"Who's Mr. Granger?"

"He lives next door. He's a neighbor of John's. Mr. Granger's a nice man and he has an automobile. Did you know only two hundred forty-three people out of a thousand in the United States own an automobile?"

"No, I didn't know that, that's very interesting."

"He asked me what happened to John's wife," Josiah said. "She's gone now. Sad."

"His wife? Oh, you mean Gertrude. I heard she spent quite a bit of time here. I never got to meet Gert, but I've heard some nice things about her. It sounds like you two were close."

Josiah shrugged and wiped sweat from his brow with the back of his hand. He was wearing a gold watch with a black alligator band. "I guess so. She told me to come over."

"I see. By the way, that's a nice-looking watch you're wearing."

Josiah looked at it and then back at Mason. "Oh, uh, John gave it to me."

"For your birthday?"

"My birthday is in July. July sixteenth. I'm a Cancer. That's one of the signs of the zodiac."

"Yes, I know."

"My sister was angry with me. That's why she wanted me to come over."

"Angry with you about what?"

"About what I did. She found out. She knew, and I was upset."

"What was it you did that she found out about?"

"It don't matter anymore, does it? She's dead. She died too young. The United States life expectancy for women is sixty-five point two years. For men it's sixty-one years, rounding up. Gert was only twenty-four. Too young. She's dead, and it don't matter anymore."

"She is dead, Josiah, but I think it may matter as to what she found out."

"Because you think I killed her?"

"Why would I think that?"

"Johnny says the police want to talk to me about it."

"Because they have questions," Mason said.

"The police question suspects in order to determine guilty parties. Guilty parties are arrested."

"But I'm not the police. I just want to know what happened. To help Charlotte."

Josiah nodded slowly. "I like Charlotte. She's pretty, and she's nice to me. She wants to be a movie star."

"Yes, she told me that. I like her, too. I hope she succeeds."

"Me too. Odds are against her, though. Statistics show that only about zero point zero four percent of the English-speaking world is famous, or what most people think of as famous. Given the current population right now in 1946, that means that only about one person in ten thousand is considered to be famous."

"Those are definitely not good odds," Mason said.

"Did you know there are just over 140 million people in the forty-eight states of America?"

"I didn't know that."

"It's true. Only 591,000 in Arizona, though. And the metropolitan population of Phoenix, Arizona, as of 1945 was 160,000."

"That's really fascinating, Josiah. But right now I want to help Charlotte. Will you tell me, please, what happened when you got to your sister's on Monday afternoon?"

"We argued. She was mad. Did you know studies show that men are generally more aggressive? But women get just as angry as men do. My sister did. She got mad at me."

"Okay. Then what?"

"I got mad, too. I shoved her pretty hard, she fell."

"And then what did you do?" Mason said.

"I don't remember exactly. I'd had a few drinks before I went over there. To calm my nerves. Alcohol is actually a depressant, not a stimulant, did you know that?"

"You pushed her and she fell down," Mason said, pressing on. "Did she hit her head? Was she knocked unconscious? Did she cry out?"

"I don't recall. I told you that. You don't listen, and you didn't answer my question. Studies show that most people only remember about eighteen percent of what they hear."

"I'm sorry, Josiah, I *was* listening, and I *did* know that alcohol is a depressant. I'm just trying to determine exactly what happened Monday afternoon and evening."

"All I remember is that I took off pretty soon after I shoved her. I was mad."

"And afraid?"

"Yes. Afraid. Fear often follows anger, though sometimes anger follows fear."

"Fear because you thought you hurt her?"

"I *did* hurt her. I shoved her down. Ain't that enough? She's dead. I killed her. Actions have consequences. Statistics show that—"

"But your sister…"

Josiah's eyes grew large and he backed up against the house.

"I thought you said you weren't with the cops?" Josiah said, his voice suddenly angry. "I should have known. Statistics show people lie over ten times a day, and I don't like people who lie to me."

"What are you talking about?" Mason said.

"The cops," Josiah said, pointing toward the street.

Mason turned his head toward the street to see a black and white police cruiser pulling up. When he turned back toward the house, Josiah was gone.

CHAPTER ELEVEN

Evening, Wednesday, May 8, 1946
Mason Adler's apartment

Mason parked his car on Encanto and walked up the sidewalk to Central, where the main entrance to the El Encanto apartments was located. He unlocked the heavy metal gate and stepped into the courtyard, tired and weary. It had been a long, frustrating, and puzzling day. He put his right foot on the steps that led to the balcony surrounding the courtyard, and as he did so, a jolting shot of pain went through his lower back, like a bolt of electricity, and he froze in agony.

"Dammit," he muttered to himself, clenching his jaw. After a short pause, he realized there was no alternative if he wished to get upstairs and into his apartment. He forced his left foot up onto the step, and then, grasping the handrail, took another step, slowly climbing upward as he grimaced in pain.

"Mason! Are you all right?" Lydia called out from behind him. "You're moving so slowly and awkwardly."

He turned his head to look at her, though it hurt to do so. "Oh, I'm fine, just peachy swell and keen. Are you just getting home from work?"

"Yes, I was on the day shift today, but I'm off tomorrow, thankfully. What happened to you?" she said, joining him on the steps and taking his free arm in hers. "You look like you're in pain."

"That's because I *am* in pain, my dear, but nothing a hot water bottle, a couple of aspirin, and a glass or two of scotch won't fix, or at least help."

"You should be in bed."

"It's only after six."

"I know, but still…"

"Still, I intend to head in the direction of my bedroom eventually once I get upstairs. I'm almost halfway now. Just a few more steps."

"Oh, my dear. Whatever did you do?" she said, as together they climbed the steps, one foot at a time.

Mason looked at her again out of the corner of his eye. "I got into a fight with a suspect."

"Mason Adler, you're kidding!"

"I'm not, I wish I was. Another new outfit?"

"What? Oh, yes, a new blouse and skirt, on sale at Penney's, and of course my discount. But what do you mean you got into a fight with a suspect?"

"You have more clothes than any woman I know, and what I mean is just what I said. I got slammed against a dresser and then put in a headlock. My back and my neck are killing me."

"You shouldn't be fighting at your age."

"Gee, thanks."

"You know what I mean, you're over fifty."

"I just turned fifty a few weeks ago, and now I'm already *over* fifty."

"Well, that's how it works, darling. There, we made it to the top. I'll walk with you to your apartment and help you inside. Have you had dinner?"

"Thanks, and no, not really. I haven't had time."

"When did this happen?"

"Yesterday, though the pain is worse today."

"It always is for some reason."

"Yes, I actually didn't feel too bad until I started climbing the stairs, then something just snapped in my back."

"If you're not better by morning, you should call Dr. Collins and have him come over to examine you."

"I'm sure I'll be fine. Here, take my keys and unlock the door, will you?"

"Of course, darling." The two of them went inside as Lydia closed the door behind them and turned on the overhead light in the living room.

"Dammit," Mason said again, mostly to himself. "Dammit to hell." He took off his hat and hung it on the hook by the door.

"You shouldn't swear, Mason. And what exactly have you been up to? I thought you'd call me last night to let me know how your meeting with Mr. Castleberry went."

"Yes, sorry, I meant to, but one thing's led to another. It's been a whirlwind thirty-six hours or so."

"Well, I want to hear all about it, of course. You really should be more careful," she said, taking off her hat and white gloves and setting them on the table underneath the telephone niche, along with her purse.

"Ugh, this injury really is most inconvenient, right in the middle of a case."

"It sounds like it's *because* of this case you're in this condition in the first place. Now, go sit in your chair over by the window. I'm going to boil some water, fill your hot water bottle, and get you a scotch, neat, just like you like it. And I'll make you a light dinner, maybe some soup and an egg sandwich."

"That sounds perfect. You're the best, Lydia, thank you," Mason said. He slipped off his jacket and draped it over the desk chair, then ambled slowly across the living room to his chair by the window.

"You're welcome. Oh, and I'll get the aspirin, too. In your medicine cabinet, I presume?"

"I actually have some in my pocket, but the hot water bottle is on the top shelf of my bedroom closet."

"Okay. Take your shoes off and loosen your tie. Sit tight, I'll just be a moment," she said, moving off toward the bedroom.

Before sitting down gingerly, he took off his shoes, removed his cufflinks, rolled up his sleeves, and took his tie completely off.

Lydia returned from the bedroom with the empty hot water bottle.

"You look better already," she said.

"I'm a little more comfortable, anyway."

"Good. You'll feel even better once I get this hot water bottle filled and on your lower back." She carried it out to the kitchen. "Where's your teakettle?"

"In the lower cabinet to the right of the stove."

"Right. Got it."

He closed his eyes and leaned back, listening as she filled the kettle from the faucet and set it on the stove to boil.

She opened the cabinet above the sink and peered inside, removing a bottle near the front. "You're running low on scotch," she said, as she also got out a clean drinking glass. "This is your last bottle."

"I know. Too bad the milkman doesn't deliver that."

"At least you still have your sense of humor," Lydia said, as she returned to the living room carrying a glass of scotch, neat. "Here you go. Something to wash those two aspirin down with."

He opened his eyes and looked at her. She was beaming and her skin glowed. "Thanks. You really love this, don't you?" He took the aspirin tin out of his pocket and removed two tablets.

She cocked her head at him, a strand of her red hair falling across her face that she brushed behind her left ear. "What?"

"Taking care of me. Mothering me."

"You need taking care of *and* mothering."

"You're right, I guess I do, at least some days. And today is definitely one of those days. Anyway, I appreciate it."

"Of course, darling, any time. By the way, I took a peek in your cupboards just now while I was looking for the kettle. You're low on provisions as well as scotch."

"Such as?"

"Well, I was going to make my vegetable soup for you. But I'd need potatoes, turnips, carrots, a leek, and some stock. All I could find was one sad potato and a couple of radishes."

"Potato radish soup it is, then."

Lydia laughed. "I don't think so. I did notice you have a couple of cans of Campbell's chicken noodle in your larder. Not as good as my homemade, but it will have to do and at least it won't take as long. Don't you ever cook?"

"I do, once in a while. But the canned items are so much more convenient. You know us bachelors."

Lydia shook her head. "Like I said, you need someone to take care of you. I bet Toby McConnell is a good cook."

"Lydia…"

"Oh stop. I'm just supposing, that's all. Anyway, enjoy your scotch and aspirin, that's the appetizer. I'll go open a can, put the soup on the stove, and fix you an egg sandwich. I did notice you have eggs and butter in the icebox and bread in the breadbox, at least."

"Yes, I don't think they've invented canned eggs yet, or instant bread."

"Funny man. I'll be right back." She kicked off her shoes and strode off toward the kitchen.

"Bring me the bottle when you come back. Oh, if you want an apron, there's one in the bottom cabinet next to the sink," Mason called out.

"Hmm? Oh, yes, I see it, thanks. That's a good idea."

"Right, can't have you spilling anything on that pretty new blouse and skirt of yours," Mason said. He put the aspirin in his mouth and washed it down with a large swallow of scotch before leaning back and closing his eyes again. He almost fell asleep until the whistle of the teakettle brought him upright and he opened his eyes, blinking.

Lydia was back in the living room again, wearing the apron and holding the red rubber hot water bottle in both hands. "Here, lean forward just a bit and I'll scooch this in by your lower back. Hopefully it won't leak."

"Hopefully not," Mason said. "Did you screw the stopper on tight?"

"I did, but you never know. If you feel any wetness, tell me."

"Believe me, I will."

"Good, there you go, now lean back," she said. "Perfect. How does that feel?" .

"Warm and squishy, but nice, thanks."

"You're welcome. Relax for a bit, I'm going to go check on the soup and start your sandwich."

"Okay, and don't forget to bring me the bottle of scotch in case I want a refill."

"In *case* you want a refill? There's a laugh."

"Only for medicinal purposes, of course," Mason said. "You know, you really don't need to do all this, though, Lydia. I'm not an invalid, I just hurt my back and my neck. I'll be fine."

"You hurt your neck, too?"

"From the headlock I was in. Strained it a bit, but the back's the worst part."

"Goodness. Well, sit tight, I'm happy to help, and I'll be back in a jiffy." She scurried into the small dining room once more and disappeared into the kitchen, but it wasn't more than a few minutes before she had returned, carrying a wooden tray with a bowl of steaming chicken noodle soup, a spoon, and a fried egg sandwich on it, along with the bottle of scotch and a linen napkin. She set the tray carefully on his lap, picked up the bottle, and poured him a refill, since his glass was now empty. "Now you're all set."

"Thanks, Lydia. But what about you? Aren't you going to eat anything?"

"Oh, I'm not hungry right now, I had a late lunch. I'll fix something downstairs at my place."

"Join me in a drink, then?"

"Not at the moment, I'm on duty."

"On duty?"

"Of course, darling. Nurse Dettling at your service. I was a Red Cross volunteer during the war, as you know. Want me to feed you?"

He shot her a murderous look. "Honestly, Lydia, I told you I'm not an invalid, so stop treating me like one. You can go home now."

"My my, you get cranky when you're not feeling well."

He sighed and took a drink of scotch. "I'm sorry. But you *can* go home. There's no need to stay and just watch me eat."

"I'll leave in due time. Once you're finished eating, I'll do up all the dishes and heat some more water."

"What for?"

"For your hot water bottle, of course. The water in it only stays hot so long, so I'll make sure it's good and hot again before I leave."

"I can do that myself."

"Don't be silly, I'm here, let me help. I'll also make sure you're all set for the night, your bed turned down, and your pillows fluffed, and *then* I'll leave."

"Honestly."

"And I'll check on you in the morning. I can make you breakfast, too."

Mason shook his head. "Nurse Dettling, you are much too much."

"Quiet, or I'll take your temperature with my rectal thermometer," she said with a wicked gleam in her eye. She sat herself down on a nearby chair, smoothing out her skirt. "Now then, while you eat your dinner, tell me all about what's happened so far with the case, and this fight with a suspect. It sounds dreadful and frightening."

He took another sip of the scotch. "Fine, but there's not much to tell, honestly. As far as the fight goes, I was at the apartment of Gertrude Claggett and Charlotte Castle, or Castleberry."

"I know the name Charlotte Castle. Her father phoned you yesterday morning and hired you to investigate that woman's murder."

"That's right."

"And I recall you saying the murdered woman was Miss Castle's roommate, so since you were at the apartment of Miss Castle and this Miss Claggett, I assume the latter is the poor victim?"

"Well done, Watson," Mason said, placing the napkin over his shirt and taking a bite of the egg sandwich.

"Thanks, Sherlock. How did she die, anyway? How did she end up in that trunk?"

"Strangulation. Pretty brutal."

Lydia's hands went to her white throat. "Oh! How awful."

"Yes. I'm assuming whoever killed her hid her body in the trunk, but I'm not certain why yet."

"I just can't imagine. So what were you doing in their apartment?"

"Having a look around. It's what I do, you know. Looking for clues or ideas."

"Okay, find anything of interest?"

"Maybe. I discovered Miss Claggett's diary, for one thing."

"And you read it, naturally."

"Under the circumstances I didn't think she'd mind. I also found the clothes that had been removed from the trunk to make room for the body."

"Simply grisly. How did you end up getting injured? You said you were in a fight with a suspect."

"Yes, I was in the bedroom of their apartment when I heard someone coming. I went to hide on the fire escape, but before I could get out I was attacked from behind. I got slammed backward into a dresser and then put in a headlock."

"Who attacked you? And how did you get out of it?" Lydia's eyes were large as she leaned forward now, resting her elbows on her knees, her chin in her hands.

"I stomped on a foot, elbowed a gut, and got in a punch to their kisser, which gave me time to draw my gun."

"You drew your gun? Oh, Mason. I hope you called the police."

"There was no need. It turns out it was all just a misunderstanding. My assailant was actually one of the building managers, who thought I was a burglar or a trespassing reporter, and I thought they may have been the murderer returning to the scene. We cleared things up, though I'm still not convinced she's not a murderer."

Lydia sat upright in surprise. "She? You mean the person who beat you up is a woman?"

"I'd rather not talk about it, and she didn't beat me up. She shoved me into a dresser and then grabbed my neck, that's all."

"And you had to draw your gun to defend yourself," Lydia said, a smirk on her face as she suppressed a laugh.

"Go ahead and laugh. It's not funny. She's a strong woman. She has five brothers she used to wrestle with."

"And now she wrestles private detectives."

"And quite successfully, I must say. She's strong enough to strangle Miss Claggett easily, I think," Mason said.

"Oh my. Do you think she did?"

"Definitely possible. She had motive and opportunity," Mason said, taking another bite of the sandwich, followed by a spoonful of soup. "The egg sandwich is delicious, but the chicken noodle needs salt."

Lydia got to her feet and retrieved the salt from the kitchen. "Here," she said, handing the shaker to him as she returned.

"Thanks."

"Sure. This woman had motive and opportunity, you say?"

"She did, definitely."

"How frightening. I'm so glad you weren't hurt even worse than you are," she said, taking a seat on the nearby chair once more.

"Yeah. Me too." He shook a little salt into the bowl and took another spoonful. "That's better," he said.

"Good. Though I only use a dash or two of salt in my homemade soup."

"You're a good cook, always have been."

"Thanks. It's been too long since I've really cooked for you. Maybe I can make dinner for you and Toby one of these days."

"I haven't even met him yet." He took a sip of the scotch and adjusted the hot water bottle on his lower back.

"Well, after you do, then, I mean. I know you two will hit it off. So, who is this woman who beat you up? Sorry, who attacked you. You said she's one of the building managers?"

"That's right. Her name's Mrs. Comstock. She and her sister, a woman who's not really her sister, I'm sure, own the Evans Comstock Residence for Young Ladies on Roosevelt, where Miss Castle and Miss Claggett lived."

"Oh, I see. I think. Her sister's not really her sister?"

"Most certainly. They're lesbians pretending to be sisters to throw off suspicion."

"Ah."

"Yes, and the younger one seemed to take a fancy to Miss Claggett, which made Mrs. Comstock quite jealous."

"So there's the motive, and since she owned the building, she probably had lots of opportunity. Did Miss Claggett return her attentions?"

"No, quite the opposite, in fact. Apparently, when she discovered the two women were lesbians, she became disgusted and even threatened to report them to the police."

"So motive number two. Is this Mrs. Comstock your strongest suspect right now, then? Pardon the pun."

Mason groaned. "Pardoned, and she's certainly one of them, along with Miss Castle, Mr. Patterson, Miss Powell, the victim's brother, and, I must admit, Mr. Brody."

"That's quite a lot of suspects," Lydia said. "Do any of them stand out more than the others?"

Mason shook his head slowly, though it pained him to do so. "I'm really not sure. They all seem to have a motive, the opportunity, and the means, every single one of them, though right now I'd say Miss Powell, Mrs. Comstock, and the victim's brother are at the top of the list, in no particular order."

"How interesting," Lydia said, picking up the scotch bottle. "Let me freshen your drink."

"Thanks," he said, holding up his glass, which was almost empty again. "Sure you won't join me?"

She got to her feet once more. "Okay, but just a short one. I'll get a glass." She breezed through the dining room and into the kitchen, returning quickly with a tumbler, which she filled halfway from the bottle.

"Cheers, Mr. Holmes," she said, holding up the glass to Mason's.

"Cheers, Watson."

"Let's start at the top. Who's this Miss Powell?"

"She worked with Gertrude Claggett at city hall in the typing pool, and through her, Gertrude met John Patterson, her boyfriend. Only at the time they met, Mr. Patterson was dating Miss Powell."

"Oh dear, so Miss Powell is the jilted woman. Always makes for a strong suspect."

"Right you are. She comes across as a tough cookie, direct, and street smart, savvy. She certainly could have done it."

"And what about Miss Claggett's brother?"

"His name is Josiah Paul Claggett. Miss Claggett called him J.P. for short. I found her diary when I was in the apartment, and in it she mentioned finding something bad out about J.P. and calling for a meeting with him the day she was murdered."

Lydia's eyes grew large again. "What did she find out?"

"I don't know for certain. Mr. Patterson believes she discovered Josiah was stealing funds from the mission he and J.P. worked at. Miss Claggett worked there, too."

"I thought you said Miss Claggett worked at city hall in the typing pool?"

"She did, but only part-time. Her full-time job was at the Lost Souls Mission. She got her brother and Mr. Patterson jobs there, too. It seems Josiah had started drinking and gambling again, and was in debt pretty deep."

"So, she got her brother a job, he embezzled money to pay for his gambling debts, she found out, he came over to her apartment, they argued, and he killed her."

"That's one theory, yes," Mason said.

"And a good one, I'd say."

"Yes. And she was strangled with a man's green necktie that had a hula girl painted on it. Josiah apparently owned and was wearing a tie like that when he visited her on Monday."

"I'd say that's enough to convict him."

"It's a pretty solid case, I must say, but I'm not one hundred percent convinced yet."

"Okay, you also mentioned Miss Castle and Mr. Patterson."

"Right, I did. Miss Castle is a possibility, but not a strong one. She had the opportunity, though, certainly. And when her father picked her up, she went downstairs to meet him rather than having him come up."

"Meaning she could have killed her roommate, put the body in the trunk, and then went down to meet her father."

"It's possible, but her motive seems weak. Just that she and Miss Claggett didn't get along."

"I admit that's weak, especially since she was moving to California anyway."

"Indeed, unless I'm missing something. Mr. Castleberry did tell me Charlotte and Gertrude had an argument about Mr. Patterson. Gertrude accused Charlotte of being interested in him or something to that effect, and Gertrude was jealous."

"Oh, well, that could be a motive, then. If there actually was something to that."

"Yes, I agree. And Mr. Patterson told me he's thinking of moving back to L.A. That's where he's from."

"And so the plot thickens," Lydia said. "He and Miss Castle both move out to L.A. together."

"Maybe. But what doesn't make sense to me is, if they *were* interested in each other, why kill Gertrude? Why wouldn't Mr. Patterson just break up with her and go off with Miss Castle to California? There would be no point in Charlotte or Mr. Patterson killing her."

"Hmm, that's true."

"John Patterson seemed to be truly in love with Gertrude, too. He told me he hoped to marry her, and he apparently gained nothing from her death, so there doesn't really seem to be much of a motive. He said Miss Claggett telephoned him at the mission on Monday to tell him she had asked her brother to come over so she could confront him, and he, worried about the brother's reaction, decided to go to the apartment and intervene."

"Okay."

"But he says when he got there, the trunk and suitcases were gone and no one was home. He didn't know where Gertrude was."

"Do you think he was telling the truth?"

"It seems likely. If he was lying, I can't put my finger on a motive, and he didn't seem to profit by her death in any way, as I said before. She left behind almost nothing."

"All right. You mentioned one other person," Lydia said, drinking her scotch.

"Yes, Mr. Brody. He worked at Union Station and is the one who picked up Miss Castle's trunk and suitcases that day from the apartment."

"You mean the trunk with that woman's body in it?"

"Yes, though he says he didn't know the body was inside."

Lydia shuddered. "Oh, that just gives me the creeps. You said he's also a suspect. Why?"

"He had the opportunity, certainly, when he went to pick up the trunk and the suitcases. Supposedly Miss Claggett was home alone, though he claims, as did Mr. Patterson, that when he arrived the apartment was empty."

"Hmm, what about a motive?"

"That's the sticky part. Mr. Brody's motive is really just a theory on some people's part."

"What do you mean?"

"Oh, some idiot who works at Union Station and even Emil, to a certain degree, think this Mr. Brody went to pick up the trunk and suitcases, found Miss Claggett alone in the apartment, made a pass at her, then attacked and killed her."

"How awful."

"Yes, if that's what happened," Mason said.

"Do *you* think that's what happened?"

"I don't know, to be honest. I had a long talk with Mr. Brody. He doesn't seem the type to go attacking some strange woman."

"But you always say there is no type when it comes to crime."

Mason nodded gently. "That's true, but he seemed genuine. I could be totally wrong, though, I suppose. He is a logical suspect."

"It seems you have lots of logical suspects. Josiah Claggett, Mrs. Comstock, and Miss Powell, as you said earlier, and I'd have to add Mr. Brody."

"Agreed."

"Who do you think did it?"

"I'm not sure, exactly," Mason said, finishing the soup and sandwich and wiping his mouth before dropping the napkin onto the now-empty plate. "I wish I was."

Lydia set her glass down and got to her feet. "Hold that thought, darling. Let me take that tray in the kitchen. I'll be right back." She picked up the tray with the empty bowl, spoon, napkin, and plate on it and carried it away along with the salt shaker, leaving Mason with his glass and the bottle of scotch on the small table next to his chair. When she returned she picked up the bottle and filled her glass halfway again.

"I thought you were only having a short one?" Mason said.

"I am. Half a glass is a short one."

"But you already had half a glass."

"And now I'm having the other half," she said, sitting down once again. "So, what did this Mr. Brody say exactly when you talked to him?"

"He said when he arrived to pick up the luggage, Gertrude was nowhere to be found, the apartment door was ajar, and the living room window was open. He went in, retrieved the trunk and suitcases, and left. So, if he's telling the truth, Miss Claggett was already dead and inside the trunk, as you mentioned earlier."

"That seems plausible. Horrible, but plausible."

"Yes, and Mr. Patterson said that when *he* arrived along with Miss Evans, Gertrude wasn't there either, and he saw Josiah hurrying away down the sidewalk, presumably escaping out the window and down the fire escape. Meaning Josiah may have killed his sister, hid the body in the trunk, and fled."

"But you said before Mr. Patterson said the trunk and suitcases were already gone when he arrived."

Mason beamed at her. "Glad you're paying attention, Watson. Yes, that's correct. But Josiah could have killed his sister and put the body in the trunk. Mr. Brody may have arrived shortly after that. He said he buzzed the apartment first and then tried Mrs. Comstock and Miss Evans when Gertrude didn't answer."

Lydia nodded. "I see, so when the front door buzzer sounded,

Josiah may have looked out the window and saw it was the man from the train station, so he hid someplace."

"Yes. The Union Station truck was probably parked on the street out front, clearly marked with the Union Station name. When Josiah saw that, he decided to go out the window and hide on the fire escape, most likely. Miss Evans let Mr. Brody into the building, and he came up to the apartment alone. He found the door ajar and the window open, but no one home. He took the luggage and left, not realizing Josiah was out on the fire escape and Miss Claggett's body was in the trunk."

"And then Mr. Patterson arrived?"

"Yes. He tried the apartment first, too, but then also had to buzz Miss Evans and Mrs. Comstock for access. Miss Evans let him in and accompanied him upstairs. Like Mr. Brody, they found the door ajar and the window open. And as I said, Mr. Patterson glanced out the window and saw Josiah hurrying away up the sidewalk."

"So, Josiah killed his sister, hid on the fire escape while Mr. Brody picked up the trunk and suitcases, and then, just after Mr. Brody left, he saw Mr. Patterson arrive."

"Seems likely."

"So then, as soon as Mr. Patterson was inside the building and on his way up with Miss Evans, Josiah climbed down the fire escape and hurried away."

"That makes the most sense, I must admit," Mason said.

"Then Mr. Brody couldn't have done it."

"Correct, unless Josiah just argued with his sister and shoved her down, knocking the wind out of her or maybe even knocking her temporarily unconscious. That scared him. He heard the door buzzer, so he hid on the fire escape. Mr. Brody came in, noticed Gertrude unconscious on the floor, and decided to take advantage of her. She comes around, they struggle, and he strangles her. He hides the body in the trunk and then leaves with it and the suitcases. Josiah, still on the fire escape, is even more scared now and decides to flee. Shortly after, Mr. Patterson arrives, finds her gone, but sees Josiah out the window on the sidewalk below."

"Wowzer," Lydia said.

"Yes, but it's *also* possible Mrs. Comstock showed up to confront Miss Claggett about her flirtations with Lucy Evans after Josiah's fight with his sister. Gertrude's knocked down, J.P. hears Mrs. Comstock coming, and he hides on the fire escape. Mrs. Comstock enters. The two women argue, Mrs. Comstock kills her, she hides her body in the trunk, and then leaves. A short while later, Mr. Brody arrives and takes the trunk and cases away, followed by the arrival of Mr. Patterson, who then sees J.P. fleeing down the sidewalk. Mrs. Comstock claimed to be in the boiler room the entire time working on the heating system, but that seems unusual."

"I must admit any and all of those scenarios are plausible," Lydia said.

"Or it may be something else or someone else altogether. I'm just not sure right now. Even Miss Powell could have dropped in after J.P., before Patterson arrived. She gets out of work at three and really had no alibi for where she went after work on Monday."

Lydia looked thoughtful. "Ah yes, the jilted girlfriend you mentioned before. Say, what's Miss Powell's first name?"

"Julia, why?" Mason said, finishing off his scotch and adjusting the hot water bottle again.

"Julia Powell, J.P., and John Patterson is also a J.P."

Mason raised his eyebrows. "I say, you're right about that, Watson. So, we have three J.P.s. Do me a favor and get my notebook from the inside pocket of my jacket, will you? I draped it on the back of my desk chair."

"Sure," Lydia said, setting down her glass and getting to her feet. She crossed the room to the rolltop desk in the corner, retrieved the notebook from the suit coat pocket, and carried it back to Mason. "Here ya go. What are you thinking?"

"Hmm? Oh, I just want to check my notes on Miss Claggett's diary." He opened it up and flipped a few pages. "Yes, here it is. This is what she wrote the day before she died, verbatim. 'J.P. is coming over tomorrow to discuss what I found out. I'm still upset and troubled and unsure of how to proceed. It goes against everything I believe to be true and right. I telephoned and arranged for a meeting here after five, after Charlotte has gone.'"

"Goodness," Lydia said, finishing her scotch also. "If her brother *was* stealing from the mission, that would certainly fit with what she wrote."

"It would indeed. But there was also an entry written three days prior that said, 'Found out something disturbing today about J.P. I almost can't believe it's true.'"

"So, when she found out whatever it was she found out, she didn't act immediately."

"No, she gave it a few days. She may have been referring to her brother's drinking and gambling, or the stealing, or all of it. She probably wanted to mull it over, maybe investigate further, to try to find out if it was really true."

"And then she confronted him, they argued, and he killed her."

"Except, if you'll notice, nowhere in her writing does she say J.P. is a man or a woman. I had assumed she was referring to her brother, but as you alluded to before, J.P. may indeed have been actually referring to Julia Powell, or even John Patterson."

"Gosh, you're right," Lydia said. "But if it *was* anyone else but the brother, what about the necktie?"

"What do you mean?"

"I mean, he was wearing the hula girl tie when he arrived, and it was then found wrapped around Gertrude's neck. So, if he didn't kill her, how would anyone else have gotten their hands on the tie?"

"Hmm, good thought, that. I suppose it's possible he took it off in the heat of the argument and left it in the apartment when he fled. Whoever showed up next saw it lying there, picked it up, and strangled Miss Claggett with it. Or I suppose it's also possible Josiah did start to strangle Gertrude, but then got scared and took off. The next person who came along just finished the job."

"Jeepers, Mason, so now what?"

"Now I have some more thinking to do, and you need to go home and fix some supper for yourself."

"Oh, all right. I imagine Mr. Zester is looking for his dinner, too." She glanced at her wristwatch. "Jeepers, it's nearly eight o'clock already. I'll leave you be, Mr. Holmes, but let's discuss this further tomorrow. I have the day off and am at your complete service."

"Come on up when you have time, then."

"I'll do that. Hopefully I can get some sleep tonight. I'll probably be up all night thinking about all of this horrible business."

"As will I, I'm afraid."

Lydia got to her feet and picked up her now-empty glass. "Finished with yours, Mason?"

"Not quite, leave it for now. I'll attend to it in a bit."

"Okay, but don't overdo it. Let me heat some more hot water for your hot water bottle, at least, and do up the dinner dishes," she said, not waiting for a reply but striding off to the kitchen, where Mason could hear her filling the kettle once more and singing softly to herself as she washed the dishes. It wasn't long before she was back, plucking the now-cool hot water bottle out from behind him and carrying it once more to the kitchen, where she dumped the tepid water into the sink and filled it with fresh hot water from the kettle. With the stopper firmly in place, she brought it back to Mason and wedged it between his lower back and the chair. "There, how's that?"

"Fine. It actually feels much better, thanks."

Lydia looked at him critically. "It's probably more the aspirin and the scotch, but I suppose the hot water bottle helps some. The apron was a tad damp, so I hung it on the back doorknob. Will you be all right tonight?"

"All right? In what way?"

"I mean, getting ready for bed and all. Do you need help brushing your teeth or anything?"

"I bet you drove the Red Cross mad, Miss Dettling. I'm fine, honestly, and I'll be just fine without you. Thank you for making dinner and doing the dishes, but go home!"

She bent down and kissed his forehead. "Fine, I'm going, but call me if you need anything. You know I'm just downstairs," she said, slipping on her shoes once more.

"I do know, and that's a great comfort. Good night."

"Good night, love. I'll play you a lullaby on my bass fiddle when I get home, after I finish eating my own dinner. With your windows open you should be able to hear it."

"That would be lovely. Preferably Brahms."

"Of course, darling. Sleep tight." She walked to the front door, retrieved her hat, gloves, and purse, and blew him a kiss before leaving.

CHAPTER TWELVE

Morning, Thursday, May 9, 1946
Mason Adler's apartment

Mason opened one eye and glanced at the alarm clock, which read twenty minutes past nine. With a soft groan, he opened both eyes and got up gingerly, sitting on the edge of the bed with his bare feet on the braided area rug. Surprisingly, his back and neck felt better, but his head hurt something awful and his tongue felt like sandpaper. He got slowly to his feet and wandered naked out to the living room, where he picked up the now-empty bottle of scotch.

"Aha," he said aloud to himself. "Back pain reliever, headache giver." He carried the bottle to the kitchen and held it over the trash can. "I thank you for your service," Mason said to the bottle before dropping it into the bin with a small salute. He made a mental note to stop by the liquor store for another and then strolled slowly back to the bedroom, where he raised the window shade, picked up the bowl of melted ice from in front of the fan, and carried it to the bathroom, dumping it down the drain.

Mason swallowed two aspirin, then washed up and shaved before getting dressed in his gray linen suit with a red tie. The day outside was clear and sunny, just another May morning in Phoenix, Arizona. He walked down the short hall into his living room, then past the sofa with his small typing table behind it, past his rolltop desk, into the dining room, and then at last the kitchen, where the sun was glaring through the courtyard side window. Mason drew the shade down and made himself some breakfast, consisting of a banana, toast with butter and blueberry jam, orange juice, and coffee. He put away the apron from last night and opened the kitchen door that led to the courtyard balcony, where he lifted the lid on the insulated metal box outside and extracted a fresh bottle of cream that had been left by the milkman. He added just a dash of the cream to his coffee, along with a spoonful of sugar, and then put the bottle in his icebox. He had just sat down at the small dining table to eat when he heard his phone ringing in the living room.

Mason took a quick swallow of coffee, got up, and walked as quickly as he could to the telephone niche by the front door.

"Mason Adler," he said, answering on the fifth ring.

"Mason, it's Emil."

"Oh, yes, good morning, Emil."

"Good morning. I didn't wake you, did I? It's already well past ten. It's actually coming eleven, as a matter of fact."

"No, you didn't wake me, not at all. I was just about to eat some breakfast."

"Breakfast? You do like to sleep in."

"I wasn't feeling well last night," Mason said, annoyed. "And I was up at nine, or thereabouts."

"I was up at six, and at the station by seven thirty."

"Bully for you, Emil. What can I do for you? My coffee and toast are getting cold."

"More what I can do for you. I have some good news."

"I could use some good news, what is it?"

"I wanted to let you know we made an arrest in the Gertrude Claggett murder."

Mason gripped the receiver tightly. "Oh? You did? Who?"

"Josiah Claggett, the brother. We picked him up late yesterday afternoon near John Patterson's house."

"So, you found him. I know you'd been looking for him."

"Yes. We brought him downtown for questioning, and he actually confessed."

"He did?"

"You sound surprised."

"I guess I am, a little."

"Or are you just surprised that for once I beat you to it? I solved the case before you did."

"I'm just surprised he'd confess. There wasn't much real evidence against him."

"It took a little coercing, but he admitted killing her."

"But he told me he only shoved her and she fell."

There was a brief pause. "Now I'm surprised. When did *you* talk to Josiah Claggett?"

"Yesterday afternoon. I was going to call you to let you know today."

"Sure you were."

"I was, honestly. I stopped by John Patterson's house yesterday to talk to him, and after we'd finished and Mr. Patterson left for work, I happened to spy Josiah around the side of the house, probably just waiting until the coast was clear so he could go inside and get something to eat and wash up."

"Okay, so then what?"

"Well, I could tell he was scared. I approached him cautiously and told him I was a friend of Miss Castle's and that I was trying to help her. He started talking to me, and he told me what happened. But then a police cruiser showed up and scared him off. They saw him go, and they went after him. And apparently they caught him."

"They did, eventually, but he gave a good chase, I hear. What did he tell you happened at his sister's place?" Emil said.

"Probably the same thing he told you. He said his sister sent for him because she was angry."

"Yeah, that's pretty much what he told us, at least initially. He said he went over there, they got into an argument, he shoved her, and she fell. He said he couldn't remember exactly what happened after that, but he fled. I guess his sister didn't like drinking or gambling, amongst a list of other stuff he does. He also confessed to us that he lost quite a bit of money recently."

"Interesting. Mr. Patterson said he thought Miss Claggett wanted to see her brother because she found out he'd been stealing from the Lost Souls Mission," Mason said.

"Probably to pay for his gambling debt."

"Yes, that's true," Mason said. "But you told me the other day his sister's cause of death was strangulation."

"So?"

"Josiah only admitted to pushing her down, at least to me."

"That's what he told us initially, too, except like I said, he claimed initially that he couldn't remember exactly what happened immediately after shoving her. I figure he knocked her down, then took off his necktie and strangled her, maybe because she was struggling, and he was in a blind rage. Then, in a panic, he tried to hide the body and settled on the trunk."

"I suppose that's possible."

"It's more than possible, it's quite likely. And there's something else, too."

"What?"

"I probably shouldn't tell you, since it's police business, but considering…"

"Yes, considering. What is it?"

"We found a button at the bottom of the trunk after removing Miss Claggett's body. It was unique, a silver unicorn. We confirmed that the button appears to have come from a green sport jacket Josiah owns. We weren't able to get any clear prints off it, but it's definitely his."

"Oh."

"That and the fact that the green tie with the hula girl on it belongs to Josiah makes for a pretty solid case against him, I must say, and I would assume you agree," Emil said.

"Certainly I agree it is pretty damning. Do you know for certain the tie and button belong to him?"

"Josiah Claggett himself identified the tie as his own when we showed it to him, and he recognized the button and admitted it must have come from his jacket. He had a motive and opportunity, and he's certainly strong enough to have done it."

"That is a pretty solid case indeed, then," Mason said. "What about the autopsy? Did it turn anything up?"

"Not really anything unexpected. The coroner confirmed the

cause of death was strangulation, but the body wasn't otherwise violated in any way. She'd been dead approximately six hours when the body was found."

"Meaning she was killed roughly around five thirty in the afternoon on Monday," Mason said.

"Roughly. We know the trunk was picked up with her body inside right around six, and Miss Castle left the apartment a few minutes before five, at which point Miss Claggett was still alive, so we're placing the time of death between five and six p.m."

"But how do you *know* she was still alive when Miss Castle left? It seems all you're going on is Miss Castle's word. She may have killed Gertrude, put her body in the trunk, then went downstairs to meet her father. When Josiah arrived he found the apartment seemingly empty. He saw Alfred Brody arrive, panicked, and hid on the fire escape. Then when Mr. Patterson arrived, he climbed down and took off."

"Josiah confessed, Mason, and Miss Castle didn't have any real motive. It's over and done with. Let it go."

Mason took a deep breath and let out a long, slow sigh. "Okay. So that's it, then, it sounds like."

"Yes, that's it. I would think you would be happy about that. Certainly your client will be happy."

"Of course he'll be pleased. Will there be a trial?"

"No need, since he confessed. There will be a hearing and a sentencing, though. Chances are his attorney will plead involuntary manslaughter, meaning he didn't intend to kill his sister."

"Yes, Emil, I know what involuntary manslaughter means," Mason said, annoyed.

"Sorry. Anyway, if that's what he ends up being charged with, he won't get the gas chamber. Chances are he won't even serve time in prison too long, if at all, though they may lock him up in a mental hospital, which is probably where he belongs."

"Maybe. Well, thanks for letting me know."

"Of course. No hard feelings?"

"Certainly no hard feelings. I'm glad the case is resolved."

"You say that but you don't sound like you mean it."

"I just still have my doubts, I guess, that's all."

"I don't see why you'd have doubts when Josiah confessed."

"But what exactly did he confess to?"

"To killing his sister, Gertrude Claggett, of course."

"But did he confess to strangling Gertrude, or to just pushing her down?"

"He claimed at first he didn't remember strangling her, like I told you, but when I showed him the tie, and he identified it, it seemed to all come back to him. He was most distraught."

"Only natural, I suppose. Well, thanks again for the telephone call, Emil. I appreciate it."

"You're welcome. And I hope the offer still stands for the use of that cabin."

"It does, of course it does. I already spoke to Mr. Blanders about it yesterday morning, and he was agreeable. He marked you down on his calendar and said he'd be in touch to get you the keys and such. I gave him your home telephone number."

"Great, thanks, Mason. After the last few days, I could really use something pleasant and relaxing to look forward to."

"Good, I hope you'll enjoy it and make Mr. Blanders a nice offer."

"It's certainly something to think about. Don't forget you said you could get me a good price, if I like it."

"Right, I haven't forgotten. Only what I actually said was I could *probably* get you a good price. I make no guarantees, Emil."

"Fair enough."

"Okay, well, I'll let you go. I'm sure you have details to wrap up."

"I do, and I know you have your, uh, breakfast to eat, and I'm sure you'll want to call your client, Mr. Castleberry, and give him the good news. And then with everything resolved, you can go back to sleeping even later, taking naps, and doing whatever it is you do when you're not working on a case."

"Yes, whatever that is. Goodbye, Emil."

"Bye, Mason. Let's have a beer together again soon."

"Sure, that would be swell."

"And I hope your toast and coffee aren't cold by now."

"Me too. Goodbye, Emil." Mason hung up the telephone receiver, lost in his thoughts. He debated telephoning Mr. Castleberry but thought instead an in-person visit would be better. He walked back into the dining room and polished off the food, coffee, and orange juice, then did up the dishes, all the while turning everything that had happened over and over in his mind. He dried his hands on a dish towel he kept hanging over the oven handle and then walked back to the living room, where he sat down at the small typewriter behind his sofa and began tapping out an itemized final bill to present to his client. He'd just finished the first line, dinner at the Cactus Café with Emil, when the buzzer on the downstairs gate sounded. Mason got to his feet and walked to the door, pressing the button on the intercom.

"Yes?" Mason wasn't really expecting anyone and couldn't imagine who it was.

"It's me, Mason," Walter said. "I've got your new clothes and a little surprise for you, so let me up."

Mason pressed the gate release button and checked his reflection in the mirror before opening the door to the balcony hall. It wasn't long before Walter was sashaying down the balcony toward him, a garment bag over his left arm and a small white Diamond's paper shopping bag in his right hand.

"Good morning, darling," Walter said as he swept into Mason's apartment and Mason closed the door behind him.

"Good morning. I thought the clothes weren't supposed to be ready until this afternoon?"

"Oh, they always say that, but they're nearly always ready early. So I stopped by on my way here to check, and sure enough, everything was all set." Walter, dressed in a seersucker suit with an orange and blue tie and coordinating pocket square, took off his dark black sunglasses and his jaunty hat and set them on the small table beneath the phone niche. "And while I was there I picked up a little gift, from me to you," Walter said, holding out the white paper bag in front of him.

"A gift? For me? Whatever for?"

"Well, I don't like to talk about it, but we both know my little birthday gift to you for your fiftieth didn't turn out so well, and I saw these and thought they would be just perfect for you."

"Well, thank you, but you really didn't need to," Mason said, taking the small bag. "Put that garment bag over the back of the sofa. I know you're dying for me to try the clothes on, but I want to see what you got me first."

"Fair enough," Walter said, draping the garment bag over the sofa as directed. He turned and looked up at Mason, who was opening the white paper bag cautiously. "I do hope you like them."

Mason reached in and removed a small box, set the bag aside, and opened the lid, revealing a stunning pair of jade and gold cufflinks. His eyes grew large, and he was truly flabbergasted. "Oh, Walter, they're beautiful, thank you so much!"

"You like them, darling? You really like them?"

"I do! They're perfect. I don't have any jade ones, you know."

"Well, now you do."

"Yes, I can wear them with my new clothes."

Walter looked appalled as he shook his head and wagged a finger in Mason's direction. "Oh no. No, no, no, darling. Your new trousers are pea green. You can't wear jade cufflinks with pea green trousers."

"Why not?"

"Because one never mixes shades of green, it just isn't done. Not tastefully, anyway. It's all about contrast and coordination."

"Contrast and coordination?" Mason said.

"The two Cs of fashion. You can't wear those with your new clothes, but they *will* look perfect with one of your dull gray suits."

"Yes," Mason said, nodding thoughtfully. "Yes, they will. Thanks again."

"You're most welcome, and I'm so glad you like them. Now then, how about a cocktail while you try on your new duds?"

"It's not even noon yet, Walter."

"A few minutes after eleven, close enough. Have any bourbon?"

"In the cabinet above the sink in the kitchen. Help yourself,"

Mason said. "I'll just take the clothes in the bedroom and try them on."

"All right, but be quick about it. I'm just dying to see everything on you again, all fitted properly. Oh, and do wear those diamond cufflinks of yours I like so much, the sparkle will be perfect."

"Sure," Mason said, picking up the garment bag. "I suppose the diamond links will *contrast* with the pea green, is that it?"

"Yes, darling, now you've got it."

"Okay. Shoes?"

"Your black cap toes, I think. Oh dear, I just realized we didn't get you any proper socks, though."

"Socks? I have plenty of socks. A whole drawer full."

"I know, but you need something colorful and fun. Yours are all black or dark brown. A pair of sunny yellow ones would be smashing with your new trousers."

"I think my standard black socks will suffice, Walter. They coordinate with the pea green."

"Oh, suit yourself, but they contrast, not coordinate. Coordinating socks would be a yellow and pea green argyle. Still, the black ones will be fine, I suppose. Maybe I'll get you some fun socks and underwear for Christmas. I just love getting and giving socks and underwear, don't you? Join me in a drink?"

"No, you go ahead," Mason said. "I'll be out in a few minutes." He took the garment bag with him to the bedroom and closed and locked the door, just in case Walter decided to pop in on him. When he emerged a few minutes later, Walter was sitting in the chair by the fireplace, sipping his bourbon over ice.

Mason, now dressed in the pea green trousers, black jacket, white French cuff shirt with the diamond cufflinks, black cap toe shoes, black socks, and burnt orange tie decorated with little black diamonds, stopped next to the sofa. "Well?"

Walter set his glass down and beamed up at Mason. "Oh, it's perfect! Absolutely perfect! Well, almost. You need an orange pocket square to go with the tie, but it has to be the perfect shade of orange."

"I thought you said not to wear colors of the same shade," Mason said.

"Dear, dear, Mason. Are you sure you're a homosexual? One wouldn't wear jade cufflinks with pea green trousers, nor a red jacket with orange trousers," Walter explained.

"I certainly wouldn't," Mason said.

"Exactly, but one *would* wear an orange pocket square to coordinate with an orange tie, as long as it was the correct shade and one of the two had a pattern. Your tie is orange but it has those adorable little black diamonds on it, you see? Like the argyle socks I mentioned before. Patterns with solids, but the pattern should have at least one of the colors of the solids in it. Does that make sense?"

"Not really, but I'll take your word for it. That's why I like my gray. Everything goes with my gray suits."

"And your gray hair and pasty white skin, darling, but we're trying to give you a little flair and color. Twirl for me, let me see it all from the back."

"Honestly, Walter."

"Please?"

"Oh, all right." Mason turned slowly around, feeling just a bit foolish.

"Brilliant! You'll be the hit of Palm Springs for sure. As soon as you solve this case you're working on, I'll contact my friend Marvin at the Triada and book us a room."

"Yes, about that…"

"Oh, I know how you are, don't worry. I'll make sure we have two twin beds so no one talks."

"Good, but I meant about the case. Emil telephoned this morning, just before you got here, actually."

"Oh? What did that old thing want?"

"He told me he's solved the case."

Walter sprang to his feet, or rather got up as quickly as he could. "You're joking."

"I wish I was. They've made an arrest and actually got a confession."

"Well, that's a surprise, I must say."

"Yes, I was surprised, too."

"Well, don't keep me in suspense. Who did it? Who murdered and dismembered that poor woman?"

"She *wasn't* dismembered, Walter."

"Fine, but who killed her? I'm just dying to know, so to speak."

"Emil arrested her brother, Josiah Claggett."

"Ohh, that's a surprise. I would have thought the roommate would turn out to be the guilty party."

"Honestly, I don't feel quite right about it."

"About what, darling?" Walter said, picking up his glass of bourbon and taking a healthy drink.

"About arresting the brother. I don't know why, but I feel he's innocent."

Walter studied him over the top of his glass. "Are you sure it's not just sour grapes because Emil beat you to the punch for once?"

"It's not sour grapes, truly. I just feel like I'm missing some clue I can't put my finger on."

"And you've such long fingers. Well, perhaps whatever it is will come to you. But in the meantime, the good news is I can now call Marvin and finally book our room at the Triada, since you're finished with the case and I'm between clients myself at the moment."

"What happened to the client who wanted you to redo her husband's law office?"

Walter cringed and held up a hand, palm out. "Let's not speak of her again. She has no taste, no imagination, and almost no budget, though I know they're loaded."

"She didn't hire you, eh?"

"No, she didn't. And it's just as well. She was extremely irritating. Anyway, since you're now available, I'm thinking next week sometime, or perhaps the week after, would be ideal for our Palm Springs sojourn. Maybe midweek when the rates are better and things aren't so crowded, say Tuesday through Friday?"

"Hmm? Oh, yes, that makes sense, I suppose. I think I'll change out of these clothes."

"Do that, darling. You don't want to spill anything on them before our trip." Walter finished off his bourbon and took the empty glass to the kitchen, where he left it in the sink before returning to the living room. Mason was still pacing back and forth in his new clothes.

"I know that look, and I know that pace. You're still dwelling on the case," Walter said, his hands on his hips.

Mason stopped. "Hmm? Oh, yes, yes, I suppose I am. Anyway, thanks again for dropping off the clothes, and for the cufflinks. They really are beautiful."

"I'm so glad you like them," Walter said. "We should do lunch soon. I've discovered a charming little café off Central you can take me to. Oh, and if I have time, I'll stop by Diamond's and look for a coordinating pocket square for you."

"You don't have to do that, you've done more than enough already. The cufflinks are wonderful."

"Oh, don't worry. If I find the right pocket square, I'll just have them charge it to your store account, now that you have one."

"You, Walter, are too much."

"Thank you, I'm so glad you noticed. I'll telephone you later after I've spoken to Marvin. I don't think he comes on duty until four," Walter said, picking up his sunglasses and jaunty hat and pulling open the front door. "Ta-ta."

"Bye," Mason said. He watched him sashay down the balcony as only Walter could, and then he closed the door with a sigh before heading to the bedroom to change back into his gray suit. He'd just finished tying his tie when a knock came from the front door. He walked back into the living room and opened it with a flourish. "Forget something?" he said. But it wasn't Walter, it was Lydia.

"What's that?" she said, surprised. "Forget what?"

"Oh, Lydia. Sorry, I thought you were Walter. He just left."

"Yes. I ran into him downstairs, and we spoke briefly. Are you feeling any better?"

"A slight headache, but overall, yes. My back and neck feel much better."

"I'm glad. Did you have breakfast?"

"I did, thanks."

"Good. I was going to pop up earlier and make you some oatmeal or something, but then my father called first thing, and after that I got to talking with Mrs. Woodburn out in the courtyard. She was out with her little dog, Scruffy. She's worried about him because he's not been eating, so I went into her place with her and we called a veterinarian. Anyway, the morning's just gotten away from me, but I haven't forgotten about you, my love."

"Thanks, but I'm fine. And I hope Scruffy will be okay. Come on in." He stepped aside and ushered her in before closing the door once more.

"I think Scruffy will be as right as rain. The vet didn't seem too concerned. He thinks it might be a dental issue of some kind, but he wants to examine him just to be certain. Mrs. Woodburn's going to take him over this afternoon, and I told her I would go with her for support."

"I'm sure she appreciates that. Do you need me to drive you the two of you?"

"Thanks, but Mr. Ferguson said he'd take us."

"Ferguson's a nice man. Want some coffee?"

"No, thanks, I had some earlier. But I wouldn't say no to some tea and a doughnut."

"Fresh out of doughnuts, but I can make some tea."

"That would be lovely. And I'll pick you up some doughnuts from the bakery on the way back from the vet's office. I'm sure Mr. Ferguson won't mind a brief stop."

"Thanks," Mason said. He crossed the living room, entered the dining room, and went on through to the kitchen, where he got out the kettle and filled it with water as Lydia made herself comfortable on one of the chairs at the small dining table.

"I'm so glad you're feeling better, Mason. I was worried."

"Not quite back to my old self yet, but I'm getting there. Ugh, my *old* self, I hate the sound of that," he said as he put the kettle on the stove.

"You're not old, love. I wish you'd stop dwelling on turning fifty."

"Easier said than done, as they say," Mason said, getting out two cups and saucers and placing them on the counter.

"Believe me, I know. I took turning forty pretty hard."

"I recall. But you still look lovely," Mason said as he put tea bags into the cups.

"So do you. Well, handsome, anyway. You're too hard on yourself."

"Maybe. Want cream with your tea?"

"Yes, please, and sugar."

"Right." He got out the bottle of cream from his icebox and set it on the table along with two spoons and the sugar bowl.

"Thanks," Lydia said. "By the way, Walter told me Emil solved your case."

"He solved *the* case," Mason said over his shoulder as he returned to the kitchen. "Apparently."

"Apparently? So you're not sure?"

"I'm not, to be honest. They arrested Miss Claggett's brother, Josiah, and got some kind of confession."

"That sounds pretty cut and dried to me. You said last night he had motive and opportunity."

"He did, but so did all the others."

"But it only takes one, and if he confessed…"

"Yes, that's what's puzzling."

"Puzzling in what way?"

"When I talked to Mr. Claggett, he admitted fighting with his sister and pushing her down, but said he doesn't remember exactly what happened next. He does remember fleeing, though."

"Okay. So?"

"So, Miss Claggett was strangled to death, apparently with a green necktie that had a hula girl painted on it, as you may recall. The tie was found wrapped around her neck and Josiah admitted the tie belongs to him. They also found a button in the trunk under Miss Claggett's body. A silver button with a unicorn on it that came from Josiah's green jacket."

"Jeepers, Mason, what more do you want, then? The whole thing on film? An eyewitness?"

Mason shook his head. "I honestly don't know, but if he *did* strangle her, I think he'd remember doing it. Emil claims it all came back to him, but I'm not so sure. And it strikes me as odd Josiah would leave behind such an unusual button and use such a distinctive tie to strangle her with, then leave it on the body to be found."

"Most likely it was just the tie he had on at the moment, and he left it in a panic and the button fell off the coat he was wearing during the struggle. He probably didn't plan on killing her, it just happened."

"Perhaps you're right. Maybe he did it in a blind rage, like Emil said, which is why he can't remember exactly what happened immediately after. Maybe he blocked it out of his mind," Mason said as the water began to boil. He turned off the stove and removed the kettle. "I have to admit it does make the most sense. All I have is Earl Grey, will that be satisfactory?"

"Sure, that's fine," Lydia said. "Need help?"

"No, I've got it." He poured water over the tea bags and set the kettle back on the stove to cool. "Sorry I don't have any biscuits, doughnuts, or anything to go with it."

"Just the tea is fine. I have to watch my figure, anyway."

"I'm sure Thad O'Connell watches your figure," Mason said through the large open doorway. He extracted the tea bags and brought the two cups and saucers into the dining room, setting them on the table.

"And I intend to make sure he keeps watching," Lydia said, adding a little cream and sugar to her cup and stirring.

"I have no doubt he will," Mason said, sitting down at the table across from her. "By the way, Walter dropped off my new clothes this morning. That's why he came by."

"Oh, how nice! I can't wait to see them. Have you tried them on already?"

"I have. I'm getting used to them."

"Used to them? Why am I not surprised you need to get used to them? What did he talk you into?"

"It's a little more color than I normally wear, but I think it will be fine. He also gave me a pair of jade cufflinks as a belated birthday present."

Lydia raised her brows in surprise as she took a sip of her tea. "Generosity like that's not typical of him. Are they to wear with your new clothes?"

"That's what I thought, but Walter told me they wouldn't look right together. He said I can wear them with one of my gray suits instead," Mason said, adding a little cream and sugar to his tea as well.

"You certainly have plenty of those," Lydia said, her eyes twinkling.

"Indeed I do, but in my defense, they are all different from one another, and different shades of gray. Hmm, that's odd."

"What?"

"A green tie and a green jacket."

"Sorry?"

"Josiah. His sister was strangled with his green tie, and the button was from his green jacket."

"I know, you said that. What's so odd about it?"

"Like Walter told me earlier, one never puts different shades of greens together, it's just not done. Coordinating, always, matching, sometimes, but never different shades of green. You wouldn't wear a lime green skirt with a jade green blouse, would you?"

"Well, no, but maybe this Josiah just didn't have the fashion sense Walter does. If you can honestly say Walter has fashion sense."

"Walter's rather colorful, it's true, but he is always well put together, and from what I understand, Josiah was, too. It seems odd he'd wear a green tie with a green jacket. In fact, if I remember correctly, now that I think of it, Miss Evans told me he was wearing a brown jacket on Monday with a yellow tie and tan trousers."

"Perhaps she was mistaken," Lydia said.

"It's possible, but she was quite detailed in her description of him," Mason said, taking a sip of his tea. "I can't believe I didn't think of that before."

"But if he *was* wearing a brown jacket with a yellow tie, where did the green tie and jacket come from?"

"That's a good question. Maybe from someone else's pocket."

"I'm sorry, Sherlock, you've lost me."

"My dear Watson, I'm just supposing perhaps the green tie and jacket were in someone else's pocket."

"But, Holmes, how would anyone fit a tie and an entire sport coat into their pocket?"

"The tie would be easy enough, and they wouldn't need the whole jacket, just the button."

"Well, that makes sense. But why? For what purpose?"

"To frame Josiah. Hmm, yes, it certainly could be. Things are falling into place."

"What things?"

"Clues. Ones that I should have picked up on before. I think the murderer is someone other than Josiah Claggett."

"Do tell, who?"

"Possibly John Patterson," Mason said.

"The woman's boyfriend?" Lydia said, surprised. "I thought he was low on your suspect list."

"He was, mainly because there didn't seem to be a motive, but maybe I just didn't see it before. As far as I know, only he would have a motive to frame Josiah, and only he had access to Josiah's button and tie. I'm not entirely sure he acted alone, either. Excuse me one moment, Lydia. I need to make a phone call to city hall."

"To Mr. Castleberry?"

"Yes. I won't be but a minute, hopefully."

Mason walked to the niche by the front door and picked up the receiver, dialing the exchange, which he now knew by heart.

"Mr. Castleberry's office," he heard Miss Gleason say after only one ring.

"Hello, Miss Gleason. This is Mr. Adler calling for Mr. Castleberry."

"Yes, sir, one moment." Mason waited a brief minute before he heard a click.

"Hello, Mr. Adler, it's good to hear from you."

"Yes, hello. Things a bit quieter at city hall today?"

"Hmm? Oh, yes, thankfully. Any new developments in the case?"

"Possibly. I wonder if you could do me a favor, though. I believe Councilman Monroe has an office at city hall, does he not?"

"He does. All the councilmen do. Why?"

"Would you be able to connect me to his office? To him directly? It's relevant to the case."

"How curious. But yes, I'm sure Miss Gleason can connect you to him, and I believe he's in today. Was there anything else?"

"No, not at the moment, but possibly later."

"All right, keep me apprised of any news. One moment while I get you back to Miss Gleason and let her know what you want."

The exchange took only a few minutes, and Mason soon heard the voice of a younger man picking up. "This is Councilman Monroe, how can I help you?"

"This is private detective Mason Adler. I'm working with Mr. Castleberry regarding the murder of that young woman found in the trunk at the train station Monday night."

"Oh, yes, I heard about Adam's daughter's involvement and connection. Adam's secretary said you wanted to speak with me directly, but I can't imagine what for. What did you need?"

"I was wondering about someone who worked on your last campaign, John Patterson, originally from Los Angeles."

There was a pause, then finally Mr. Monroe spoke. "What about him?"

"You recall the man I'm speaking of?"

"Yes, I most certainly do. Why?"

"I understand he did fund-raising for you."

"How is this related to that woman's death, Mr. Adler?"

"I'm not entirely sure yet, but Mr. Patterson was the woman's boyfriend."

Another pause, slightly longer than the first. "Oh, I see. Most unfortunate. Mr. Patterson *did* work on my campaign for a while, but he was discharged before the election even took place."

"For what reason, may I ask?" Mason said.

"I'm really not at liberty to say. No charges were brought against him as nothing could be proven."

"Nothing could be proven in terms of pilfering those funds he raised, or a portion of them?"

"Again I'm not at liberty to say, Mr. Adler, but I will say you appear to be fairly astute."

"Thanks, and thank you for your time, Mr. Monroe."

"You're welcome. I hope you are able to determine the guilty party in that poor woman's death. Good day."

"So do I," Mason said, "Good day." He hung up the receiver and turned to see Lydia, who had followed him into the living room and had been watching him intently.

"What was that all about?" she said.

"Just confirming a theory, more or less. I think I may know a motive now."

"For John Patterson? Well, spill the beans already, please."

"I think Mr. Patterson was embezzling a good portion of the funds he raised for the mission."

"Really? And Miss Claggett found out about it?"

"That's my theory."

"If you're right, that most certainly would give him a motive."

"Yes. After all, he'd had lots of experience embezzling funds, I'm willing to bet, out in L.A., and with Councilman Monroe's campaign. Mr. Monroe all but confirmed it. Most likely when Patterson first heard from Julia Powell, who heard from Miss Claggett, that they were looking for someone to help with fundraising at the mission, his eyes lit up like a pinball machine."

"So, Mr. Patterson, probably running low on funds, decided to apply for the job at the mission," Lydia said.

"Yes. He got Miss Powell to introduce him to Gertrude Claggett. He wanted to get in good with Gertrude so she would use her influence to get him the job at the mission. And perhaps he thought breaking up with Julia and dating Gertrude would open even more doors for him, or at least make her look the other way if she discovered anything funny."

"Which she did."

"I think so, unfortunately for her. Like the mission elders, she probably figured something crooked was going on, and she suspected Mr. Patterson but waited to confront him until she was sure."

"And she didn't go to the police or other members of the mission because they were dating, and she cared for him."

"Correct, Watson, just as he had planned and hoped. She wanted to give him a chance to clear himself or make things right. He told me an elder at the mission alerted him to the missing funds, and they may have informed Gertrude, who did some investigating of her own."

"But how did he think he could get away with embezzling?"

"I'm not certain what methods he employed, exactly, but most likely he got people and corporations to donate large amounts of money to the mission, just like he did with Monroe's campaign, and other places in L.A., I'm sure, most likely using a different last name. Only the mission job seemed like taking candy from a baby to him, I bet. After all, people like to be generous, to help those in need, feed the hungry, clothe the poor, and take care of the sick."

"That's true. I always try to donate to worthy causes when I can."

"As do I. In fact, I had planned to send a check to the mission after speaking with Mr. Patterson," Mason said. "He's very persuasive."

"But that's just it. Most people write checks made out to the mission, not to Mr. Patterson. So, how did he get his hands on the money?"

"I suspect, with Gertrude's help, he had control of the finances, with check writing privileges. Perhaps he told her he needed to spend money to make money. So if a company gave Patterson a check for a hundred dollars, he deposited it but changed the amount in the ledger to read ten dollars or something to that effect, and withdrew the rest for himself."

"Devious, underhanded, and awful."

"I agree. And worse, I think he made it appear like Josiah was the one cooking the books and stealing the money. It was Patterson's idea to get Josiah to work with him in the office. Patterson probably gave him lots of access to the accounts and the books, with the intention of framing him should anyone get wise."

Lydia shook her head slowly. "Poor Josiah."

"Yes. If I'm right, Mr. Patterson certainly planned it all out well. He knew by dating Gertrude, she'd be hesitant to expose him. And if she *did* expose him, he could blame it on Josiah instead, pointing to the evidence he carefully planted."

"Would Gertrude have believed Josiah was capable of that?" Lydia said.

"I don't know. Certainly she would want to believe her boyfriend was innocent, but after doing a little investigating on her own, I suspect she came to the realization he wasn't."

"So, she confronted Mr. Patterson," Lydia said.

"I think so. I'm sure she was heartbroken, and she didn't want to turn him in to the authorities. Perhaps she told him he should confess to the police himself, or at least confess to the higher-ups at the mission, and then resign and set up a repayment plan. No doubt neither one of those ideas would have appealed to Patterson, though perhaps he agreed to the latter one initially, to appease her. But since she was the only one who knew the truth about him, he decided to kill her. I'm sure he felt he could convince the mission elders that Josiah was to blame."

"So it was premeditated?"

"More or less, yes."

"But what about Miss Claggett's diary? She wrote that she found something awful out about J.P. Do you think she was referring to John Patterson, then?"

"I don't know for certain, but it's possible. Or the first entry may have referred to Patterson and the second to her brother."

"Or maybe both entries were about Josiah, about his gambling debt as well as the fact that he'd been drinking again."

"I think that's the most likely," Mason said. "Since she called her brother J.P., I don't think she'd use the same nickname for her boyfriend."

"That *would* be confusing."

"Definitely. I think she asked Josiah to come over to her apartment sometime after five on Monday so that she could scold him. Josiah most likely told Patterson about this, and Patterson saw it as the perfect opportunity to kill Gertrude and frame Josiah for the missing money and her death."

"That's horrible," Lydia said.

"Yes. I remember John Patterson telling me Gertrude telephoned him on Monday around five o'clock. But according to Gertrude's diary, she had found out about what Josiah was up to at least the day before, and possibly three days prior, and arranged for the meeting. So, why would she telephone John upset and angry about it on Monday afternoon?"

"That's a good question."

"Yes. I think he lied about the telephone call, but he did go over there. He took Josiah's green hula tie and a button off Josiah's green jacket, as it had the most distinctive buttons, and went to work at the mission, as usual, at two in the afternoon. He probably told Gertrude he was going to resign that day and come clean, setting up a repayment plan, but of course he never did. After Gertrude was dead, he'd have no reason to."

A shiver ran down Lydia's spine. "He went to work at the mission that day, all the while planning to kill Gertrude and frame her brother?"

"Correct. That's my theory, anyway."

"Oh, Mason. I just can't believe someone would do something like that."

"People have done worse, unfortunately. And of course, I'm merely speculating at this point. I may be wrong about everything. What time is it?"

"A quarter after twelve, why?"

"Just wondering. I want to have a word with John Patterson. I seem to recall he's off on Thursdays, so he's probably home. He rents a little house over on Third Street. I'm pretty certain he's the murderer, but there's only one way to find out for sure."

"You're going to his house to confront him? Now? Alone?" Lydia asked, her voice dripping with concern.

"Yes, yes, and yes."

"But don't you think you should call Emil and let him know?"

"Not just yet. I may be barking up the wrong tree, after all."

"Oh, Mason, let me go with you."

"Whatever for?"

"To protect you. Your back is better but it's still bothering you, I can tell. And you said this Patterson is a young man."

"I'll take my gun and I'll be fine, but thanks for the offer."

"All right, but I'll be a nervous wreck the whole time."

"Don't forget about Scruffy," Mason said.

"Oh yes, that's right. I suppose I'd better get changed and get ready to go with Mrs. Woodburn, Scruffy, and Mr. Ferguson to the vet."

"Tell them hello for me, and don't worry. I'll give you a ring when I get back."

"I will, and you'd better."

"I promise. I have to make one quick call to the Lost Souls Mission, and strap on my gun and holster, grab my hat, and then I'll be off."

CHAPTER THIRTEEN

Afternoon, Thursday, May 9, 1946
John Patterson's house

Once more Mason eased himself behind the wheel of his blue 1939 Studebaker Champion and steered it toward McDowell and then east to Third Street, parking in front of the small beige adobe house with the sand and gravel yard and the large tree. He left his car windows down and walked up the narrow, cracked cement path to the front door, which this time was closed. Mason rapped on it and waited what seemed a long time before Patterson opened up, dressed in dark brown trousers, an open at the neck cream-colored shirt, and a tan two-button jacket.

"Well, Mr. Adler, this is a surprise," he said.

"How do you do, Mr. Patterson. I suppose you heard about Josiah?"

"I did. Detective Hardwick telephoned me earlier today to give me the news. Such a shame, but I can't say I'm entirely surprised, given Josiah's temperament and everything."

"Yes. And everything."

"Still, it's hard to believe, and so sad. I just kept hoping it would turn out he was innocent. That the murderer would have been a stranger off the street. Still, given Josiah's mental state, I'm sure he won't get the death penalty."

"Yes, well, do you mind if I come in? It's awfully warm out here."

"Hmm? Oh, yes, I suppose so, though it's not much cooler inside. The fans help some, I guess." He stood aside as Mason entered the living room and John closed the door behind him. "I'm afraid I only have a few minutes, Mr. Adler. I was just getting ready to head out on some errands."

"This should only take a few minutes, Mr. Patterson." He removed his fedora and placed it on the small table behind the sofa.

"Okay, well, what can I do for you? Are you dropping off that donation check for the mission you mentioned the other day?"

"No, not just yet." Mason stood with his back to the front door and surveyed the living room, the kitchen to his right, and the small hall directly ahead of him. The bathroom door, he noted, was closed. The rest of the place looked pretty much like it had the last time he was here, unkempt and messy. "I just wanted to go over a few facts so I can conclude my investigation and type up my report for my client."

"Okay, but I think I already told you everything I know."

"I want to make sure I remember the details correctly." Mason took out his notebook and read aloud from one of the pages. "You told me when you first arrived at Miss Claggett's apartment on Monday afternoon with Miss Evans, the door to 3A was ajar and the living room window was open."

"Yes, that's right."

"And you and Miss Evans subsequently entered the apartment, and you looked out the window, where you saw Josiah on the sidewalk below, hurrying up Roosevelt away from the building."

"I did. He was moving pretty fast, like he was running away from what he'd done. It's so hard to believe."

Mason looked up from his pad directly at John Patterson. "It *is* hard to believe, because all he had done was have a fight with his sister. He pushed her and she fell, probably knocking the wind out of her. That scared him. He may have even *thought* he'd killed her, so he took off, though I suspect all of that happened far earlier, long before you entered the apartment with Miss Evans. Perhaps thirty to forty-five minutes earlier. By the time you arrived with Miss Evans,

Josiah was long gone to places unknown, so you couldn't have seen him scurrying away."

John gave Mason a strange look. "That's crazy. I saw him out the window, like I said."

"And that was a little after six, is that right?"

"Yes, that's right."

"Why did you go to Gertrude's apartment that evening? You left work to do so."

"Because Gert called me at the mission and told me Josiah was on his way over to her place, and she planned to confront him. I was worried he might do something to Gert. I only wish now I'd gotten there sooner."

"Actually, you *had* gotten there sooner, hadn't you? When you heard she wanted to talk to him privately, because she was angry with him about his gambling and drinking, you decided that was a perfect opportunity."

"What do you mean by that?" John narrowed his eyes, his lips pursed.

"I mean she found out about her brother's gambling and drinking. She even mentioned it in her diary," Mason said, closing his notebook and putting it back into his inside coat pocket.

Patterson looked surprised. "I didn't know Gert even kept a diary."

"She did. She wrote in it that she found out something awful about J.P. I wonder if she'd found out those things about him from you? Though I can't quite figure out why you'd tell her about the drinking and gambling and the debts he had incurred."

"Because she had a right to know. She was his big sister, and she was responsible for him."

"Or was it really because you wanted to set him up?"

"Meaning what?"

"Meaning the heat was on, and you needed a pigeon to cook. An elder at the mission suspected something was off with the finances and mentioned it to you and probably to Miss Claggett. You told Gertrude that Josiah was drinking and gambling again, and heavily in debt, which would be a good motive for embezzling, though I'm guessing you stopped short of accusing Josiah. You placed the pieces in front of her and let her put them all together. I imagine she was pretty upset by the news, probably not even wanting to believe it, so she waited a few days to confront him. In the meantime, she did a little further investigating on her own, and much to your chagrin, she found out that *you're* the one who had been stealing money, not Josiah."

"Don't be absurd," Patterson said.

"I try not to be absurd, but sometimes it can't be helped. This is not one of those times, however. She confronted you, and you denied it, pointing out the evidence you'd planted. But Miss Claggett saw what you'd been trying to do, and as difficult as it was for her, because she loved you, perhaps, she told you that if you didn't resign from the mission, confess what you'd done, and set up a repayment plan, she *would* go to the police."

"Utterly ridiculous. Josiah confessed to killing Gertrude, and I'm sure he'll confess to taking the money, too, if he hasn't already."

"Maybe, but it would be a false confession on both counts, under duress."

"A confession's a confession. He was seen on the property just before her death. He clearly did it, and there's plenty of proof."

"Meaning the tie and the button. Clever of you. But getting back to Gertrude's ultimatum, you realized you didn't have much choice, so you agreed to Gertrude's terms, telling her you'd resign and confess to the elders at the mission on Monday evening during your regular shift. I imagine you begged her forgiveness, maybe even with crocodile tears in your eyes. In the meantime, Gertrude asked her brother to come over to her place sometime after five on Monday, after Miss Castle had left, so she could discuss his drinking and gambling, which she discovered was indeed true. Josiah, nervous and feeling he could trust you, told you about it. He probably sought solace with you, maybe even hoped you'd come with him, but you told him you had to work, which you did. But of course, you planned to go over to Gertrude's apartment anyway, arriving sometime shortly after Josiah left."

"Why would I do that?"

"Because you wanted to make sure you had a pigeon, as I said earlier, not only for the theft of money but for Gertrude's death. You figured by the time you arrived, Josiah would probably be good and agitated, and the two of them would argue, hopefully loudly enough so the neighbors could hear, like they did when he was staying there and he and his sister would fight. And his fingerprints would be all over the place."

"You're crazy, old man."

"So I've been told," Mason said. "I'm guessing you actually got to the building around a quarter after five. You waited outside until you saw Josiah leave through the front door around five thirty or so, and then you went in, probably with a little help, via the back door. By the time you got up to the third floor, Gertrude was shaken up over the fight with her brother. She was naturally surprised to see you, but perhaps pleased, thinking you'd come to tell her you'd confessed and resigned. But you strangled her instead, using a distinctive necktie that belonged to Josiah, planning all along to frame him. Once she was dead, you needed to buy some time until you could make your exit and reappear. But perhaps you heard the front door buzzer about a quarter of six, so you panicked, broke the lock on the trunk, removed the clothes, and stuffed Miss Claggett's body inside along with the unicorn button, maybe with the thought of framing Miss Castle if framing Josiah didn't work out. Then you went down the fire escape, catching your blue jacket on it and tearing it."

"How would you know that?"

"Because I found a piece of the fabric still clinging to a corner of the fire escape. I imagine you'll have a ripped blue sport coat in your closet, unless you were smart enough to dispose of it, which I doubt, and it will be a match to the piece I found. You were wearing a blue coat that night because you came right from the mission, supposedly because you were worried about what Josiah would do to Gert."

"I was worried, and rightly so. Gertrude telephoned me at the mission and told me he was coming over. I could tell she was upset. Josiah had a terrible temper, and he killed her, and he stole the missing funds. That's what happened, despite what you may believe."

"Still sticking to that story, eh?"

"Yes, because it's the truth."

"Your version of it, anyway. I highly doubt she ever phoned you at work or anywhere that night. After all, she thought you were confessing and resigning that day. And I don't imagine she expected much trouble with Josiah. She was used to dealing with him and had actually discovered he was drinking and gambling days earlier. But it made a good story. After killing her and hiding her body in the trunk, you went down the fire escape unseen as the man from the train station was coming up the inside stairs. You had to waste some time until he left again, so you probably took a long walk around the block, and then you waited just out of sight until you saw him load the trunk and suitcases into his truck and drive off at just a few minutes past six o'clock."

"Utter nonsense," Patterson said, almost spitting out the words as he clenched his fists.

"I don't think so. What I do think is once he'd left, you walked casually up the front walk and buzzed the managers. You told them your little story about the supposed phone call from Gert to you, and how you were worried about Josiah possibly harming Gertrude. Miss Evans then told you she saw Josiah arrive earlier, and that the man from the train station told her there didn't appear to be anyone home in Gertrude's apartment. So, you and she went and had a look, and indeed the place seemed empty. You glanced out the window and pretended to see Josiah hurrying up the block, and you made sure to mention to Miss Evans that you saw him, and that he wasn't wearing a tie."

"I did see him, and he definitely was *not* wearing a tie."

"Really? How could you have known Josiah wasn't wearing a tie if you saw him, from a third-floor window, hurrying *away* from the building, up the street, his back to you?"

"What? Oh, well, I guess he turned around when I called out to him."

"That's not what you said before. You clearly said you called out to him, but he never looked back. And I'm sure Miss Evans would testify that is what you said as well."

"I guess I was mistaken, then. I think you should leave now."

"I guess you were mistaken, and I will leave, soon enough. You took one of Josiah's most distinctive ties from your house earlier that afternoon, along with a button from his green jacket, and had them with you in your pocket. You used the green hula girl tie to strangle Miss Claggett, then put her body in the trunk, along with the tie, still wrapped around her neck, and the button."

"You've no proof, Adler. None at all."

"I know from Miss Evans's testimony that when Josiah arrived, he was wearing a yellow tie and a brown jacket. I imagine if we make inquiries, we'll find others to corroborate that, including Mr. Granger, who lives next door to you. I'm sure you weren't aware he gave Josiah a ride to his sister's apartment on Monday afternoon."

"Oh, did he really?" John looked suddenly worried.

"He did, and I'm sure he'll remember Josiah was wearing a brown jacket and a yellow tie that afternoon. Why would Josiah bring a green hula tie along to strangle her? Indeed, why a tie at all? If he planned all along to kill her, why not use his bare hands? Surely he was strong enough, and Miss Claggett was a small woman."

"I don't know, maybe he just had the extra tie along, or he'd left it behind from when he was staying there, and she had it out to give it back to him, so he used it."

"My, you are a quick thinker, Mr. Patterson. But you said yourself he was wearing the green tie and green jacket on Monday."

"I guess I may have been confused."

"I guess you were, as Miss Evans and Mr. Granger will swear to."

"Well, er…"

Mason held up one of his hands. "There's something else, too. One last thing, but an important one, Mr. Patterson. The button found in the trunk was from Josiah's green jacket, but he was wearing a brown jacket that day, again according to Miss Evans and, I'm sure, Mr. Granger. But if by some chance they were both mistaken, and he *was* wearing the green one, I doubt Josiah would have chosen a green tie to go with it. He was far too fashion conscious for that, as you yourself attested to. Oh, and I almost forgot, you stated the other day that Miss Claggett phoned you at the mission a little before five on Monday, and you left immediately. The mission is less than a mile away from here, yet Miss Evans states you didn't arrive until after six. What were you doing during that time?"

"I may have been mistaken as to the time Gert called."

"Or you may have gone up to Gertrude's apartment shortly after five, say around a quarter past, then, around five thirty, strangled her and put her body in the trunk. You climbed down the fire escape when you realized the man from the train station had arrived, and you walked around the block to kill time, so to speak, until he left. I imagine that all would have taken you about forty-five minutes or so."

"I guess I didn't leave the mission as early as I'd thought, that's all."

"I took the liberty of telephoning there before I came here. The woman I spoke with confirmed you left at just a few minutes past five and didn't return until nearly seven. She was most concerned because you'd told her your foolish story about being worried about Gert and her brother, both of whom she knew."

"I, uh, made a few stops before I got to the apartment building. Yeah, that's what I did."

"Even though you were supposedly worried about Gert and in a hurry to get to her apartment? Rather strange to make a few stops in that case, but the police will want a full list of the places you claim to have visited. Oh, by the way, I also telephoned Councilman Monroe's office. Though he wasn't at liberty to say outright, he did suggest that I was right about you embezzling funds from his campaign. I imagine if the police investigate, they will find similar patterns of missing funds from other places you've worked."

Patterson scowled, shoving his fists into his pockets. "You had no right to telephone Monroe's office. That's none of your business."

"It is when it leads to murder, Mr. Patterson. Oh, yes, and one other thing. You stated the other day Miss Castle's trunk and two suitcases had already been picked up by the time you arrived with Miss Evans. Is that right?"

"Yes, that's correct, why?"

"And you had not been in the apartment that day prior to when you showed up with Miss Evans?"

"No, I had not, despite what you keep insinuating."

"Then how did you know she had two suitcases? Which she did, by the way. She could just as easily have had just one or three or four. It wasn't stated in the newspaper article."

"I never said two, exactly. I just said suitcases."

"Actually you *did* say two, and you were quite specific. But according to you, the bags had already been picked up by the time you arrived, so there's no way you would have known that. There is one thing I can't figure out, however."

"Oh? And what, pray tell, is that?"

"I can't figure out how exactly you got into the building the first time. Oh, I know myself that it's not *too* difficult to gain access, but you needed to keep it quiet, without arousing attention to yourself. You couldn't just buzz the apartment because you wanted to slip in the back door unnoticed. You certainly wouldn't want to take a chance on being seen in Miss Claggett's apartment building *before* you killed her."

"And why would I care about that?"

"What if someone saw you? What if Miss Evans or Mrs. Comstock came out of their apartment while you were in the hall, before you killed Gertrude? They both know you by sight. That would certainly throw a wrench in things as far as your timeline, wouldn't it? You needed to get in the building and upstairs unseen to kill her and back down again. You couldn't risk being seen coming into the building, going up, *or* coming back down. It would ruin your plans. And you also had to be certain neither Miss Evans nor Mrs. Comstock saw Josiah leaving through the front door. You needed help to get inside the building and keep the managers occupied."

"I don't know what you're talking about."

"No? Maybe Miss Powell does, then. That is her perfume I smell, isn't it? Goût de Minuit, or Taste of Midnight, as it's otherwise known. A lady friend of mine wears that, too. It's quite distinctive."

"I'm sure lots of women wear that, Mr. Adler," Patterson said.

"But not lots of platinum peroxide blondes. Mind if I use your bathroom?"

"It's out of order."

"Is it? Or is it occupied by someone in hiding? I notice the door is closed."

Patterson stared hard at Mason, but Mason stood his ground, unwavering. Finally, Patterson turned his head slightly and called out over his shoulder. "You might as well come on out, Jules."

Slowly the bathroom door opened, and a platinum blonde dressed in a tight-fitting red dress stepped across the small hall and into the living room, looking cautiously at the two men.

"Well, if it isn't Julia Powell," Mason said to her.

"And if it isn't the big dick with a little gun," she said, moving over to where John was standing.

"Oh, right, thanks for reminding me," Mason said, unbuttoning his coat and drawing his Colt, which he pointed at the two of them.

"You never called me," she said, staring at Mason.

"Sorry about that, but you're really not my type."

"Yeah, I figured that. My women's intuition is seldom wrong."

"I'm sure," Mason said. "Aren't you supposed to be at work at city hall today, Miss Powell?"

"I quit this morning. I hated that job. I only took it to pay the bills until Johnny could make enough off that stupid mission. We're headed to L.A. in a few days."

"Oh? You're leaving the mission right away, Mr. Patterson?"

"I figure it's time. They'll be on the alert now that they know about the missing funds, even though they think Josiah took them. So, on to greener pastures. L.A.'s a big city with lots of opportunities."

"Nice of you to wait until after Miss Claggett's funeral tomorrow, at least," Mason said.

"It wouldn't have looked right if we hadn't," Patterson said.

"Indeed. And what will you do in Los Angeles, Miss Powell?"

"Maybe I'll try my hand at acting, like Charlotte. I think I could do just as good a job as her, maybe even better."

"Certainly better on the casting couch," Mason said.

"What's that supposed to mean, smarty pants?"

"I don't have time to explain it. Anyway, I must say you tried to think of everything, Mr. Patterson. Miss Powell here was the pretty peroxide blonde who stopped by the Evans Comstock Residence for Young Ladies Monday afternoon to look at apartments, using the name Audrey Allen."

"That's right," Patterson said.

"Audrey Allen was my idea," Julia said. "It has a nice ring to it, don't you think? Maybe I'll use it as my stage name."

Mason ignored her for the time being. "Did you also arrange for the meeting between Gertrude and her brother?"

"More or less. It was her idea to confront him after I told her about his drinking and gambling, but she wanted to come here to my house to see him while I was at work. I convinced her to have him go over there shortly after Charlotte left around five, so she'd have the home court advantage, so to speak."

"And of course, Mr. Patterson, you knew Miss Evans waters her flowers a little after five every day, so she'd see Josiah arrive, which was important. She'd probably notice he looked nervous and upset."

"Because he was. He was worried his big sister was angry with him," Patterson said.

"So, Josiah arrived and Miss Evans saw him. Meanwhile, I'm guessing Miss Powell was waiting nearby, watching until Josiah was inside and upstairs and Miss Evans had gone back in. Then she walked up the walk, buzzed the manager's apartment, and pretended to be looking for a place. All she had to do was keep the two women in their apartment until Josiah left and you could get upstairs and back down again, is that right, Mr. Patterson?"

"Yeah, that's right," Julia said, answering for him. "It wasn't too hard to keep the young one busy. I think she's a bit queer, personally, and I'm sure you know what I mean by that. The only problem was the old one. She was supposed to be there, too, but she was working on the boiler or something. I was worried she'd come back before Johnny had a chance to get to the third floor and down again, but fortunately she didn't."

"Besides keeping the women busy, you also had another task to do, didn't you? You asked to see the building, and while Miss Evans was showing you around, you slipped a piece of tape or something over the back door lock, allowing Patterson here access a short while later, is that right?"

"I pretended I wanted to see out back, is all, to make sure the neighborhood's safe for a young lady like me. Miss Evans made a big deal of telling me how both the front and back doors were kept locked. She never noticed me rigging it."

"All went according to plan, except you weren't counting on the man from Union Station arriving, were you?"

"No, I wasn't," Patterson said. "I admit that was a surprise. I had originally planned on just leaving the body on the floor, with the tie around her neck and the jacket button next to her. When I came back later with one of the managers, we'd discover Gert, and I'd pretend to see Josiah hurrying away on the street below."

"But then the front door buzzer buzzed, and you panicked. You looked out the window and saw the Union Station truck out front and figured someone was there to pick up the trunk and suitcases. You probably thought about fleeing and leaving the body, but that would blow your plans as far as coming back later and claiming to see Josiah out the window."

"Yeah, I didn't know what to do, exactly. But then I looked at the trunk and I figured it would be better to hide the body inside it and buy me some time, so I did. I figured when the body was discovered later, they'd finger either Charlotte or Josiah, or maybe even the train station man."

"Rather devious and clever."

"Thanks, but I admit I didn't really think about that part until later. Anyway, I went down the fire escape, just like you said, then waited a short while until the train station man left before making my appearance at the front door of the building."

"And you, Miss Powell, were still with Miss Evans in her apartment. Was Mr. Patterson supposed to give you a signal once he was outside and the task completed so that you'd know it was safe to leave?"

"Not a signal. He was supposed to come back downstairs, then act like he'd just arrived. He'd ring the manager's bell and say he'd come to see Miss Claggett, and I'd leave, only the train station man arrived before he was finished. I didn't know what to do, as I figured Johnny was still upstairs, but I figured he'd hide some place, and he did. It all worked out. Johnny's a clever fellow. Still, I was relieved when he did finally buzz the manager's office shortly after the man left."

"You played your part well. And you played the part of the jilted girlfriend admirably, too, I must say, Miss Powell. Academy Award winning, in fact. Maybe you do have a future in the movies."

"Thanks. And you're smarter than I gave you credit for."

"Thanks," Mason said. "Did you two know each other in California?"

"Yes, we've been together a while now," Julia said. "We're a team. We came to Phoenix when the cops got a little too close out in L.A. I took the job at city hall to pay the bills while Johnny looked around for a gig after the one with the councilman ended."

"And you rented this house as Mr. and Mrs. Patterson, I would imagine, though I suspect Patterson isn't your real name," Mason said, looking at John. "Mr. Granger next door asked Josiah what happened to your wife, and at the time I assumed he was referring to Gertrude, who was over here often. But he meant Miss Powell here, who had been posing as your wife."

"That's right. You're a smart cookie, for a dick. Jules had to move out and get a cheap apartment when I started dating Gert, and then Josiah moved in with me."

"I didn't like it," Miss Powell said, "But it had to be done, and at least Josiah was paying a little rent here and I still had my job at city hall."

"Originally we figured we'd just lay low in Phoenix for a while, then go back to L.A. after the councilman job, only this Lost Souls gig came along, and it was too good to pass up," Patterson said.

"I see. You, know, Mr. Patterson, you really had me believing you broke up with Miss Powell and that you saw her only as someone to have some laughs with."

"We do have laughs," Julia said. "Lots of them."

"Yes, Jules is a laugh a minute, but I must say I'm getting a bit tired of her cackling."

"What's that supposed to mean?" Julia said, whipping her head in Patterson's direction.

"Shut up," Patterson said.

"Oh dear, it doesn't sound like either of you will be laughing much anymore," Mason said.

"Oh, I don't know," Patterson said, "It's all about who has the last laugh, isn't it?"

"What do you mean by that?" Mason said.

Patterson swiftly plucked a small revolver from his pocket and held it up to Julia's temple. "I'll blow a hole in her head to match the ones she's already got if you don't drop your gun."

Julia flinched and tried to get away, but he held her right arm tightly with his left.

"What are you doing, Johnny? Let go of me, this isn't funny." She looked suddenly terrified, the color draining from her face.

"I think it's hilarious," Patterson said. "And don't think I wouldn't blow your brains out if I need to."

"What would that accomplish, Patterson?" Mason said. "If you shoot her, then I'll shoot you. Then you'll both be dead."

Julia struggled and squirmed. "You're hurting me, let me go, Johnny, stop it."

"Shut up and stop moving, or I *will* pull this trigger."

"You do, and you'll both be dead. I'm an excellent shot."

Johnny stared hard at Mason. "So what? We're as good as dead, anyway. This state has the death penalty, in case you didn't know. But our blood will be on your hands, Adler. Unless you want to live with that, drop your gun and let us go."

Mason snorted. "Drop my gun so you can shoot me instead? I *thought* you were volunteering information a little too freely. Miss Powell said I'm smarter than she gave me credit for. Perhaps I'm smarter than you give me credit for, too, Patterson."

"I'd say we're at a stalemate, then," Patterson said, perspiring profusely now. "I didn't want to kill Gert, you know. Even though she was annoying, I actually kind of liked her. But ultimately I had no choice. She would have turned me in to try and reform me, and I'm not fond of prison."

"That's too bad. By the way, I wasn't aware God-fearing men like yourself carried guns."

"Praise the Lord but trust in Smith and Wesson, I always say." Patterson released Julia's right arm and moved his left hand squarely onto her lower back. He shoved her forward as hard as he could into Mason. Mason, taken by surprise, reached out instinctively to catch her and keep her from falling as she crashed into him. Unable to get a clear shot, Patterson rushed toward him, grabbing the gun from Mason's hand. Mason let go of Julia, who struggled to regain her balance, as he swung at Patterson, connecting with Patterson's chin. Patterson reeled backward, dropping Mason's gun, which clattered to the wood floor.

Mason acted quickly to get it, but out of the corner of his eye, he saw a female hand picking it up before he could get to it. He shut his eyes and braced for impact as a shot rang out. Seconds went by as Mason hit the floor hard. He rolled instinctively away and opened his eyes. Strangely he didn't feel as though he were shot. Maybe he was dead, he thought. Maybe this was what it was like. He finally noticed Patterson lying against the wall by the front door, unconscious, blood pouring from his right shoulder. Surprised, Mason looked up toward Julia in her tight red dress. She was even more pale now and looked as though she might be sick. She held her hands up, palms out. Odd. Mason managed to sit up then and looked behind him, where he saw Lydia standing in the doorway from the kitchen to the living room, shakily holding his revolver on Julia Powell.

"Lydia, what on earth are you doing here?"

"Saving you, I'd say," she said, but her voice was quavering as she kept her gaze locked on Julia Powell. "Are you okay, Mason?"

Mason got slowly to his feet, making sure he wasn't standing in the line of fire. "Yes, more or less. But how did you get here, and how did you get in?"

"Mr. Ferguson drove me. He, Mrs. Woodburn, and Scruffy are out in the car. We're on our way to the vet's office, but I convinced them to stop by here first. I found the address in the phone book. Fortunately he's the only Patterson on Third Street."

"But how did you get in Patterson's house?"

"The side door off the kitchen. It was unlocked. I took the precaution of peeking in one of the windows when I arrived and quickly assessed what was happening."

"And you didn't think to call the police?" Mason said. "You just came in here by yourself?"

"If I hadn't, you'd probably be dead by now, Sherlock."

"Good point, Watson, thanks. Nice shooting, by the way. Looks like you got him square in the shoulder."

"Thanks, but I was aiming for his head."

"Nice. He appears to have passed out, and he's losing a fair amount of blood. I suppose we should call an ambulance and the police."

"What about me?" Julia Powell said.

Mason looked at her, her hands still raised. "I'm sure the police will be happy to give you a ride downtown, Miss Powell. And for the record, I don't think Mr. Patterson ever intended to shoot you. If he had, he would have shot you and me both when he had the chance, after he shoved you toward me. But he couldn't get a clear shot at me without shooting you, too, so instead he went for my gun."

"Gee," Julia said softly. "He really does care."

CHAPTER FOURTEEN

Late afternoon, Friday, May 10, 1946
The Cactus Cantina

Mason, Lydia, Walter, and Emil all sat around a four-top near the front window of the small, colorful restaurant and bar, with their various drinks in front of them.

"How are you feeling, love?" Lydia said, looking at Mason.

"Stiff and sore," he replied, taking a swig of his scotch.

"You really shouldn't be fighting at your age," Walter said over the top of his martini. "I was just shocked when I'd heard what happened. A fistfight with a woman, and then a brawl with that nasty fellow with a gun."

"It really wasn't a fistfight, Walter, and I didn't have much of a choice either time," Mason said. "But I'm paying for them both today. At least it all ended well. Or well enough, anyway, thanks to Lydia. If not for her, who knows what might have happened with the brawl with Mr. Patterson."

"I don't want to think about it," Lydia said. "It makes me shake, and I don't want to spill my martini."

"Well, as you said, all's well that ends well, and another case solved by you, darling," Walter said.

"Apparently so," Emil said, slightly annoyed. He picked up his beer and took a long, hard drink.

"Oh, Emil, don't feel too bad that you've been bested yet again by Mason," Walter said.

"What are you, Walt? Mason's best friend all of a sudden?" Emil said, looking sideways at him.

Walter shot Emil a foul look back. "You *know* I hate it when you call me Walt. And I don't know about my being his best friend, but I am his friend. Aren't I, Mason?"

"Yes, of course," Mason said. "You're *both* my friends. And honestly, Emil, this isn't a competition between me and you, at least not on my end. I don't intentionally try to solve cases before you do."

"Just like you don't intentionally try to make me look bad to my chief," Emil said, setting his beer down and lighting up a Lucky Strike.

"I truly don't."

Emil inhaled and then exhaled a cloud of cigarette smoke toward the ceiling. "Eh, I know that, I suppose, but I wish you'd take a vacation once in a while."

"That's a splendid idea, Emil," Walter said. "In fact, we're in the process of making plans for a Palm Springs getaway very soon, aren't we, Mason?"

"Um, yes, that's the plan, anyway."

"I haven't had a chance to telephone Marvin at the Triada yet, but I will, don't you worry," Walter said.

"Who's Marvin? And just the two of you are going?" Emil said.

"Marvin's a friend of Walter's who works at one of the Palm Springs resorts, and yes, just the two of us, I guess, unless you'd like to join us, Emil. Or Lydia?" Mason said.

Walter held up a hand, palm out and shook his head. "Oh no. No women allowed."

"Fine by me," Lydia said. "I don't have any paid time off coming at the store yet anyway."

"Oh, that's too bad," Walter said, quite insincerely. "And I'm sure Emil wouldn't go anywhere without Shirley."

"Unless it was to that mountain cabin. Mr. Blanders telephoned me and gave me all the details, by the way. I can hardly wait," Emil said.

"That's wonderful," Mason said. "I do hope you like the place."

"I think I will. Just don't go solving any more cases while I'm gone."

"I'll see what I can do. Or can't do, as the case may be."

"Right. Anyway, good job on the Claggett murder case, Mason."

"Thank you, Emil, that means a lot coming from you. Lucky it turned out as it did, in more ways than one. I really didn't have any solid evidence against Patterson. Just conflicting accounts about what Josiah was or wasn't wearing, mostly, and that piece of blue cloth I found on the fire escape."

"That blue cloth was a perfect match to Patterson's blue blazer, by the way. The lab confirmed it," Emil said.

"That's good, but that probably still wouldn't have been enough on its own. Especially with Josiah having confessed. Not to mention the evidence Patterson planted against him, both in the trunk and at the mission," Mason said.

"True," Emil said, taking another drag on his cigarette. "I suppose I should be thanking you, Mason, or at least Josiah Claggett should. We released him last night, all charges dropped."

"I'm glad to hear it," Mason said.

"Yeah. To think he could have gone to jail. I can't figure out why he'd confess to strangling her if he didn't," Emil said.

"Because you coerced him into it, of course," Walter said, lighting up a Camel cigarette from the candle in a wine bottle on the table. "I can just see poor Josiah, sitting at a table in a small, dark room at the police station, under a hot, bright lamp, as you and your cronies berated him about the necktie."

Emil blew a puff of smoke at Walter. "We don't operate like that, Walt. You watch too many movies."

"Nonetheless, I'm sure he didn't just volunteer that information, especially since he was innocent," Walter said, blowing a cloud of his own cigarette smoke back at Emil.

"Well, not entirely innocent," Emil said. "He did knock her down hard enough for her to fall and get the wind knocked out of her. He did admit to that willingly."

"Still, I highly doubt he would have admitted to strangling

her if the suggestion wasn't planted in his brain by you brawny, thickheaded policemen."

Emil scowled. "Listen, Walt. Us brawny, thickheaded policemen could run you in for all those nasty things I've been hearing go on down by the canal after dark by you and fellows like you."

"Boys," Mason said loudly to the two of them. "Let's not argue, please."

"Yes, please," Lydia said. "We're here to celebrate, not aggravate."

"That's right. And I would be remiss in not giving my hearty, heartfelt thanks to Dr. Watson once more," Mason said, raising his glass. "Our own Lydia Dettling, who literally saved my life. A toast to Lydia."

"To Lydia," Emil and Walter said, raising their glasses.

"Glad to be of service, Holmes," she said with a smile as the other three drank to her.

"Say, what do you suppose will happen to Miss Evans and Mrs. Comstock?" Lydia said, picking up her martini again and taking a sip.

"Happen to them? I imagine they'll live happily ever after, unless some pretty young thing moves in that catches the eye of Miss Evans again," Mason said. "Otherwise, I think their secret's safe, and I think they truly love each other."

"That's good, I'm glad to hear it. And what of Charlotte Castle, or Castleberry?" Lydia said.

"Her father tells me she's still planning to go to L.A. as soon as the trial is over. She may be called to testify, so she can't leave yet," Mason said.

"Do you think she'll make it in the movies?" Walter said. "It's a tough business."

"Impossible to say, but stranger things have happened. I certainly wish her well," Mason said.

"Me too," Lydia said. "And Josiah?"

Mason looked at her softly. "That's even more impossible to say. I think he'll be like a stringless kite in the sky on a windy day without his sister to ground him, but I hope he'll be okay. Working at the mission is bound to help, and I suspect the people there will watch out for him and hopefully take care of him once the trial is over and his name's been officially cleared."

"That just leaves Alfred Brody," Emil said.

Mason looked across the table at Emil. "Yes, not so difficult to say about him. He's bright, articulate, hardworking, and energetic. I think he'll be just fine. I stopped by his place this morning to give him the news, since he doesn't have a phone. He gave me some news of his own."

"What?" Emil said, grinding what was left of his cigarette into the ashtray.

"He's applied for a teaching job at Paul Quinn College in Dallas, Texas, along with a couple of other places, and I suspect he'll be offered at least one of the positions."

"That's wonderful," Lydia said. "I never met any of these people, except for Patterson and Julia, but I feel like I know them all, hearing you talk about them over the last few days. Speaking of, what will happen to those two now?"

"To John Patterson and Julia Powell?" Mason said.

"Yes," Lydia said.

"You can probably answer that better than me, Emil," Mason said.

"They'll stand trial," Emil said, taking a swig of his beer. "Patterson, whose real name we now believe is John Price, will most likely be found guilty, based on the evidence, Mason's testimony, and everything that's happened, and will get the gas chamber. Julia Powell will likely be found guilty as an accomplice and serve time in prison."

"I hope they lock her away for a long time," Lydia said. "Poor Miss Claggett. You said you went to her funeral this morning, Mason?"

"Yes, it was a small service, but nice. Miss Castle and her father were there, and Josiah, of course, along with Miss Evans and Mrs. Comstock and a few others."

"May she rest in peace," Lydia said.

"Yes. I propose another toast. To Gertrude," Mason said, raising his glass once more.

"To Gertrude," the others said, also raising theirs.

MYSTERY HISTORY

- This story is inspired by the real-life murders of Agnes Anne LeRoi and Hedvig Samuelson in 1931, by their friend Winnie Ruth Judd. Winnie Ruth Judd was found guilty, but then later committed to the Arizona Insane Asylum, from which she escaped multiple times. Winnie Ruth Judd hid the bodies, one of them dismembered, in trunks, and took them with her from Phoenix to Los Angeles, where the bodies were discovered when a baggage handler noticed a foul odor and leaking fluids.
- Diamond's Department store in Phoenix was founded by Jewish immigrants Nathan and Isaac Diamond in 1897 and was first called the Boston Store. Oddly, that same year a store called the Boston Store opened in Milwaukee, WI, but as far as the author is aware the two were not related. The one in Phoenix wasn't actually renamed Diamond's until 1947. It was among the first stores to install air conditioning, in 1931. The chain was eventually sold to Dayton-Hudson and then Dillard's. J.C.Penney's was located at the same intersection.
- The Union Station train depot in Phoenix opened in 1923 at 401 West Harrison Street. It was an Amtrak station until 1996 and now stands vacant, used for storage as of this writing.
- The Triada Palm Springs Hotel was built in 1939 and did indeed attract huge movie stars of the time, including Tyrone Power, Lana Turner, Jimmy Durante, and Howard Hughes.
- The Racquet Club Palm Springs opened in 1934, founded by

actors Ralph Bellamy and Charles Farrell. It was quite popular with the Hollywood elite.

- Cary Grant, a very popular movie star, was married to Barbara Hutton from 1942 to 1945. Randolph Scott and Cary Grant lived together, on and off, for twelve years and have been rumored to have been a gay couple, though it has never been proven.

- "What's your name? Puddin' Tane, ask me again and I'll tell you the same. Where do you live? Down the lane. What's your number? Cucumber!" is an old children's rhyme, first appearing in the U.S. in the late 1800s, often recited by the author's maternal grandmother, who was born in 1906, as well as her daughter, the author's mother.

- Jack Benny, born 1894, died 1974, was a hugely popular radio, television, and film star, known for being "forever 39," among other gags, such as his stinginess and poor violin playing, when in reality he was fairly generous and played the violin quite well.

- Dagwood Bumstead is one of the main characters in the long-running comic strip *Blondie*, which first debuted in 1930. *Blondie* can still be found in newspapers and online today.

- Popeye and Olive Oyl are cartoon characters in the comic strip *Popeye*. Olive Oyl is known for being extremely thin and flat chested.

- Hedda Hopper was an American gossip columnist known for her outlandish hats. At one point her readership was over 35 million.

- Sherlock Holmes and Dr. Watson are fictional characters created by British author Sir Arthur Conan Doyle. They were well known for solving crimes, with Sherlock being the brains and Dr. Watson the sometimes befuddled assistant.

- Camelback Mountain is a famous mountain in Phoenix whose name came about because its shape resembles that of the hump and head of a kneeling camel. Though you can't drive to the peak of the mountain, you can park very close.

- Gertrude was actually the name of the author's first hamster.

- Goût de Minuit, or Taste of Midnight, is a fictitious perfume, first created by the author in *Death Takes a Bow*, a Heath Barrington mystery, where the character of Verbina Partridge wore it.
- Paul Quinn College in Dallas, Texas, was founded in 1872 and is still in operation today. It is affiliated with the African Methodist Episcopal Church. It's the oldest Black college west of the Mississippi.
- Fort Huachuca, located in Cochise Country, Arizona, had quarters for over 24,000 enlisted soldiers during World War II, including the 92nd and 93rd African American Infantry divisions.
- Spencer Tracy (1900–1967) was a popular actor, often paired with actress Katharine Hepburn both on screen and off.

About the Author

David S. Pederson was born in Leadville, Colorado, where his father was a miner. Soon after, the family relocated to Wisconsin, where David grew up, attending high school and university, majoring in business and creative writing. Landing a job in retail, he found himself relocating to New York, Massachusetts, and eventually back to Wisconsin. He and his husband now reside in the sunny Southwest.

His third book, *Death Checks In*, was a finalist for the 2019 Lambda Literary Awards. His fourth book, *Death Takes A Bow*, was a finalist for the 2020 Lambda Literary Awards.

He has written many short stories and poems and is passionate about mysteries, old movies, and crime novels. When not reading, writing, or working in the furniture business, David also enjoys working out, and studying classic ocean liners, floor plans, and historic homes.

David can be contacted at davidspederson@gmail.com or via his website, www.davidspederson.com.

Books Available From Bold Strokes Books

Murder at Union Station by David S. Pederson. Private Detective Mason Adler struggles to determine who killed a woman found in a trunk without getting himself killed in the process. (978-1-63679-269-9)

A Champion for Tinker Creek by D.C. Robeline. Lyle James has rescued his dad's auto repair business, but when city hall condemns his neighborhood, Lyle learns only trusting will save his life and help him find love. (978-1-63679-213-2)

Heckin' Lewd: Trans and Nonbinary Erotica, edited by Mx. Nillin Lore. If you want smutty, fearless, gender diverse erotica written by affirming own-voices folks who get it, then this is the book you've been looking for! (978-1-63679-240-8)

Inherit the Lightning by Bud Gundy. Darcy O'Brien and his sisters learn they are about to inherit an immense fortune, but a family mystery about to unravel after seventy years threatens to destroy everything. (978-1-63679-199-9)

Pursued: Lillian's Story by Felice Picano. Fleeing a disastrous marriage to the Lord Exchequer of England, Lillian of Ravenglass reveals an incident-filled, often bizarre, tale of great wealth and power, perfidy, and betrayal. (978-1-63679-197-5)

Murder on Monte Vista by David S. Pederson. Private Detective Mason Adler's angst at turning fifty is forgotten when his "birthday present," the handsome, young Henry Bowtrickle, turns up dead, and it's up to Mason to figure out who did it, and why. (978-1-63679-124-1)

Three Left Turns to Nowhere by Jeffrey Ricker, J. Marshall Freeman & 'Nathan Burgoine. Three strangers heading to a convention in Toronto are stranded in rural Ontario, where a small town with a subtle kind of magic leads each to discover what he's been searching for. (978-1-63679-050-3)

One Verse Multi by Sander Santiago. Life was good: promotion, friends, falling in love, discovering that the multi-verse is on a fast track to collision—wait, what? Good thing Martin King works for a company that can fix the problem, right...um...right? (978-1-63679-069-5)

Fresh Grave in Grand Canyon by Lee Patton. The age-old Grand Canyon becomes more and more ominous as a group of volunteers fight to survive alone in nature and uncover a murderer among them. (978-1-63679-047-3)

Loyalty, Love & Vermouth by Eric Peterson. A comic valentine to a gay man's family of choice, including the ones with cold noses and four paws. (978-1-63555-997-2)

Bury Me in Shadows by Greg Herren. College student Jake Chapman is forced to spend the summer at his dying grandmother's home and soon finds danger from long-buried family secrets. (978-1-63555-993-4)

A Different Man by Andrew L. Huerta. This diverse collection of stories chronicling the challenges of gay life at various ages shines a light on the progress made and the progress still to come. (978-1-63555-977-4)

Busy Ain't the Half of It by Frederick Smith and Chaz Lamar Cruz. Elijah and Justin seek happily-ever-afters in LA, but are they too busy to notice happiness when it's there? (978-1-63555-944-6)

Pursuit: A Victorian Entertainment by Felice Picano. An intelligent, handsome, ruthlessly ambitious young man who rose from the slums to become the right-hand man of the Lord Exchequer of England will stop at nothing as he pursues his Lord's vanished wife across Continental Europe. (978-1-63555-870-8)

Best of the Wrong Reasons by Sander Santiago. For Fin Ness and Orion Starr, it takes a funeral to remind them that love is worth living for. (978-1-63555-867-8)

Coming to Life on South High by Lee Patton. Twenty-one-year-old gay virgin Gabe Rafferty's first adult decade unfolds as an unpredictable journey into sex, love, and livelihood. (978-1-63555-906-4)

Death's Prelude by David S. Pederson. In this prequel to the Detective Heath Barrington Mystery series, Heath discovers that first love changes you forever and drives you to become the person you're destined to be. (978-1-63555-786-2)

His Brother's Viscount by Stephanie Lake. Hector Somerville wants to rekindle his illicit love affair with Viscount Wentworth, but he must overcome one problem: Wentworth still loves Hector's brother. (978-1-63555-805-0)

The Dubious Gift of Dragon Blood by J. Marshall Freeman. One day Crispin is a lonely high school student—the next he is fighting a war in a land ruled by dragons, his otherworldly boyfriend at his side. (978-1-63555-725-1)

Quake City by St John Karp. Can Andre find his best friend Amy before the night devolves into a nightmare of broken hearts, malevolent drag queens, and spontaneous human combustion? Or has it always happened this way, every night, at Aunty Bob's Quake City Club? (978-1-63555-723-7)

Every Summer Day by Lee Patton. Meant to celebrate every summer day, Luke's journal instead chronicles a love affair as fast-moving and possibly as fatal as his brother's brain tumor. (978-1-63555-706-0)

Everyday People by Louis Barr. When film star Diana Danning hires private eye Clint Steele to find her son, Clint turns to his former West Point barracks mate, and ex-buddy with benefits, Mars Hauser to lend his cyber espionage and digital black ops skills to the case. (978-1-63555-698-8)

Royal Street Reveillon by Greg Herren. In this Scotty Bradley mystery, someone is killing the stars of a reality show, and it's up to Scotty Bradley and the boys to find out who. (978-1-63555-545-5)

Accidental Prophet by Bud Gundy. Days after his grandmother dies, Drew Morten learns his true identity and finds himself racing against time to save civilization from the apocalypse. (978-1-63555-452-6)

Counting for Thunder by Phillip Irwin Cooper. A struggling actor returns to the Deep South to manage a family crisis but finds love and ultimately his own voice as his mother is regaining hers for possibly the last time. (978-1-63555-450-2)

Of Echoes Born by 'Nathan Burgoine. A collection of queer fantasy short stories set in Canada from Lambda Literary Award finalist 'Nathan Burgoine. (978-1-63555-096-2)